"Sibyl was lying on her back, looking at me, her eyes wide open. Her lips were parted, her black hair was spread out in the snow. She stretched out her arms to me. I wanted to help her to get up, but I slipped and fell on her. She kissed me. Her lips were hot and wet. Her teeth sank into my lips, blood ran across my tongue . . ."

Was Sibyl a monstrous mistress of evil—or its helpless victim?

Did her body offer paradise—or hell?

Investigative reporter Paul Holland did not know.

He only knew that he had to continue having her —no matter what the perverse price. . . .

THE SIBYL CIPHER

a novel by
Simmel

Translated from the German
by Catherine Hutter

POPULAR LIBRARY • NEW YORK

Original German title: *GOTT SCHUETZT DIE LIEBENDEN*

THE SIBYL CIPHER

Published by Popular Library, a unit of CBS Publications, the
Consumer Publishing Division of CBS Inc., by arrangement with
Paul Zsolnay Verlag GmbH.

Copyright © 1957 by Paul Zsolnay Verlag Gesellschaft m. bH.,
Wien/Hamburg
English translation copyright © 1979 CBS Publications,
The Consumer Publishing Division of CBS Inc.
All Rights Reserved

ISBN: 0-445-04395-4

Printed in the United States of America

10 9 8 7 6 5 4 3 2 1

For Lulu with love

When we say to someone, "I can't live without you," what we really mean is, "I can't live feeling you may be in pain, in want." That's all it is. When they are dead our responsibility ends. There's nothing more we can do about it. We can rest in peace.

Graham Greene, *The Heart of the Matter*

BOOK ONE

1

The telephone was ringing.

I sat up in bed, startled, and groped in the dark for the switch on the bed lamp. It wasn't my bed and it wasn't my room, so I didn't find the switch easily. The illuminated face of a small clock read 5:00 and the telephone was still ringing. Sibyl didn't hear it. She went on breathing evenly as I leaned across her. We had slept in the same bed, close, she still in my arms. My hand fumbled in vain for the switch but found the receiver. "Hello."

"Is that 87-1348?" The voice of the young female operator sounded wide-awake.

"Yes."

Sibyl moved. She sighed, a long sigh.

"You asked to be called," said the fresh young voice. "Five o'clock, Herr Holland. Have a nice day."

"Thank you."

I put down the receiver and lay back. From far away I could hear the sound of an airplane engine being revved. Sibyl, I was pretty sure, didn't hear it anymore. She had been living in this part of Berlin for far too long; but for me the sound, which grew louder and louder, was a constant reminder, an inexpressible threat, that depressed me. The windowpanes rattled as the four-engine plane roared over the house.

My days in Berlin were over again, I had to leave. Nothing was lasting, not grief nor joy. And there was no peace. Two lines of a poem came to mind: "And constantly I hear behind me the rushing steps of the times, that go on and on. . . ." Who wrote it? I couldn't remember. Now the noise grew less. Every day, at least four times an hour, a plane flew over Sibyl's house, either arriving or departing. The Tempel-hof airport lay to the south. During the blockade, according to Sibyl, the windows had never stopped rat-tling, in good weather or bad.

Another fifteen minutes and I'd get up. No. That was cutting it too fine. Ten minutes. Now the noise of the plane was muted, like a loving murmur, then I didn't hear it anymore. Another plane was already ap-proaching Berlin, still somewhere up in the clouds, in the first rosy light of this winter day. It was coming closer, getting ready to roar over our heads, to cause the air to tremble, powerful, dominant, yet just as un-sure and hovering between life and death as the people on board and we humans down below.

"Paul?"

"Yes, beloved."

Sibyl turned on her side, and I could feel her soft warm lips on my breast. She was shorter than I, and very slim; she had long legs and narrow hips. Her breasts were small and firm. Naked, she looked almost like a boy. Men who didn't like women said, "Thank God, Sibyl isn't a real woman." But they could only say that because they didn't know her. I knew how much of a woman she was, how sentimental she could be, how tender and caressing.

We slept naked. Now Sibyl pressed her body against mine, and for no reason I could explain I was filled with an infinite sadness. "We have to get up, don't we?" she whispered.

There was nobody in the apartment besides us, yet she was whispering as if she had secrets with me that she wanted to keep from her books, her pictures, her narrow bed. I had to clear my throat. "My poor darling," she said. "Whenever you have to leave, you get hoarse."

"I'm absolutely miserable," I said.

"Don't talk like that." She was stroking me with her cold, pale hands. Mine were damp with excitement and exhaustion. "What do you want me to say?" she whispered, nuzzling my armpit. "You'll fly away, but I—I have to come back to the apartment, to this bed that will still smell of you, to this room where everything reminds me of you. You want to know something? Once I beat up your pillow because it wouldn't stop smelling of your hair!"

I answered, all the time listening for the roar of the plane, "I love you, Sibyl."

"And I love you, my sweet."

"I'll be back in ten days."

"Yes, Paul."

"And then I'll stay longer."

Now the bed lamp was on and I could see Sibyl. She

looked like a beautiful, passionate cat. Her eyes slanted
a little and were just as black as her hair, which she
wore short. Her nose was small and upturned. You
could see her nostrils, which quivered a little when she
was nervous. Her red lips glistened, velvety and wet.

"We're going to be very happy," she whispered. "I'll
wait for you, I'll play our records and read the books
you brought. And I'll play Rachmaninoff—our
concerto."

"Invite your friends."

"I will."

Her eyes dimmed suddenly. When Sibyl was sad, a
strange curtain of melancholy always fell across her
eyes.

"And go out evenings."

"No. I don't want to do that."

"Go. Please. To the theater. Or to Robert's." Robert
was the owner of a bar on the Kurfürstendamm, where
Sibyl and I often went when I was in Berlin.

"I don't want to go to Robert's," she said, "and all
you want is to hear me say so!"

"True, beloved."

The quiet is lasting too long, I thought. It's too
peaceful. What's happened to the next plane?

"When I come home," I said, "they've got to give
me some time off from the office."

"Yes," she said softly.

"I'll have enough money. We'll go south, to Naples.
From there we'll take a boat across the Mediterranean,
to Egypt. Four whole weeks!"

"Promise?"

I slipped one hand between her legs because I

wanted to swear on something I could believe in, and I said, "Promise."

"Four weeks," she said. "And you won't write any articles?"

"Not a line."

Sibyl was quiet a moment and then said, "Since I've known you, I've begun to pray again. I pray to God to let us stay together, and that we should stay happy."

She propped her head on one hand, her slanting cat's eyes concentrating on my lips. "You don't believe in Him, do you?"

"No."

"Did you ever believe in Him?"

"Yes. Long ago. Before the war. During the war I stopped."

"We love each other," she whispered. "That's what I tell God all the time. I say: look at us, dear God. We are faithful to each other. Please, dear God, let it stay that way. Don't let either of us grow uneasy or restless or hungry for someone else. . . ."

I lay on my back and saw her little breasts, her beautiful narrow wrists and long thin fingers, but I said nothing.

"I pray whenever you're flying," Sibyl whispered. "I pray for your success in your work, and that you may go on loving me as you have done all this year, and that you don't find another woman who excites you as I do. . . ."

And I was thinking: we have just lived through war. A new one is on its way. A few years more, a few years more of peace! Sibyl was lucky. She could speak to God.

I wished I could believe. Then I would have been able to pray right now for divine protection. I stroked Sibyl's hand, still waiting for the roar of the next plane to rise out of our peace. But it didn't come. . . .

"You're flying to Brazil, Paul," Sibyl murmured in my ear, her voice almost inaudible. "They say the most beautiful women in the world are in Rio."

"You are the most beautiful woman in the world."

"If you feel you have to, Paul, then be unfaithful to me in Rio. I don't mind."

"I won't," I said, "if for no other reason than out of superstition."

"You're smart," she whispered. "You know that it would never be the same again if one of us were to be unfaithful."

I thought of how I had slept with many women in my life, and Sibyl with many men. But I had left every one of these women, or they had left me, and Sibyl had had the same experience. Both of us had been filled with restlessness before we had met. We had drunk too much, smoked too much, and not been at peace with ourselves. Since we had found each other, we slept well and the early morning hours had lost their terror. We didn't mind waking up when it was still dark because we slept in the same bed, in each other's arms. The bed was so narrow that only those who truly loved each other could be happy in it. "Of course we wouldn't leave each other right away, the first time one of us was unfaithful," whispered Sibyl.

"No. But it wouldn't be the same."

"Our trust in each other would be gone," said Sibyl.

"And we can only love each other so much because we trust each other. Paul?"

"Yes."

"If it's very hot in Rio and you've had a lot to drink and you're feeling very—very restless . . . go ahead."

"I don't want to."

"That's wonderful. But if she has long exciting legs and black hair and firm little breasts . . ."

"Stop it!" I sat up, held her close, and kissed her. She sighed softly and felt very fragile in my arms. She whispered, "They say God protects lovers . . . so, dear God, protect us, too. Please, dear God. Please."

At last I heard the plane, far off, on its way to the airport. I held Sibyl close, my lips on hers, and could feel my heart beating, and we were one as the roar of the plane came closer. Mercilessly it tore into our peace. The windowpanes rattled. I closed my eyes. It was a stern reminder.

"We must get up," I said.

"Yes, my sweet."

"Give me the prosthesis."

She slipped out of bed and ran naked across the room to the chair where my artificial limb was lying. It was a prosthesis for my left leg, from the knee down. I still had my right leg.

She came back with the prosthesis and knelt down in front of me, and I sat up so that she could strap it to the stump. It hurt. "It's going to rain," I said.

It was a very modern prosthesis and I could move easily with it. At first, right after the war, I had used crutches until the wound had healed. Then I had been given a prosthesis which had been attached to a stiff left shoe; the right shoe came with it. The fact that the left shoe was attached irritated me. I stayed in hotels a lot, and in the evening I was always faced with the same problem when I wanted to leave my shoes in front of the door to be cleaned. I either had to put out both, with the prosthesis, or only the right one, and that looked as if I were crazy or drunk. So I invested in another prosthesis, this time with a left shoe that was removable. It had cost a lot but it was made of the best leather and chrome.

Sibyl strapped it on deftly; the stump rested on the foam rubber pad. "Is that all right?"

I got up and did a few knee bends. "Yes," I said. "It's fine."

2

I have just read what I have written and wonder if I have the strength to go on. About two months have gone since that clear, cold morning when the phone rang at 5:00 A.M. I am writing in a comfortable room on the fourth floor of the Ambassador Hotel in Vienna. It is decorated in red, white, and gold; the drapes are red, too. It is a bright day. People's voices and the sound of cars rise up to me from the Neue Markt below. A window is open.

It is Tuesday, April 7, 1956, and it is already quite warm in Vienna, for April. The flower women at the entrance of the Capuziner crypt, opposite the hotel, are selling small bunches of primula, snowdrops, and violets.

I was dismissed from the hospital a week ago, but my doctor, Gürtler, insisted that for a few days, at least, I should have complete rest. "But the wound is healing!" I protested. "Everybody is optimistic, and I've been off critical for a long time."

"Why do you want to get up?"

"I've got to write something."

"It's too early for that."

Dr. Gürtler is an elderly, white-haired man who was recommended to me by the Vienna representative of the Western Press Agency. He takes care of me in a way I find touching. Since leaving the hospital he has been to see me every day. When I told him yesterday that I simply had to get up, he shook his head and said, "That's very unreasonable of you, Herr Holland. Five centimeters higher, and the bullet would have penetrated the heart and you wouldn't have been in the position to write another line."

"You see," I said, "what a difference five centimeters can make. Please let me write, if only an hour a day. I know I can manage that. I have a small portable typewriter. I've been doing all my own typing for years. And I've got to get this down on paper!"

Whereupon Dr. Gürtler, who knows everything that

has happened to me in the last two months, said, "You are about to do something foolish."

"What?"

"You intend to look back, into the past. You are still thinking of this woman."

"How do you know?"

"The night nurse told me."

I have a night nurse here at the hotel. The Western Press Agency insisted on it. And since the attempt on my life I feel for the first time that I am an important and valuable employee.

Dr. Gürtler went on. "You talk in your sleep. Sometimes you cry out."

"Does it make sense?" I asked. "I mean, what I say and scream."

"You talk only about her," said Dr. Gürtler. "About this woman." He paused in a deprecating fashion before the last two words.

"I loved her."

"You must forget her. You must get well, Herr Holland. And when you're well enough, you should go away, a long trip, on the Mediterranean perhaps, to Egypt. And on the ship you can write all about it and rid yourself of everything that happened."

"I always wanted to cross the Mediterranean to Egypt," I said.

"Well, there you are!"

"But I wanted to do it with *her*."

"You can't travel with her anymore. You know. She is dead."

I had hidden a bottle of whiskey under my bed, and I had a second one in the closet. I had had to bribe the waiter because I wasn't supposed to drink whiskey. But if I didn't, I couldn't sleep, and when I couldn't sleep, Sibyl appeared and sat down on my chest and I couldn't breathe. The whiskey was stronger than Sibyl. It was the only consolation I had left. . . .

"For the present I strictly forbid you to get up or to write anything," said Dr. Gürtler, rising. The minute he had gone, I got up, put on my robe and poured myself a whiskey. The wound under my heart smarted. I still felt groggy. Quite possibly I was running a temperature. Still, I walked over to the window and sat down and inserted a sheet of paper in my portable. I could feel Sibyl was in the room. The scent of her skin and perfume stupefied me. I drank some more whiskey. It was a marvelous relief to put down the first words of this report and to recall that snowy, bitter cold night in Berlin on which everything began. I wrote for about two hours, then I stopped.

The perspiration is running down my neck, into my collar. My hands are wet, making the typewriter keys slippery. My ears are buzzing, my lips are dry. I can feel my heart beating fast. God protects lovers. That's what Sibyl said. But did He protect them from each other? The wound under my heart hurt with every breath, the wound from which Dr. Gürtler had extracted a 7.65 MM bullet not long ago.

It's no use. I have to go on writing. Only that way can I hope to forget what happened during these last two months, and how it all began in Berlin, a city four times divided, in a Germany partitioned into two parts, in a Grunewald apartment at Lassenstrasse 119 on a winter's day at 5:00 A.M.

3

The house was big. A rich man had built it at the turn of the century. I think he was the personal attorney of the German Kaiser. It stood in the middle of an old park, and it had a pond that froze over in winter. In good weather, children played on the ice. Their cries and laughter could be heard in Sibyl's apartment.

After the Second World War, the house had been divided to create four apartments, all of which were soon rented. The tenants were for the most part people who kept to themselves: a couple, an industrialist and his girl friend, two young artists. One saw them only in the park, because each apartment had its own entrance. There were no neighbors in the real sense. The house on the left had been gutted in the war and stood there now—a bleak, weathered ruin that was being slowly swallowed up by vines and weeds—and on the right there was the pond. I mention the comparative isolation of the house because it plays a role in the events to come.

The superintendent's name was Wagner. He was a

short, pale man, married to a big, slow woman. They had a daughter, age sixteen. A severe case of scarlet fever had left the girl mute. Maria—that was her name—was only able to utter hoarse, barking sounds. One got the impression that she was choking on them. She was blond and well developed for her age. For a year now she had been fooling around with boys. Sometimes she would stay out all night. Her mother was in despair about it. She told me once, "The boys know she can't tell on them." Maria was standing beside her, eyes half closed, flicking her lips with her tongue, then she let out a few shrill, high-pitched sounds and ran away.

"There's no wind," said Sibyl. She was standing at the window when I came out of the bathroom, and now she had on a robe. "You'll have a good flight." She was looking out into the dark park. "I think it's very cold." She went on talking, short sentences followed by pauses. "And it's going to be slippery." Her big black eyes avoided mine. "I hope they've cleared the runways."

I grasped her by the shoulders and turned her around. "My darling," I said. She kissed me on the cheek and sighed. I slipped one hand under her robe and touched her soft shoulder. She stepped back. "No. Please. It makes me feel quite ill when you touch me and I know there's no time."

"There is time." My hand slipped lower. "A little time."

"We're both much too nervous," she said. "Get dressed. I'll make coffee."

While I got dressed, Sibyl was busy in the kitchen. I

packed my few belongings and put my typewriter on my suitcase. I could hear Sibyl in the bathroom. I sat down beside the bookcase. She had a lot of books, most of them in Italian. She had lived in Italy for a long time, but whether before the war or during the war I didn't know. She used the books in her work; she taught languages.

Sibyl spoke about Italy often, and I imagined she had been very happy there. She had thrown a lot of coins in the Trevi fountain in Rome. They say one will return to the Eternal City if one does.

I took a slim volume off the shelf and found out that it was a critical essay on Anaximander of Miletus. Did Sibyl read things like that? She had a strange assortment of books—I'd noticed this before—books that didn't seem to go with her at all. I leafed through the book as I listened to her cleaning her teeth, and read some lines that were marked in pencil: "The origin of all things is boundless. They perish of necessity out of that which formed them because they are penitent, and retaliate toward each other for their injustices according to the order of their times."

"Paul?"

I looked up. She was standing in front of me with nothing on but her stockings and garter belt. I saw her beautifully proportioned boyish body, the narrow buttocks, the wide shoulders, the little breasts with the protruding nipples. She stretched out her arms and I saw the birthmark under her right armpit. It was dark brown and about an inch in diameter.

"What shall I wear? My green suit or the black one?"

"The black one. It's warmer."

"Look at me," she said. "Look at me once more so's you don't forget what I look like."

"I can close my eyes any time and see your face and your body just the way you are."

"I can do that, too."

"Because we love each other."

"I'll get ready. We can have breakfast in ten minutes," she said, and ran back into the bedroom. I felt tired and spent. My head ached and my hands were cold.

4

We only drank the hot coffee, neither of us felt like eating anything. The toast remained untouched, the soft-boiled eggs in their cups, the red jam, the yellow butter.

"It's no use," said Sibyl. "I can't eat."

"We've known each other for a year, and every time we have to part we go through the same thing," I said.

I went to the phone and called a taxi. Sibyl put on

her heavy coat. I took my suitcase. She said, "Let me take the typewriter."

She had on a gray felt hat that looked like a tropical helmet. Her coat was gray, too, and had large pockets. We went downstairs and out the front door. It was so cold, the air froze in our nostrils.

"Look out, darling," I said. "It really is slippery."

She walked cautiously to the gate on her high heels. When we got out into the street, the taxi hadn't arrived yet. A baker's boy was delivering bread and rolls with his bicycle, but he was wheeling it. It was too slippery to ride. The boy was walking hunched over because he was cold, and he was hanging his bag of rolls on the gate handles.

The taxi arrived soundlessly, like a ship at sea. Suddenly we were standing in its headlights. The driver stopped, got out, and put my suitcase in the trunk. "To the airport," I told him.

I had difficulty getting in. The prosthesis felt heavy, the stump was still hurting. There was going to be a change in the weather. In the car I felt for Sibyl's hand. She took off her glove and her fingers clasped mine. It was very cold in the car, which smelled of gasoline and leather. It skidded on the curves.

"Please drive more slowly," I said. "We're not in a hurry." The driver didn't reply.

Now we were in the city. People on their way to work were standing at the bus stops, freezing. It was still very quiet.

I said to Sibyl, "When you get home, go back to bed and try to get some more sleep. Take something." She nodded. We were driving across a bridge. I could see a maze of railroad tracks below. Far away a locomotive was letting off steam. A white column of smoke rose into the gloom and was lost in the leaden sky. A plane roared over our heads, deafening. It was about to land. I could see the red and green navigation lights. "We're there," Sibyl said in a dull voice.

We had arrived at the square in front of the main building. In the light of dawn I could see the concrete arch of the monument commemorating the air shuttle, a thing of the past now. I asked Sibyl, "Did a lot of planes crash during the blockade?"

"A few," she said. "It was difficult for the pilots, with the airport in the middle of the city. They had to land and take off between the houses."

The driver, who until now hadn't said a word, spoke. "I saw one."

"You say a crash?"

"Yes, sir." He gestured with his unshaven chin toward a ruin. "Over there. I was working here at the time."

He spoke with his back turned to us as he drove cautiously across the icy square toward the airport lights. "I helped to unload the planes. And one evening—it was cold like today—one of the Amis was landing with a cargo of flour, see? Comes down on the runway a little too much to the left and wham! Straight into a house! What a bloody mess!" He shook his head, apparently still horrified by the ghastly memory. "Six dead, many injured. Before we could do anything the flour was on fire."

"Were you able to put it out?"

"The heat was so great, sir, the wreck glowed white.

But there was a tree in front of the house, an old chestnut tree. Snow all around it. As I said, it was just as cold as today, around the middle of January. And next morning, what do you think had happened?"

"What?"

"The tree had started to sprout."

"No!"

"As I live and breathe," said the driver, and now he turned around, nodding his head. "It was the heat. The leaves began to open, the buds started to swell. It was creepy. Wreckage and blood and flour all over the place, and in the middle of all that shit, an old chestnut tree starting to bloom!"

A porter opened the door of the taxi. "Pan Air do Brasil," I said, "to Rio. If you'll take the suitcase, please, I'll take the typewriter. The lady is going back to Grunewald in the taxi."

The driver was about to say something but Sibyl stopped him in a cutting tone I had never heard her use before. "No, thank you. I'll take another taxi, or the bus."

I looked at her, she looked away. I shrugged and paid the disappointed driver. Meanwhile, Sibyl had walked on ahead. I caught up with her at the entrance of the main building. "What was wrong?"

"Where?"

"In the taxi?"

"Nothing." Her laugh sounded artificial. "I didn't like the driver."

"But that story of his about the tree—"

"Just because of the story about the tree."

"I don't understand," I said, surprised at the vehemence of her reaction.

"But the story isn't true," she said. There was a deep frown now between her eyebrows, and her nostrils were quivering nervously. "The man was lying just to make a point. I hate people like that!"

She had stopped, her voice was raised. I had never experienced anything like this with her before. "The buds *and* the leaves!" she cried bitterly. "As if just the leaves wouldn't have been enough! Exaggerating and showing off! Life rises out of the ruination of death, there is no finality—all this symbolic nonsense! It's revolting!" Her lips were trembling. "What's dead is dead! It never comes back! Not in any shape whatsoever!"

"Sibyl!" I said in a loud voice, and took her arm, and she stared at me like someone awakening from a deep sleep, a look of incomprehension in her wide eyes, which soon changed to an expression of embarrassment. "What on earth's got into you?"

"It's nerves," she said, turning away. "That's all. Come," and she took my hand and led me into the lobby. Her fingers dug into my hand and I understood that she didn't want me to mention the outburst again.

The fluorescent lighting in the lobby made everybody look ill. More than the usual number of employees were busy behind the counters of the various airlines. The girls looked tired, their eyes were tiny; and the men, in their blue uniforms, were nervous. I was astonished to see so many people. Men, women, children. "What's going on here?" I asked the porter.

"Refugees from the East Zone." He sounded contemptuous. "They're being flown to the West." He put my suitcase on the scale beside the PAA counter and shrugged. "That's what it's like every morning. And they say it's going to get worse."

I looked at the refugees. They were sitting on their bundles and suitcases, shabbily dressed, deprived, humble. They spoke to each other softly. The women were wearing bandanas, the men were dressed like peasants. Many of them were wearing collarless shirts, no ties. Their hands were calloused by hard work and red with the cold. A small child began to whimper.

"That'll be fifty pfennigs," said the porter, tipped his cap and went off. Sibyl clung to me. Suddenly I held her close because I was reminded of the refugees I had seen in Saigon, in Seoul, and on the island of Quemoy. They always had a label strung around their necks with their names and a number on it, and they were called out by their numbers, not by their names.

"Attention, please!" said a voice in the loudspeaker. "Air France Clipper 767 to Munich is ready to take on passengers at Gate 2. Women and children first, please. We wish you a pleasant flight!" This was followed by a commotion among those waiting. They moved forward, those belonging together held hands. Somebody yelled, "Let the children go first," but no one listened.

I held Sibyl closer. A man from the East was having an argument with a PAA employee. I was standing behind him. He held a hat in his hand. In spite of the cold he wasn't wearing a coat, and his shirt had no collar. The man was unshaved and pale. He spoke German with a Saxon accent. He was a simple man who couldn't comprehend what was happening to him.

"Herr Pilot," he said humbly, "please try to understand. We are from Dresden. My wife, my two children, and the cat." Now I saw the cat, lying in a basket on the counter, covered by a blanket, a fat, reddish-brown cat. It looked sleepy. "From Dresden, Herr Pilot!"

"I am not a pilot," said the employee, a choleric looking fellow with hair that was thining. "I'm afraid I can't help you."

"Herr . . . what is your name, please?"

"Klar."

A line was forming behind me. Everybody was nervous and everybody was listening to the conversation between the man from Dresden and the PAA employee.

"Herr Klar, please try to understand—the cat left Dresden with us. It's a long way from Dresden to Berlin. It took us three days to get here. We got into the West Sector illegally. We can't go back."

"I know, Herr Kafanke. I—"

"We are political refugees. All of us were in the Kuno-Fischerstrasse. Six weeks. The cat, too. All of us have our papers. . . ."

"Not the cat," said Herr Klar.

"But she left with us, Herr Klar! We put bromide in her food so that she would be quiet. What are we going to do, Herr Klar? We can't leave her in Berlin!"

"Attention, please. British European Airways Viscount Flight 342 to Hannover and Hamburg is taking on passengers at Gate 3. We wish you a pleasant flight!"

"Herr Kafanke, please try to understand the situation! We don't allow animals on board! Those are the regulations. Please, Herr Kafanke, there are a lot of people in line behind you and they are in a hurry."

The man from Dresden looked back and saw the people waiting in line behind him, looked at them humbly and bowed low like a Russian postmaster faced with a Tsarist general. "Please forgive me, ladies and gentlemen, and don't be angry. It's about our cat. Please excuse the delay."

Nobody said a word, a few nodded.

"Attention, please! Passenger Thompson, repeat, passenger Thompson, with PAA to New York. Please come to the ticket counter. There is a message for you." Meanwhile the man whose name was Kafanke was saying, "It's murder if you don' let me take the cat, Herr Klar. Don't you understand? Murder!"

"Please, Herr Kafanke!"

"What's to become of the animal?"

"Cats can look after themselves very well. They always find their way home."

"Home? To Dresden?" Refugee Kafanke's eyes were brimming with tears of rage. "Through the Brandenburg Gate perhaps?"

"Herr Kafanke, please!" Beads of perspiration were forming on employee Klar's forehead.

"So this is why we fled, Mother." Kafanke addressed a fat woman sitting on a suitcase to one side. "For this we left home."

"Won't they let Mitzi come with us?"

I gave employee Klar a sign. "Just a moment," he told Herr Kafanke, and turned to me. "Where are you flying to, sir?"

"But listen, please," Kafanke protested weakly, then was abruptly silent, stroking his reddish-brown cat. "My beauty, my pretty one, don't be afraid. We won't abandon you. Even if I have to talk to an American general!"

"Calling passenger Thompson! Passenger Thompson! Please come to the PAA ticket counter!"

The cat mewed softly.

"I'm flying to Rio," I told Herr Klar. "With Pan Air do Brasil." The Brazilian airline didn't have an office in Berlin. Pan Am took care of their business. I laid my ticket on the counter.

Employee Klar looked at the red-brown cat bitterly, wiped the perspiration off his forehead and found the right list. "Herr Paul Holland?"

"Yes."

"Where do you reside, Herr Holland?"

I hesitated. It was a question that I always found awkward. I lived in many places, in many cities, but I wasn't really at home anywhere. "Frankfurt am Main," I replied. "Parkstrasse 12." Parkstrasse 12 was the Astoria Hotel, where I had a room the year round. A picture of Sibyl hung in it. It also had a closet with my underwear and suits in it, a few books and a lot of old manuscripts. It contained everything I possessed in the world and that wasn't much.

"Why are you flying to Rio?" asked Herr Klar.

"That's on my entry permit," I said curtly, furious with Herr Klar but really furious with myself, with the way I lived.

"Your permit says 'on business.'" Herr Klar wasn't friendly anymore. "What is your business?"

"I'm a correspondent for the Western Press Agency," I told him, while Sibyl's soft hand, stroking mine, was trying to calm me down. "We are putting new people in our Rio office. I know Rio very well; the new employees don't. I'm to make the start easier for them."

"Thank you, Herr Holland." Now he was formal. Sibyl smiled at him. He said, "I'm only doing my duty, *gnädige Frau*."

"Herr Holland didn't mean to offend you."

"All of us are nervous," said Herr Klar.

The cat meowed.

"Attention, please! British European Airways Flight 452 from Düsseldorf is arriving . . ."

"And now may I see your immunization card please, Herr Holland?"

I gave him the card. I had had to be inoculated for this flight. There were two places on my arm that still hurt from the injections.

"Thank you, Herr Holland. And your medical report."

I gave it to him. It informed whomever it might concern that I did not have tuberculosis, Egyptian eye disease, leprosy, or syphilis. Then I gave him the paper I had signed with the assurance that I would not join any movement in Brazil that was agitating against the existing government, nor would I beg on the streets or in any way become a public burden.

"Thank you, Herr Holland. Is that all the luggage you have?"

"Yes."

"You have time. We'll call your flight."

I took my typewriter, nodded to him, and tried to make a path for Sibyl and myself through the crowd around us. "Excuse me," I said to Herr Kafanke. He looked at me with tired, discouraged eyes. "You are a reporter, sir. I heard you say so. Couldn't you do something for my cat?"

I looked at all the people waiting in the lobby and again saw the children in Seoul, the old men in Saigon, the hysterical women on the island of Quemoy tearing open their blouses to show their willingness to do anything to be taken along, to get away. . . .

"I can't help anybody," I said softly, and clung to Sibyl's arm as if it were the only thing I had to cling to.

5

In the airport restaurant the waiters greeted us like old friends. I had been there often with Sibyl. They could always read on our faces whether I was leaving or had just arrived.

The restaurant was almost empty. We could look through the big dark windows at the waiting planes being fueled in the gray dawn. That morning it didn't seem to want to grow light. I sat down on Sibyl's left. She didn't hear well with her right ear. An old man had struck her on the street when she was twelve and had damaged her eardrum.

"Coffee, sir?"

"Mocha," I said.

"Yes, sir." The waiter smiled. Whenever I went I tipped too lavishly.

"A melange for me," said Sibyl.

"Yes, *gnädige Frau*." He left us.

Behind us another waiter was spreading a fresh cloth on the table, and outside they were fueling the Super Constellation of Pan Air do Brasil, on which I was flying.

"You've got to get out of Berlin," I said. There wasn't much time left. I wanted to talk about practical matters. The business with the cat had been the last straw.

"Where do you want me to go, darling?" Her hand was on mine; her hand was always on mine, wherever we sat.

"You're coming to me, to the West."

"To Frankfurt?"

"Yes. I have enough money. We'll take an apartment." I was getting all excited. "Anything can happen here any day. What are going to do if there's another blockade? If there are no more planes going back and forth? If I can't get to you?"

"Dearest," she said softly. "We've talked this over so often. I can't just take off and leave my work and my friends, my whole small world here, and join you in Frankfurt and live there as your mistress."

"Attention, please! Calling passengers Collins, Crawford, Hitchcock, and Ribbon with Air France to Stuttgart! Your aircraft is about to take off! This is your last call!"

I said, "Would you marry me, Sibyl?"

Of course the waiter had to come just then, with our coffee. Sibyl was clinging to my hand, tears in her eyes. "Answer me. Please, Sibyl, answer me." I didn't have much time left. They'd be calling my plane any minute."

She said hoarsely, "It's because of the cat."

"No!"

"Or because you don't feel at home anywhere. Because you don't have a home anywhere."

"No." I leaned forward and kissed her hand. "It's because I love you, because I want to be with you always, and because I'm so afraid of losing you."

I said, "We've known each other long enough, a whole year. I don't want any other woman. Do you want another man?"

She shook her head.

"We'll take an apartment. We'll use your furniture and your books." I was talking fast now. "I have a few books, too. Everybody in Frankfurt will love you. It's a good city. You'll like it there. And I'm going to write that book this year, I swear I am. If you're with me. I can write it. And then we'll buy a little house outside the city, or we'll build one. And just think, Sibyl, we'll be together all the time. We'll sleep together and wake up together. We won't have to send each other any more telegrams, or phone."

"But I can't have any children," she said in a whisper I could scarcely hear, and she took a sip of her coffee.

"I don't want any children."

She looked at me silently.

"I shouldn't have any children anyway," I said. "I've drunk too much in my life. I'd sire nothing but idiots!" I kissed her hand again.

Time was running out, I could feel it hanging over me like a threat. "Tell me that you'll marry me when I get back."

She nodded. Now the tears were streaming down her cheeks, into her mouth. She licked them away with her tongue and threw her arms around me. The waiter who was setting the table behind us turned away discreetly. "I know it's only because of the cat," she whispered.

"It's not!"

"But I don't care. Yes, I want to marry you, Paul. And we'll be so happy."

"It won't be long now, darling," I said, and kissed her. To hell with the waiter!

"When you're married to me, you won't be able to get rid of me so fast, like the bar girls you sleep with."

"I know that."

"I'll never leave you," she whispered in my ear. "Never!"

And I was thinking: can the love of two people be stronger than the intrigues of Mao Tse-tung, Foster Dulles, and Bulganin? Was there any hope of happiness in this century? Was there such justice for cats, mutes, and Jews? *Did* God protect lovers?

6

But now it was 7:00. My plane left at 7:15. As usual I saw Sibyl off, an old superstition of ours. *I* wanted to be the one to see *her* go. I paid and walked with Sibyl through the garishly lit lobby to the exit. The day was finally dawning, slowly, tortuously, a gloomy day. The two women in the tax-free shop that sold reading matter and liquor greeted us politely as we walked past them.

Herr Kafanke from Dresden was still trying frantically to make his point at the PanAm counter. I looked away. Herr Kafanke didn't have much more time. His plane left at 7:30. The cat was sleeping comfortably in her basket.

"And play the Rachmaninoff concerto," I said, as I led Sibyl out the glass door.

"Every evening, my sweet."

"Play it after ten. I'll try to figure out the time difference and be thinking of you."

"But it may be daytime in Brazil and you could be

in the middle of a conference," and that made her laugh like a child.

The snow in the street was dirty and trodden flat. I hailed a taxi. It stopped in front of us, its brakes screeching. The driver was hunchbacked and looked at us suspiciously. "Where do you want to go?"

"Lassenstrasse 119, Grunewald."

I embraced Sibyl. The gigantic radar screen on top of its tower began to revolve above us, silently, eerily, its sound waves seeking far-off planes somewhere above the clouds, calling out to them, accompanying them, invisible sound waves, invisible planes. . . .

"God bless!" I said.

She freed herself abruptly and got into the taxi. The door closed, the driver settled down behind the steering wheel. Sibyl tried to put down the window on her side, but it wouldn't open. The taxi drove off. I saw Sibyl's white little face with the slanting eyes pressed against the icy glass, and I waved.

The taxi drove an almost complete circle around the square. I watched it pass the firehouse and police station and continue in the direction of the Kurfürstendamm. Now Sibyl was looking out of the rear window. As we had embraced and kissed, a few people had stopped to stare at us. They were still staring at me. In France, in similar situations, nobody stares. In Germany they do.

I could see the red taillights of the taxi as the driver stepped on the brake and the right turn signal lit up. The car was nothing now but a small black speck. I couldn't see Sibyl anymore, but she could probably see me, so I waited until the taxi made the right turn and disappeared behind the first house. In the lobby the loudspeaker was announcing, "Pan Air do Brasil Flight 182 to Rio do Janeiro via Düsseldorf, Paris, Lisbon, Dakar, Recife! Taking on passengers at Gate 4."

I had a few minutes left and went over to the flower shop beside the branch post office. The salesgirl knew me. The main shop was on the Kurfürstendamm. I always bought flowers there or here for Sibyl. I said, "My plane leaves in a few minutes. Please send a dozen roses every other day—"

"To Frau Loredo." The young girl was smiling. She knew that I was in love with Sibyl Loredo, everybody in Berlin seemed to know it, and it seemed to make everybody smile.

"Yes, please. Until my return."

"We'll attend to it, Herr Holland."

"I'll pay when I get back."

"Of course, Herr Holland. Have a pleasant trip."

"Thanks."

Just outside the door I bumped into Herr Kafanke. I wanted to hurry on but he clutched my sleeve. There was a look of crazy determination in his eyes. "You've got to help me, sir."

"Please let go! I'm in a hurry!"

"You're flying via Düsseldorf, aren't you?" he gasped, the basket with the fat cat swaying on his arm. "I get there fifteen minutes before you do. I asked." He was still clinging to me. "You have an hour in Düsseldorf. Take the cat under your coat. Nobody will notice."

"No!"

"Please, sir. Please! They'll be watching me now,

but nobody's going to notice you. We left the East," he cried, "because they told us in the West there was freedom! But what kind of freedom is it if they won't let me look after an innocent animal?"

"Herr Paul Holland! Herr Paul Holland! Please come immediately to the passport counter. Your plane is waiting!"

"Give it to me," I said.

His pale face glowed. He lifted the fat cat out of its basket. I unbuttoned my coat. "God will reward you," he said, as he tucked the animal under my left sleeve in a way that enabled me to hold it from the outside. It really was a good cat. It didn't object to anything. For a moment I wondered if it was still alive! I said, "I'll be waiting for you in Düsseldorf, in the restaurant."

He watched me as I walked away, his hands folded. He was praying for his cat.

The clerk at the passport counter stamped my passport. I hurried to Gate 4. The glass door was open. I could see my plane waiting on the tarmac outside. A stewardess was standing at the top of the stairs. When she saw me, she waved me to hurry. I couldn't wave back because I had the typewriter under one arm and the cat under the other. Just as I reached the door, a man stepped out of the shadows—Herr Klar, with the balding head.

"Give me the cat," he said softly.

"What are you talking about?" I tried to hurry past him but he blocked my path. "Let me pass! Don't you see, my plane's waiting." My stump was beginning to hurt again.

"The cat, Herr Holland."

"I don't have a cat."

"Under your coat."

I stared at him, he stared back at me, expressionlessly. "I'm only doing my duty, Herr Holland. No animals are allowed on the refugee transports."

I opened my coat, he took the cat. In his arms it began to purr. He said, "I didn't invent the Iron Curtain."

7

There were only seven of us on the huge plane. A few more passengers would get on in Paris and Dakar, the stewardess told me, but the flight was by no means full. Seven passengers and a crew of nine. I kept on my coat and put my seat back. The stewardess brought me a blanket and arranged the seat in front of me so that I could stretch out my legs. I fell asleep before takeoff. I was scarcely aware of our arrival in Düsseldorf. When I finally woke up, it was midday and we were circling over Paris.

In Lisbon it was very warm. In the restaurant a man tried to sell me some hideous dolls in Schwarzwald costumes. I wrote Sibyl a postcard and bought a bottle of whiskey, because all you could get on the plane was Brazilian cognac, which I found too sweet. Then I sat down on a bench outdoors and looked at the green mountains. There were a lot of flowers in bloom and the women were wearing colorful summer dresses.

A new crew took over the plane. Right after takeoff, we were served a meal. It seemed as if we were being served some kind of meal constantly. When we were flying over the Straits of Gibraltar, the captain asked me to join him in the cockpit. I had flown with him several times. He was a big Portuguese with short black hair and he laughed a lot. His name was Pedro Alvarez. His copilot stretched out for a nap, and I took his seat beside Alvarez. We smoked and drank coffee while the African coastline became visible below us. It was a beautiful day, sunshine, a cloudless blue sky. Alvarez didn't speak a word of German, but fluent English. He lived in Rio. Happily married. His wife was pregnant again. Did I remember how he'd told me what tiny breasts she had? I remembered. Well, now they were swelling and getting big and hard, her stomach, too. Alvarez found all this very exciting.

It was a seven-hour flight from Lisbon to Dakar. I wrote a few letters, slept some more, and when it began to get dark, I drank whiskey. We were flying too high to recognize anything below us, but I watched the light change and the hills of Africa, green at first, grow brown, then violet, and saw the color of the sea change as the sun below us went down. We reached Dakar at midnight and set our watches back five hours. Alvarez gave me a sleeping pill when we took off again and the stewardess dimmed the lights in the cabin. It took us five hours to cross the Atlantic.

In Recife the palms were swaying in a morning breeze and I could see orchids in the trees. The moment the engines stopped and the air conditioning quit, we began to sweat. We were not allowed to leave the plane. A huge Negro in police uniform came in and sprayed a caustic liquid out of an aerosol bomb on us one by one, a germ and insect killer that almost choked us. Then we were allowed to get off the plane. I took a bath and shaved. In the waiting room I saw a friend from the Associated Press who was on his way to Madrid. His plane was having engine trouble. He'd been waiting in Recife for eleven hours. I gave him what was left of my whiskey.

From Recife to Rio took another seven hours. We were served an enormous breakfast. Six English farmers and a few blacks had boarded the plane. An old Negress read my palm. She prophesied me a lot of money and a blond woman who would give me three children.

We flew over a river bed. An hour before Rio the sugar plantations became visible, vast red-brown acres in the dark green of the jungle. The river looked muddy. Punctually at 12:00 Brazilian time, we landed in the international airport of the city that is supposed to be the most beautiful in the world. I went at once to the post office and sent Sibyl a telegram that I had arrived safely and that I loved her. This was February 2, at midday.

8

I spent eight days in Rio. I checked in at the Miramar Hotel on the Avenida Atlantica, where I had stayed twice before. The Copacabana beach was situated on the other side of the avenida. When it was windy, a little cool spray from the ocean penetrated my bedroom. The weather remained beautiful.

I introduced my colleagues—three pleasant gentlemen—to the Brazilian authorities and took them to see our diplomatic representatives. The press attachés knew me and seemed happy to do whatever they could for the new man from WPA. Our offices were in the Rua de Misericordia 213, in a skyscraper that had been built recently with the same error of construction as all skyscrapers in Rio: namely, when it was very hot the water didn't reach the top floors. Sometimes there was no water at all and one had to shave with the contents of a soda bottle.

In the afternoon we drove to the Jockey Club for tea, or my colleagues went down to the beach to swim and sunbathe. I showed them whatever I thought would interest them: the cafés, the bars—Venus and Circe—the Shelton and Ritz restaurants, the golf course, the football stadium, the Holy Virgin Church, and the bordello on the Avenida Presidente Antonio Carlos. In the evening we were always invited somewhere.

We met a lot of important people. Toward the end of my stay, Senator Carioca Darcas gave a reception for us. The senator was one of the most powerful men in the city with political influence everywhere. He had married a very ugly but extremely wealthy heiress. Senhora Darcas had a huge dog. It was generally known in Rio that the Darcases had separate bedrooms. Senhora Darcas and the dog slept in the big double bed, Senhor Darcas by himself next door.

On my last day I rented a car and drove my three colleagues up Corcovado, the mountain with the famous statue of Jesus on top. I knew that there was a restaurant halfway up, in the forest, and I invited my guests to lunch there. A pleasant meal. We drank beer and sugar schnapps, and tame parrots in the bushes watched us. Then we went for a walk in the woods.

There were a lot of small caves and niches, and I showed my friends the many macumbas. Although the macumba is a native superstition, I know quite a few Europeans who make their own, mainly women. They are a protection against the spirits that live in the jungles of Corcovado, spirits that could harm human beings if they wanted to. To placate them, one offers them cigarettes and sugar schnapps. In the niches we saw little schnapps bottles, considerately opened, with cigarettes lying beside them, even matches to light

them. We had brought along a few little bottles ourselves to please the invisible spirits. It was the custom
to make a wish at the same time.

I wished that Sibyl and I might stay together, that
we should continue to love each other, and that no
misfortune should befall either of us. I prayed to the
gods of the jungle, not to the Christian god of Bethle-
hem. And I didn't care which one of them heard me, if
only he was able to protect Sibyl and me, and our love.

9

On the flight back, the plane was full. A famous
football team was flying to Zürich. I had cabled my office in Frankfurt that I had completed my assignment
and wanted to take a few days off in Berlin, to which
they had agreed. This time we flew from Lisbon to
Berlin via Madrid-Rome-Zürich-Düsseldorf. In Rome I
sent Sibyl a telegram in which I told her I would be arriving that afternoon. This was at 8:00 A.M. on February 12, 1956. The plane was on time, 4:30 P.M. at
Tempelhof-Berlin. From Zürich on it had been practically empty.

I felt cold, although I was wearing my winter coat again. On the plane I had taken Vasanthron to prevent a possible attack of diarrhea. Every time I came back to Europe after a stay in a hot climate, I suffered from dysentery.

The moment I stepped out of the plane, I had a feeling something was wrong. I walked through the heavy rain that had washed away all the snow, to the stairs that led up to the main building, with its galleries on either side, where Sibyl always waited for me when I arrived in Berlin. Today I couldn't see her. What could have detained her?

As I passed through passport control and customs I tried to reassure myself—Sibyl was late, probably caught in a traffic jam. But I really didn't believe any of it. I became increasingly anxious but tried to control myself and waited. Though Sibyl didn't come, my luggage did. A porter carried it to a taxi for me. I told the driver to wait while I walked through the entire building, looking for Sibyl—the lobby, the restaurant, the post office. No sign of her.

I went to the telphone booth and dialed her number. It rang and rang. The sound of the unanswered ring became unbearable. I hung up and went back to the taxi. "Lassenstrasse 119."

The car drove off. Suddenly I was so cold, my teeth chattered. "What's the matter?" The driver turned around to look at me.

"Nothing."

I was thinking: perhaps she didn't get my telegram. Or she stayed at a friend's house and hasn't been home yet. "Please drive faster!"

"Faster!" The driver was a man who talked with his hands. "The gentlemen are always in a hurry. And if something happens, whose fault is it? Always ours!"

"All right, all right," I said.

I had a key to Sibyl's apartment. "Please wait," I told the driver when he stopped in front of the gate. He didn't reply. I hurried in the rain across the gravel path. Not a soul in sight. As I opened the front door I called out, "Sibyl!"

No answer.

I took the stairs to her apartment as fast as I could. "Sibyl!"

Silence.

I unlocked the door to her apartment—that is, I tried to unlock it, but the key wouldn't turn. My heart began to beat fast when I saw why it wouldn't turn. The door wasn't locked!

I pushed it open and ran into the dimly lit foyer. The first thing I saw was six vases of roses, the roses that had been sent to Sibyl at my order. They stood on the floor. The little hallway was filled with their scent. Although I was still cold, I began to sweat. "Sibyl!" I shouted for a third time.

No sound. Nothing moved. Only the rain drummed monotonously against the windows.

I ran into the living room. It was empty. I looked into the kitchen. Nobody there. I wanted to go to the bedroom next, for which I had to go back into the foyer. The door was still open, but now a man was leaning against it, a short man with short brown hair. He was wearing knickerbockers and a sports jacket.

"Are you Herr Holland?" asked the man.

"Yes," I stammered.

"I've been waiting for you," he said. "I've been waiting for three days."

"Who are you?"

"My name is Albers." He showed me his identification. "Walter Albers from homicide."

"Homicide?" I repeated over the roar of an approaching plane.

"May I see your passport, please?" said Police Officer Walter Albers, stretching out his hand. My passport. In Germany the first thing they always wanted was your passport. The drumming of the rain was now drowned out by the roar of the plane which had almost reached the house.

"Where is Frau Loredo?" I yelled.

"She has disappeared," he answered coldly.

The panes rattled, the plane streaked over the treetops in the park, the scent of the roses was stupefying. Then the noise faded, I could hear the rain again, steady and hopeless now. Police Officer Albers added, "We think she has been kidnapped."

10

He spoke with constant spasms of hesitation which any listener would have found irritating. At every s sound he paused as if he had to swallow something, and every time he did, his jaw moved as if he were chewing. "Your passport," he said again, with a pause after the s's.

I handed him my passport and he examined it carefully. "You've come from Rio?"

"For God's sake, Herr Albers, act human! Tell me what happened! What do you mean, she was kidnapped?"

"There was a struggle in the apartment and shots were fired."

"Who shot?"

"We don't know."

"When did this happen?"

"Three days ago. Toward evening. About six-thirty."

"How do you know?"

"The girl gave us the information." He gestured in the direction of the super's apartment. "The superintendant's daughter, Maria. She heard the shots. Then she heard Frau Loredo screaming for help. She ran to the apartment, and when she saw the destruction in the bedroom she ran for her father. And her father called us."

"And?"

"Nothing. Frau Loredo had disappeared."

"But the shots? Do you think she was shot?" Everything was beginning to revolve around me. I felt sick.

"It's possible. There was blood on the carpet in the bedroom, Herr Holland. But that doesn't tell us very much. Perhaps she was only wounded before she was dragged away," he added helpfully.

There was a buzzing sound in my ears. The roses smelled rotten, fermented, sickly sweet. I couldn't breathe. I went to the bathroom and vomited. Then I washed out my mouth and my face with cold water.

Under the mirror I saw my comb, my shaving cream, my toothbrush. Only Sibyl was gone. They had found blood on the carpet in her bedroom. . . .

I cleaned my teeth, rinsed my mouth and rubbed eau de cologne on my forehead. As I went back to Albers, I was afraid my knees might give way.

Albers had gone into the bedroom, which looked as if an earthquake had struck it. The bed was a shambles: a small table and all the chairs had been toppled. The bed lamp lay shattered on the floor. Albers was staring down at the shards. Because I felt weak, I wanted to sit on the disheveled bed but hesitated for a moment. "Is it all right?"

He nodded. "Everything's been photographed. The people from the crime lab were here, too."

"And?"

"Nothing. No clues. A lot of fingerprints. Frau Loredo's. Probably yours, too."

"Probably."

"Did she have a cleaning woman?"

"Once a week."

"Well, as I said, a lot of fingerprints."

I stared down at the bed. There was a faint trace of her perfume, of the scent of her body. I could smell Sibyl. I got up quickly and walked to the other side of the room.

Albers was watching me. "By the way," he said, "I called the superintendent just now"—he hesitated tactfully—"while you were in the bathroom. He's coming over. With his daughter."

"Why?"

"I want him to tell you what happened. It should interest you. The man said you and Frau Loredo were friends."

"We were going to get married."

"Horrible business." The last word almost choked him.

"Do you have a cold?"

"No. Why?"

"You seem to have difficulty speaking."

"I've got new dentures. I only got them a week ago. You have no idea how much they hurt. I can't eat a thing. Only liquids." He went on bitterly, "And in this condition I have to do patrol work. No consideration. No consideration for their fellow men." He collected saliva in his mouth and swallowed visibly. "You have no idea how much they hurt."

I thought: Sibyl has disappeared. Somebody has taken her away from me, although I made a macumba. Although I have prayed to every god there could possibly be, in none of whom I believe. But I believed in Sibyl. I found in her what other people find in religion or a political doctrine. A magician's assistant doesn't believe in his master's tricks, but he may believe in his master. And everything had gone so smoothly, I had thought all would go well for us. My eyes fell on a dark spot on the carpet. "Is that the blood?"

Albers nodded. "It's been examined. "It *could* be her blood. It's always the same in these kidnapping cases. A revolver, or chloroform, or a blow on the head." I was staring at him. "I'm sorry," he said, "but one gets accustomed to things like this." He touched his jaw gingerly, full of self-pity. Outside I could hear steps, then the super's voice, calling for Albers, who cried out, "Here!"

Superintendent Wagner came into the bedroom with his mute daughter. Her eyes were downcast as she curtsied. She didn't look at me, she didn't look at anybody. "How do you do, Herr Holland," said Wagner. He had thrown a loden coat across his shoulders. "I'm terribly sorry," he said, and it sounded sincere.

There he was with his condolences, as if were already established that Sibyl had not only disappeared but was already dead, as if there could be no doubt anymore that she was no longer alive. I said weakly, "Hello, Maria."

The girl emitted a barking sound. Albers said, "I shall now tell Herr Holland what you wrote down for us, and when what I am telling him is correct, you'll nod your head. All right?"

Maria nodded. She was wearing a pink and green faded pullover and a blue jumper. She had outgrown both. Her little breasts stretched the stitches of her pullover. She stood there, shoulders hunched, and was ashamed of her body. Her long, gangly legs were bare above the knees. She had on rolled-down silk stockings and worn-out sandals. For just a moment she lifted her head and looked at me. Her eyes were shifty, with dark circles underneath them; her face was ashen.

"You often came to see Frau Loredo, didn't you, mostly in the afternoon?"

The child's pretty mouth with its paralyzed throat tried to form words, gave up, and answered with a nod. Yes. Sibyl had read aloud to her, played records for her. Maria was very fond of Sibyl.

Albers went on talking, letting Maria nod her assent after every statement. According to his account, Maria had been playing on the frozen pond late in the afternoon of February 9. Suddenly, she had heard three shots. "Is that right, Maria?"

"Ar—arr—arrhh!"

It was right.

The shots had been followed by screams in a woman's voice. Maria recognized the voice at once—it was the voice of her beloved Frau Loredo. She ran as fast as she could across the ice to the house. The door to Sibyl's apartment was open. Maria made straight for the bedroom. It was empty. Sibyl was gone. "Is that right, Maria?"

The girl let out a tortured cry and suddenly clung to

me. She went on screaming convulsively and nodding her head. Such pain, such misery, and no way of expressing it in words!

Wagner said quietly, "Well . . . and then she came and got me, Herr Holland. I was sure at once, the minute I saw the bedroom, that Frau Loredo had been kidnapped."

"Why did you think so right away?"

"I used to live near the Potsdamer Platz. There was a kidnapping in our house one day, a man called Lebrecht. It happened just the same way. Screams, shots, and blood on the staircase." He was lost in the memory. "But they shot Lebrecht right away." He nodded, horrified in retrospect. "Yes, yes . . . dear God . . . yes. . . ."

"And there was no one in sight? What did you do?"

"I locked the door and ran to the police station."

"Why didn't you use the phone?"

The superintendent looked at Albers.

"What's the matter?" I asked.

"Herr Wagner couldn't use the phone. It had been torn out of the wall."

"But only an hour ago—" I began, but Albers interrupted me. "The connection was restored yesterday."

They had an answer for everything. Sibyl had disappeared, whatever I asked; Sibyl had been kidnapped, they kept coming up with more proof. They seemed to have come to some sort of agreement about it all.

"I ran to the Bismarckplatz station," Wagner was saying. "That's very near, as you know, Herr Holland. First to Johannesplatz, then around the corner on Casper-Theyss Strasse and—"

"For God's sake, man, I know where the station is! Go on!"

"Two officers ran back with me, Herr Holland."

A noise startled me. Maria was crying. Her crying was worse than her screams. "Please," I said, "please, Maria, stop crying!"

I was reminded of a story I had read once about a mute whom a tyrant had tortured until he screamed. What man had that been? What tyrant? I couldn't remember. Perhaps I had only dreamed it or seen something like it on the stage.

I said, "But this—all this simply isn't possible! Who could have wanted to kidnap Frau Loredo?"

"That's what we're asking you," said Albers.

"But I have no idea!" I cried. "Why are you looking at me like that? You don't think I had anything to do with it?"

"We are in Berlin, Herr Holland," said Albers. "Things like this happen here all the time. Of course we haven't got to the bottom of it yet, but we will." He said this as if to himself, solemnly.

"There was blood on the staircase," said Wagner. He seemed to like the word *blood*; he said it with feeling.

"On the wall," said Albers.

"And you haven't found a clue?"

"We were waiting for you, Herr Holland. We hoped you could help us."

There was a noise outside. A man's voice cried out, "I'd like to know how much longer I'm supposed to wait!" The taxi driver. I had forgotten all about him. "Bring up my things!" I called down to him.

"If it's all right with you," said Albers, "we could take the taxi to the police station."

"Why?"

"The chief wants to speak to you. We were to take you to him as soon as you turned up."

So we left Sibyl's apartment after the driver, grumbling, had brought up my suitcase and typewriter. I walked along the gravel path in the rain, as I had walked so often with Sibyl. The keys to her apartment jingled in my coat pocket. It was growing dark slowly under a low cloud ceiling. Somewhere above the clouds a plane was heading toward the divided city of Berlin. I could hear the roar of its engines.

11

A bright desk lamp burned on Chief Hellwig's desk in the Berlin-Grunewald police station. His office was on the second floor of a red-brick building and was furnished simply. The windows looked out on a wildly overgrown garden. Officer Albers wasn't present during the interview, only a man who took down what I was saying.

"How long have you known Frau Loredo?"

"About a year ago. No. A little longer. I met her for the first time a year ago last November."

"Where?"

Hellwig was a man of about 60, calm, formal, with gray hair, and he was wearing tortoiseshell glasses that made him look like a scholar. He smoked a pipe. I got the feeling that the pipe helped him to give the impression that he was in complete control. He reminded me of a night reporter I had worked with once, a man whom nothing could ruffle because in the course of his hardworking life he had arrived at the conclusion that everyone on this earth was despicable, with one exception, and that was his fat old wife. For her he would have done anything, any meanness, any betrayal. I had always admired him. I had tried to be like him, without success.

I told Chief Hellwig, "I met Frau Loredo in the Maison de France, at a press reception held by the French colony."

Hellwig sucked on his pipe. I was pretty sure he was happily married and that he had a cozy little apartment somewhere in Grunewald where his white-haired wife was waiting for him. They were old, all passion spent, only love remained, true love. I was sure that they ate well and drank good wine together and that he was affectionate with her. Suddenly I realized I was crying.

The stenographer leaned discreetly over his pad. He was pale and thin. There was a long silence. The rain was beating against the window and melting the snow in the garden. As it had when I left for Rio, my stump was hurting. Meanwhile it had grown dark, and I was afraid of the night that lay ahead.

"But you weren't with Frau Loredo all the time?"

"No. I'm a reporter. My office sends me out on assignments. I had to leave Berlin frequently, but whenever I could, I came back. I'd say I spent half the year in Berlin."

"And you were going to get married?"

"I loved Frau Loredo," I said, and my voice sounded strange to me. How could I express what I really felt?

"It's hard for you," he said, and his glasses glittered in the strong light. "It's not easy to find a truly compatible partner, is it?" It didn't sound sincere; his tone was all wrong. Was he probing for a reaction from me? Evidently he was, because he went on. "Do you consider it possible that Frau Loredo was working for a foreign news agency?"

"Are you crazy!"

"Just a question, Herr Holland. Or perhaps for a spy organization in Germany,"

I was puzzled at the question until I understood. "You're asking that," I said, "because you've found out that newsmen from the East came to her apartment sometimes. Am I right?"

His face remained expressionless but he nodded.

"Well, I can clear you up on that," I said, pleased with my intuition. "They came to see *me*."

"Is that the truth, Herr Holland?"

"It certainly is," I said. "Every news agency of any importance has its contacts in the East. There is nothing unusual about mine. Frau Loredo had nothing whatsoever to do with them."

"It was only a conjecture." He sighed as if he were sorry for me. "Then I'll have to rephrase my question. What do you know about the woman you intended to marry?"

"I don't know what you mean!"

"Herr Holland—a crime has been committed. We are looking for the perpetrator. We are looking for a motive. We haven't found one, but there must be a motive, don't you agree?"

"Of course."

"So . . . would you please answer my question?"

I had been trying to think of an answer to the question and had come to the embarrassing conclusion that I really knew very little about the woman I had chosen to play an important role in my life. I had wanted to have someone to believe in because I had come to the conclusion that one had to believe in someone or something if one was to survive, and now . . .

But did one have to know all about a woman to love her? Did one have to hear her talk in her sleep to know she was faithful? Did one have to be her master to believe in her? Whose concern was it except mine whom I loved and what I believed in?

I said, "I know the essential things. Frau Loredo was single, born in Munich, lived for a long time in foreign countries, had no children. . . ."

"What did she live on?"

"She taught languages. Private tuition."

"And she was able to live on *that*?"

"Occasionally I gave her money."

"Large amounts, Herr Holland?"

"Yes. No. Yes. . . ."

"Did you know any of her pupils?"

"She used to talk about them."

"Do you know any of their names? Their addresses?"

"Of course not."

He leaned back, cleaned his pipe and said sadly, "Not even their names?"

"I know a few names, Chief Hellwig. They were mostly women. I believe Sibyl had a lot of friends who wanted to learn Italian and French, well-to-do people. . . ."

"You *believe* she had friends?"

I leaned forward. My shirt was wet with perspiration. When I moved it stuck to my body clammily. "Chief Hellwig," I said, "don't talk to me like that. I did not kidnap Frau Loredo. I loved her. This—this is a ghastly evening for me. You talk as if Frau Loredo had committed a crime, but as far as I can see, a crime was committed against Frau Loredo."

He waited until the plane that had been flying over the building while I had spoken had flown on, then he said softly, "We are looking for the truth, Herr Holland. That is our profession, just as it is yours."

"I don't seek the truth."

"You mean to say you don't care if the stories you write are true or not?"

"Of course not, as long as they're good stories."

"You can't mean that! Are you a Catholic, Herr Holland?"

"Yes," I said, "but let's not go into that! What business is it of yours?"

He looked at me silently, then he handed me a sheet of paper. "Here are the names and addresses of all Frau Loredo's pupils. Tell me how many you recognize."

I looked at the list. There were twenty-four names. "About ten," I lied. I knew five, and I had never set eyes on any of them. I think he knew I was lying.

"And here," said Hellwig, handing me a second sheet, "are the names of friends and acquaintances, all that we could find."

This second list was longer. It included about fifty names, among them actors, painters and writers, also a few journalists.

"How did you get this list?"

"For the most part the persons mentioned contacted us, we found the rest. Do you think that among these people there could be anyone who would have a motive in kidnapping Frau Loredo?"

"I don't know!"

"Are you—I'm sorry to have to ask this, but are you aware of any men friends, any affairs Frau Loredo might have had?"

"She told me about all her affairs." Suddenly I was furious. He was talking about the woman I loved, in whom I believed. "When she and I fell in love, she stopped seeing her other men friends, but she made sure there were no hard feelings."

"Yes," he said. "We've found that out in the meantime, too. And you know what that means, Herr Holland?"

"It means there is no motive."

"Exactly, Herr Holland."

It was 6:58. The plane approaching now was the PAA plane from Frankfurt, arriving at 7:00 P.M. I had arrived often on that plane while Sibyl had been there, and she had always met me at the airport. First we had gone to Robert's for a schnapps, after that we had dined there, then we had driven home to Sibyl's apartment. And we had been happy to be reunited, as if it had been the first time. When I fell asleep toward morning with her in my arms, I had felt as if I had been to confession and received absolution for my sins. I had felt so secure with Sibyl, so at home. . . .

"You may come back tomorrow morning," said Hellwig, "and sign your statement. I take it you'll be staying in Berlin a few days?"

I nodded. I was still disoriented.

"And there's one more thing, Herr Holland."

"What?"

He looked at me for a long time, then he came closer and I could smell the tobacco on his breath. "We found no documents in her apartment. Her passport, ID card—everything was missing."

"And nothing else was taken?"

"Nothing."

"And what happens now?"

"I'm afraid nothing much will happen very soon, Herr Holland. If Frau Loredo has been kidnapped, then she has left our jurisdiction."

He shrugged again. "We can try to find the perpetrators, if they are still in Berlin. Needless to say we'll do our best, however . . ." Then both of us were silent.

Before leaving I asked, "Are you married, Herr Hellwig?"

"I knew you were going to ask that," he said quietly. "My wife died a year ago. We were very happy."

"For how long?"

"Forty-one years."

I don't know how a boxer feels who has just been hit below the belt, but I used to play football, and I was kicked once, hard, in the genitals. They carried me off the field and I felt as if my guts were spilling out, and I couldn't walk for three days. I thought of this most humiliating experience of my life as I left the Grunewald police station. I had promised not to leave the city without leaving an address. I had said I wanted to stay in Sibyl's apartment, although I had perhaps decided that a little too hastily. As I staggered along Bismarckstrasse, which was still wet in spots with snow and ice, I felt as if I had just been kicked in the balls. I managed to reach the first icy bench in Johannesplatz, and sat down.

"Look, *Mammi*," said a little girl. She was wearing fur boots and her mother was pulling her along. "Come, pet. The man is drunk."

That brought me to my feet again, and I walked on painfully. A light fog had rolled in with the darkness and the streetlights were framed in a soft mist. As I walked up the stairs I asked myself what I should do with the apartment, with the furniture and books, with Sibyl's clothes. To whom did it all belong now? According to my knowledge, she had no living relatives, but, I thought bitterly, what did I really know about her?

By the dim light on the staircase I could see a dark spot on the wall, just above the banister. It was long and smeared. Somebody, probably the police photographer, had circled it with chalk. So it was blood. Only three days ago it had coursed through the veins of a beautiful woman, through a body that was soft and warm, alive and desirable. Now it was smeared on a dirty wall. Sibyl had disappeared. Perhaps she was dead. Three days ago I had still been on the other side of the earth, sipping gin and tonic on the terrace of the Miramar Hotel. I shook again with cold.

A note was affixed to the door of Sibyl's apartment with a thumbtack. It read, "I forgot to tell you that they're coming to collect for the electricity tomorrow. Respectfully, Emil Wagner."

The apartment was overheated because the windows had been closed for such a long time. I couldn't stand the scent of the roses. I opened the door to the terrace and threw them out. They lay there, bright red on the white snow, with the rain falling on them. I looked for some whiskey.

There was a bottle in the refrigerator. The refrigerator was working. Sibyl had regulated it. She liked to fiddle around with the thermostat, it amused her. I corrected myself. She *had* liked to fiddle around with the thermostat, it *had* amused her. . . .

There was food in the refrigerator—vegetables, meat, soda water, beer. I mixed myself a strong drink and went into the living room with my glass. The record player was open. There was a record on the turntable. Rachmaninoff's Piano Concerto No. 2. Like in a bad movie. . . .

I turned on the player and let the record run, but I couldn't stand it for long and turned it off. Now all I could hear was the rain beating against the windows. Letters that hadn't reached Sibyl lay on an old pewter plate. Three days' mail. My telegram from Rome among them. I looked at them. Postcards from England and Austria. "You'll never guess who's with us! Old Peter Joli! We just met him in Piccadilly. . . ." A few bills. According to tailor Adolf Jacobs, Berlin-Wilmersdorf, Athenerstrasse 32a, the gray dress was ready for a second fitting. I drank and wondered what I should say to tailor Adolf Jacobs. What would he do with the gray dress?

What was I to do? I thought for a moment. Mechanically I opened another letter. "My dear Sibyl! Tommy and I are delighted with your letter and we wish you a Happy New Year, too. How wonderful that you are so happy with Paul! We always hoped you would find that kind of happiness. Of course we'll come to Berlin for your wedding. We are *so* curious to meet him. . . ."

I couldn't go on reading. I walked into the bedroom, back into the living room. I paced up and down because I was much too nervous to sit still. Then I pulled myself together and went over to the big wardrobe and opened it. I decided to search the entire apartment, every closet, every drawer, every corner. Perhaps I would find some lead.

Her dresses hung side by side on hangers, her underwear lay neatly folded on the shelves. It smelled of her perfume. I rummaged through piles of lace slips and panties. Nothing. The pockets of her suits. Empty. There they were, side by side, the black and the green suit. I could hear Sibyl say, "What shall I wear? My green suit or the black one?" And I could see her standing in front of me in the cold weak light of our last morning, naked, only her stockings and garter belt on. "Look at me once more so's you don't forget what I look like."

"I'll never forget what you look like. I can close my eyes any time and see your face and your body just the way you are." Oh, dear God, dammit, dammit, dammit. . . .

I found nothing helpful in the wardrobe.

I opened a drawer of the bureau. There were small boxes and folders in it, old drawings, pictures, a photograph album. Strangers were standing beside Sibyl in the pictures. Mostly they were smiling. Sibyl in a bathing suit. Sibyl at the theater. Sibyl in the Bavarian Alps. Old pictures. I found my letters in a Bally shoe box. I read two, then put them away.

A pair of old evening shoes. A fan. Seven dried forget-me-nots. A dirty doll. A little red calendar for 1955. I leafed through it. Beside some of the dates there were a few notes in Sibyl's handwriting. "April 15—red roses." "April 17—letter and carnations." "April 22—letter." "April 24—telegram." I went on. "May 11—orchids and a letter." "May 19—roses." "May 25—roses." "May 27—at last! For a whole week! Am so happy!"

She had noted the arrival of every one of my letters, of every time I had sent flowers. On May 27 I had come to Berlin for a week.

I leafed through the calendar to the end of the year. The entries were concerned only with us. "December

31—Thank you, dear God." She had written that not quite three months ago. I put the calendar back and closed the drawer. Just then the phone rang. It startled me so, I spilled my whiskey.

The phone rang again and again, an inhuman sound in the deathly still apartment.

The phone was in the hall. I walked over to it, then hesitated. Who could it be? The police? Somebody looking for me? But who could be looking for me in Sibyl's apartment? My hand was sweating when I picked up the receiver and said, "Hello?"

A high woman's voice said, "Who is this?"

"This is 87-1348."

"May I speak to Frau Loredo?"

The rain was beating against the glass door that led to the terrace. I could see the roses lying outside, in the snow. I said, "I'm sorry, you can't."

"Isn't she home?"

"No."

"Who's speaking, please?" The voice sounded bright.

"My name is Holland."

"Oh, Herr Holland! How nice to hear your voice! Sibyl has told me so much about you." There was no stopping her. "This is Helga Maas. I'm a very old friend of Sibyl's. She may have mentioned my name. We have known each other for so many years." She spoke very fast and I made no further effort to interrupt her. "You see, Herr Holland, I've just come back from Kitzbühel, with my husband. We were there for the winter sport. It was heavenly! And we met such nice people. I only wanted to say hello. Please tell her I called, and I'll call again tomorrow."

"Yes, *gnädige Frau*, I'll tell her."

"Good night, Herr Holland."

"Good night, *gnädige Frau*."

"And you *must* come and have tea with us, you and Sibyl."

"I'll be happy to, *gnädige Frau*."

By now it was quite clear to me that I couldn't stay there. The telephone could ring again. I called for a taxi and put on my coat. I left all the lights on in the apartment and locked the front door. The taxi was waiting for me when I got downstairs. I drove to Robert's.

12

There was no more snow on the Kurfürstendamm; it had been washed away. The asphalt glistened in the rain. The street and its shops were brilliantly lit, neon signs glowed and gave a false impression of a hectic life and American-type prosperity, but in the side streets it was dark, and the ruins of 1945 rose up starkly in the nocturnal haze.

Very few people were out. The whores stood in house entrances. They wore fur coats and were cold. Some hopped from one foot to the other to keep warm.

When I walked into Robert's bar the man playing the piano nodded and began to play "C'est si bon." He had played the song when I had come here with Sibyl for the first time, and the tune had become a greeting of sorts. The old song had always made us feel sentimental. The piano player had begun to play the tune out of habit, then he realized what he was doing and stopped. As I passed him on the way to the bar he said, "I'm sorry, Herr Holland. I wasn't thinking. . . ."

"It's all right," I said, and shook hands with him. "Go on. I don't mind." He hesitated, then nodded, a little embarrassed, and began with "C'est si bon."

Robert's bar was decorated in red. There were small tables, booths, a dance floor, and a semicircular bar. I sat down in one of its two corners. The lighting was intimate—candles on the tables—the guests were conversing softly, there was no orchestra, only the pianist. That was what Sibyl and I had liked about the place.

There was a new bar girl, a voluptuous platinum blond who showed all her capped teeth when she smiled; her hips swayed when she walked. She was quite young and apparently took her job seriously. "Good evening, sir."

"Good evening. A double whiskey, please."

"Herr Holland!" Robert came across the bar to me. He was stocky and his head was almost completely bald. There were heavy bags under his sensuous eyes and he had a big hooked nose. All this, combined with a mouth that was always friendly, made for one of the kindest faces in the world. He was elegantly dressed, as usual, and smelled of Knize 10 toilet water. He shook my hand. "I've been waiting for you to turn up."

"Good evening, Robert," I said. We addressed each other with *Sie*. Sibyl and he had said *Du* to each other. They had known each other much longer.

Robert Friedman had been forced to emigrate in 1933 and had lived in London until 1946. He had done very well there, but as soon as it had been possible he had returned to the Berlin of 1946, with its cold, starvation, and poverty. He always said that Berlin was the only city he could live in. On Sunday mornings he drove out into the country in his little car, with his dog. He would walk for an hour, then drive back to a tavern in Grunewald where he would meet friends— a couple, a woman and a few bachelors. There they sat between eleven and one, lunching, drinking beer and Steinhäger, and the dog got ground meat. Robert smoked cigarillos and chatted with his friends. They told the latest jokes, exchanged the latest scandal, and discussed anything else that might come up. Robert said these were his best times; for these hours, if for nothing else, he would have come back to Berlin. In exile he had dreamed about these Sunday get-togethers. "Here in Berlin you know where you belong," he said. "You have friends. You aren't a stranger." He lived alone. His wife was dead. She had stayed in Berlin until it was too late because she had felt she couldn't bear to leave the city.

"Herr Holland," Robert mumbled, as he slid onto the barstool beside me. "Nothing has touched me so much since the death of my wife as the disappearance of Sibyl. Tell me, what can I do? I'll do anything to help. Herr Holland, anything!"

The bar girl put my whiskey down in front of me, left us discreetly and began washing dishes at the other end of the bar.

"Who could have done it, Robert? Someone from the East? Who?"

"I don't know. That's what's so terrible."

"Did she have enemies?"

He shook his head.

I downed my drink and gave the bar girl a sign and she poured me another. Robert said, "Bring the bottle over here, Coco, and bring me a glass, too. Don't pay any attention to us. Whatever the gentleman drinks is on the house."

When she had left us and Robert was pouring his drink, I said, "You've known Sibyl longer than I have."

He nodded, his face troubled. "I met her in 1946."

"That's just it, Robert. You know I loved Sibyl. I'm not asking out of jealousy, but I've got to find the bastard who did it. Tell me, what men were there in Sibyl's life, I mean, before me."

He didn't answer. The pianist played "April in Portugal." That had been one of our songs, too. A few couples were dancing, close, in love. We had danced like that.

"Please, Robert."

"Of course there were men," he said. "Sibyl was alone, and she wasn't happy."

"Why?"

"She must have suffered a lot during the war." He took a cigarette from his pack. His fingers were nicotine-stained. "And in 1946 things were wild in Berlin. It affected all of us. Yes, Herr Holland, there were quite a few men, all of them good fellows, though. But after Sibyl met you, there were no more. No one but you."

"Yes, yes, I know. I told you I wasn't jealous."

"Wait a while, Herr Holland."

"What do you mean?"

"Right now all Berlin is talking about it. There are a lot of stories going around. You'll hear them—that there were too many men in Sibyl's life, that she was unstable, things like that."

"That's not going to make any difference; she was faithful to me."

"Yes, Herr Holland. Yes." He was looking at me seriously. "If I didn't love my wife so much, I might even have asked Sibyl to marry me."

"Do you still love your wife, Robert?"

"Of course."

"But she's been dead for years."

"That doesn't make any difference," he said. "In London, yes, there I began to forget a little. But since I've been back in Berlin, Sarah is with me all the time. And I think I'll stay with her. Look how old I am. Why should I start something new?" He was still looking at me. "Herr Holland, *you'll* understand me. I don't think Sibyl was a very typical woman, I mean deep down inside her. In that respect she was a lot like a man, don't you agree?"

"Yes."

"She reacted like a man. And when she went off with a man—I'm speaking now of the time before you—then she did that, too, like a man. She did everything like that—loving, drinking, smoking, thinking. . . ."

"Yes," I said. "Above all, thinking. That's why we were so compatible. Not only because of sex, Robert, but because we always agreed about everything. Sometimes we didn't even have to speak. We would look at each other and know what the other was thinking."

"It was like that with Sarah, too," he said.

"Do you think Sibyl was in some way connected with a news agency?"

"Every third person in Berlin is in some way connected with a news agency, but in her case—no. I don't think so."

"We were going to get married."

"Yes," he said. "I know. Sibyl told me I was going to be one of the witnesses."

We drank. The bar was filling up. I felt a nagging, burning sensation in my stomach and knew what that meant. The Vasanthron hadn't helped. I was in for an attack of diarrhea, I hoped not a bad one. Whiskey usually helped; hopefully it would now.

"Did the police come to see you, Robert?"

"Yes. A nice fellow called Hellwig. He showed me a list of people Sibyl knew. I added a few."

"Any who could have had a motive?"

"Not that I know of. I think they all liked Sibyl."

"But what about those who are speaking badly of her now?"

"Those are people who didn't know Sibyl, strangers, gossips."

I was back to square one. "Who saw her last? Do you happen to know that?"

"Frau Langbein," he said promptly.

"Do you know her?"

"Yes. Very well. Vera Langbein is a good friend of Sibyl's," he sad slowly.

"I must talk to her. Perhaps she can help. Do you have her address?"

He nodded and wrote it down for me, with the telephone number. "Call her in the morning, but not before eleven. She sleeps late."

Now I had stomach cramps, and groaned. "What's the matter?" he asked.

"It's the change of climate. It always upsets my stomach. Nothing serious."

"Wouldn't you like to stay with me? In my apartment? I can take care of you."

"No, thanks." I finished my whiskey. "I'd rather be alone."

My stomach was burning as if on fire. I had to get home fast.

"Listen, Herr Holland, if you are going to see Vera Langbein tomorrow, I'd better explain the situation at her place, so that you don't say the wrong thing. It's rather complicated."

I said, "These days a lot of people in Berlin find their situation complicated."

He sighed. "It's because of this goddamn isolation,"

he said. "As if we were living on an island. All of us have an erotic foxhole complex."

"Not only erotically," I said.

"So listen. There is also a Herr Langbein. He's a wealthy jeweler. And there is a couple called Hansen. Herr and Frau Langbein love each other, Herr and Frau Hansen don't. Although Herr Langbein loves his wife, he finds it impossible to have sex with her. This has been going on for years. Herr Hansen, however, has no difficulty in sleeping with Frau Langbein. That's why Herr and Frau Langbein have separated and aren't living together anymore. Herr and Frau Hansen have separated, too. Frau Hansen is living alone, but Herr Hansen is living with Frau Langbein."

"And Herr Langbein?"

"He's taken an apartment."

"So the man I meet when I go to see Frau Langbein will be Herr Hansen."

"Exactly."

"Well, that's not so complicated," I said. "Why did you go into such detail about it, Robert?"

"It's going to be the talk of the town that you've been to see Vera Langbein. Everything gets around in no time. So Frau Hansen will find out about it and she'll call you up and ask questions. She always does. She calls up everybody who has had anything to do with Vera. I just want you to understand the situation when she calls."

"I take it that Frau Hansen hates Frau Langbein."

He shook his head. "No. The two are good friends. Frau Hansen hates Herr Langbein."

"But he's being cheated, too! It's not his fault."

"That's what you think. But Frau Hansen says it's all his fault, and everybody else seems to think so, too."

"Berlin is a crazy city," I said.

"And still it's the only city to live in, Herr Holland. The only city in the world." He smiled, his wry Jewish smile, and the bags under his eyes looked puffier and darker than ever.

13

The night passed as expected. I barely closed my eyes despite sleeping pills. I lay on the narrow bed in which I had always slept with Sibyl, because it was the only bed in the apartment. I should have remembered this, not that it made that much difference. I was too distraught and drugged to think things through.

Toward dawn I fell into an uneasy sleep, only to be awakened at 7:30 by the man from the electric company. "Morning."

A young man was standing in the doorway, tipping his hat. Sleepily I said, "Frau Loredo—"

"She's been kidnapped," he said. "I read about it in

the paper. Do you want to pay the bill? It's twenty-
four eighty." I paid and he gave me a receipt. "What's
going to become of the apartment?" He was looking
around curiously. "I had a look at it once when Frau
Loredo was still here. Nice place. I know somebody
who'd snap it up. A shame for it to stand empty. I
could—"

"Get out!"

"*What?*"

"I said get out!"

I slammed the door in his face and could hear him
muttering angrily all the way downstairs. I went into
the kitchen and made myself a cup of tea. The attack
was over, but I still felt very weak. When I took a few
steps, everything began to swing around me. After I'd
drunk the tea, I put in a call to my office in Frankfurt.
It came through quickly. "Hello?"

"Western Press Agency." The voice belonged to the
nicest girl on our switchboard.

"Holland speaking. Good morning, Marion."

"Good morning, Herr Holland. I'm terribly sorry
about what happened."

So they knew all about it already in Frankfurt, too.
"May I speak to the boss?"

"Right away, Herr Holland. We've been expecting
you to call."

A click in the wire and Werner was on the phone.
He was the office manager. "Morning, Paul. I'm terribly sorry about what happened."

Why did they all say the same thing? But I had to
be fair. What else could they say?

"I'd like some time off, Werner."

"Of course, Paul. How long?"

"I don't know yet. Two or three weeks."

"It's okay. Kalmar will substitute for you."

"Thanks."

"What are you going to do?"

"I don't know yet."

"Do you need money? Want us to send you some?"

"Yes. No, thanks. I'll call you if I need anything."

"Not a trace of her?"

"No."

"We haven't heard anything, either. If there's anything we can do for you, Paul . . ."

"Thanks, Werner. I don't know what to say. . . ."

"Don't be silly. We have your Berlin address. Call us if there's any change."

"I will."

I felt better after the conversation, as if I had somehow made progress. I waited until eleven, then I called Frau Vera Langbein and asked if I could see her. She lived in a suburb of Berlin, on the Avus highway, near the Zehlendorfer Kleeblatt, which was right next to the East Zone border. Before taking a taxi, I went to see Chief Hellwig to sign my statement. He wasn't there, but I was allowed to sign it anyway. "Any news?" I asked the man who was taking Hellwig's place.

He shook his head.

Vera Langbein was a beautiful, nervous woman of about forty. She had very blond hair and very black eyebrows. Her skin was white, her eyes were a limpid blue. She received me in the salon of her big luxurious house. Her right foot was in a cast and she was hobbling around with the help of a cane. She told me that she had fallen from her horse and broken a bone in her foot, but it was healing nicely. She offered me vermouth and cigarettes and looked at me quizzically. I got the impression that she didn't like me.

"Sibyl and I were old friends," she said. "I took Italian lessons from her."

"For a long time, *gnädige Frau*?"

"Not so often lately," she said. "But about two years ago, when things weren't going well for her, I thought it would help her out if I took some lessons. Neither of us really took them seriously. Most of the time we chatted, or Sibyl taught me slang expressions."

"I see."

"As I said, I took the lessons mainly to help Sibyl a little, financially, which wasn't difficult for me."

Our feelings were mutual—I didn't like Frau Langbein either.

"Lately," she went on, folding her arms across her chest and looking at me with ill-disguised contempt, "we didn't see much of each other, in fact none of her friends saw much of Sibyl during the last year."

"I hope that wasn't my fault."

"Well, in a way it was, Herr Holland. Sibyl lived a fairly withdrawn life after she met you."

I said nothing but let her go on, with the feeling that she would eventually say something relevant. "For instance your phone calls."

When I wasn't with her I had called Sibyl daily all last year, from wherever I was. I hadn't done so from Rio for financial reasons. "What about my phone calls?"

"Well . . . you couldn't do a thing with Sibyl in the

evening anymore. She had to be home at eight o'clock because that was when you called."

I nodded.

"Although sometimes you didn't call until midnight, or one o'clock." Her smile was sour.

"*Gnädige Frau,* I frequently called from a foreign country. Sometimes I had to wait hours for a connection. Or I was in a conference."

"I'm not reproaching you, Herr Holland," she said, although it was exactly what she was doing. "That's how it was the last time we saw each other, the day before—" She hesitated and looked down. "I simply cannot understand who could possibly have done it, Herr Holland."

"Nobody can."

"But *somebody* must have done it!"

"Exactly. Would you mind telling me what took place the last time you saw Sibyl?"

"Of course not. I picked her up after lunch and we drove out to see my horse."

"Your horse?"

"My husband gave me a horse for Christmas. I imagine you've heard that my husband and I don't live together."

I mumbled something unintelligible.

"There's a lot of gossip going around in Berlin, Herr Holland. My husband and I are devoted to each other. The present of a horse is proof enough of that, isn't it?"

"I should say, *gnädige Frau.*"

"To say nothing of all the other presents he's given

me," she went on. "Modern people find modern ways to surmount their difficulties."

I nodded.

Suddenly she asked clear and loud, "Who told you about me? Was if Frau Hansen?"

I shook my head.

"Then who was it?"

"I can't remember, but it certainly wasn't Frau Hansen."

She looked at me distrustfully and I tried to bring the conversation back to the only topic that interested me. "So you went to see your horse. . . ."

"Yes. Sibyl took him *lebkuchen*. Sweet of her. By the way, we talked about you all the time," she said plaintively. "Sibyl was so happy. Were you really going to marry her?"

"Yes."

"Sweet," she said again, absentmindedly. She was thinking of something else, probably of Frau Hansen.

"And after you'd gone to see the horse, *gnädige Frau*?"

"What? Oh, yes. We drove back to the city and had tea together."

"Where?"

"At the Wagenseil Konditorei."

I knew the *konditorei*. "Were you there a long time?"

"About half an hour. It wasn't pleasant."

"Why?"

"Oh, it was so full. And then there were some Italians. They kept staring at us. It was a nuisance."

Italians. Sibyl had lived in Italy. She had talked about it often. I asked, "Did you know any of them?"

"Of course not! They were absolute strangers. Impudent strangers, to stare at two women like that! Even the waitress was annoyed."

But I was interested in the Italians. "How many were there?"

"Oh . . . six or seven. I can't remember. Why?"

I answered with a question. "Did you get the impression that Sibyl knew any of them?"

"Herr Holland! Whatever gave you such an idea!? Of course not! They were just some very fresh fellows."

"So you left the *konditorei*," I said.

"Yes. I brought Sibyl home early. She said it was past six-thirty."

"But the day it happened, I was in Rio, and I didn't call from Rio. That day she needn't have gone home so early!"

"She said your letters from Brazil always came with the evening mail."

That was true. My plane, which also carried mail, arrived in the early afternoon, and I had written to Sibyl every day.

"And she was absolutely calm?"

"Absolutely, Herr Holland."

And a day later she had disappeared. . . .

"None of us can find any explanation for it, Herr Holland," said Vera Langbein, as if she had read my thoughts.

The door opened. A stocky man with restless eyes came in. His color was poor, he looked sick, and he didn't look in the least like an adulterer. "I'm sorry," he said, "I didn't mean to . . ."

"Peter, this is Herr Holland. Herr Holland, this is Herr Peter Hansen." She blushed a little.

"My condolences, Herr Holland," Herr Hansen said promptly, and I wondered what Herr Langbein looked like.

"I only wanted to ask you for the car keys, darling," Herr Hansen said softly. "I have to go to the city again."

"I must leave, too," I said. "I've kept you much too long, *gnädige Frau*."

"May I take you along?" asked Herr Hansen.

"Thank you," I said, "but I have a taxi waiting for me." And I left.

As I walked out onto the street, I looked around suddenly, just in time to see the curtain at the salon window fall back into its folds. Somebody had watched me go. For the first time since yesterday afternoon I was filled with a happy restlessness. I was sure I was on the right track.

"To the Wagenseil Konditorei," I told the driver.

"Yes, sir."

As we left the Avus and passed the radio tower, a plane was flying over it, very low. "One day they'll hit the damn' thing," said the driver.

14

This time, to save time, I used my press pass. I was lucky—the place was almost empty, and I got hold of the right girl at once. Her name was Ellen. She was dark and looked sleepy.

"I'm a journalist, Ellen," I said. "I have to write a piece on the kidnapping of Frau Loredo. You've heard about it, I suppose."

"Of course, Herr Holland." She spoke with a Saxon accent. Her hands were big and red, and she kept trying to hide them. "A few men from the police were here already. Frau Loredo had tea here the day it happened."

"And you waited on her, didn't you?"

She nodded solemnly and looked worried. She was standing in front of mounds of cake, large trays of pastry—Schwarzwald cherry torte, cream puffs, yellow custard Napoleons, glistening yellow fruit tarts—her red hands behind her back. I had sat down in a corner and ordered a cognac. Meanwhile it had grown dark. Fog was beginning to blanket the city. If it got any thicker, there would be no more flights that night. Meanwhile, Ellen, the waitress, was saying, "There was a lady with her."

"Did they stay long?"

"No. There were some men here who annoyed them."

"What kind of men?"

"Italians, I think. They kept staring at Frau Loredo and her friend, and making remarks about them."

"What did they say?"

"I don't understand Italian."

"And what happened when the ladies left?"

"Nothing. The Italians left, too."

"All together?"

"Yes. They were together. One of them asked me if I knew who the ladies were."

My heart began to beat fast, but I asked perfectly calmly, "And did you answer?"

"I said I only knew one of them—Frau Loredo."

"Did the man ask for her address?"

"No."

I thought, if he had her name, he didn't have to ask for her address. Loredo wasn't a common name, and there was always the telephone book.

"What did the man look like, Ellen? Can you remember?"

"Very thin and tall. He wore tortoiseshell glasses and had black hair. He spoke a little German."

"Would you recognize him if you saw him again?" It was the standard question in all detective stories, but then, hadn't I decided to behave like the people in the books?

"I think . . ."

"How many men were there?"

"Five."

"Are you sure?"

"Quite sure. They sat over there. That's a table for four and I had to bring them an extra chair."

Five Italians. That was all I knew. But twenty-four hours ago I had known nothing.

I gave the girl a lavish tip and left. The minute I got outside, I saw Sibyl on the other side of the street.

15

"Sibyl!"

I screamed the name at the top of my lungs, once, twice. People stopped and stared. I ran out into the street, a man pulled me back. "Are you out of your mind?" And a car shot by, so close I could feel the draft it created.

The Wagenseil Konditorei is on the Meineckestrasse, near the Kurfürstendamm. By now Sibyl had reached the big show window of the Modehaus Horn and disappeared around the corner. I was absolutely sure it was Sibyl, regardless of how impossible this might seem and despite the fact that she was wearing a fur coat I didn't recognize. But for a moment I had seen her face by the light of a street lantern, and it had sufficed. But a prosthesis is only an artificial leg, however ingeniously constructed and however much it may have cost. There are certain things one shouldn't do when one is wearing a prosthesis, it tells you about them in the instruction leaflet. First among them is running. The artificial leg won't take it. I thought of that as I started to run. I thought, For God's sake let it hold out! The leg creaked, I could feel the little rubber foam pad shifting. . . .

When I got to the Kurfürstendamm I stood still for a moment, then I saw her again. She was walking toward the illuminated ruin of the Gedächtniskirche, and she was walking fast. There were a lot of people between her and me. I couldn't move quickly enough on the sidewalk so I ran out into the street again. Now my stump was rubbing against the leather. The pain brought the tears to my eyes. I yelled Sibyl's name again, and now quite a lot of people stopped. The driver of the car behind me was blowing his horn furiously. I had to get back on the sidewalk.

Here I kept bumping into angry pedestrians. "What's your hurry, man?" "You must be nuts!"

"Excuse me, please, I've got to get through. There's a lady I have to catch up with."

They let me pass, but it had cost me time. I couldn't see Sibyl anymore. I hurried on, gasping, toward the street lantern in front of the Berliner Kindl. Where was she? Only a moment ago I'd seen her. . . .

There! Crossing the street on the green light in the direction of the Zoo Station. I ran out into the street again. This time I paid no attention to the cars blowing their horns. When I got to the crossing, the light changed. But I had no intention of losing sight of Sibyl again. I ran across the Kurfürstendamm although the cars that had the green light had already started to move. My prosthesis buckled under me, I stumbled but managed to remain upright.

A whole strident symphony of automobile horns! Tires screeching on the frozen asphalt! Headlights and car bumpers coming at me. I jumped from side to side like a hunted rabbit. A policeman was blowing his whistle. As I rushed past his tower I saw him starting to come down. And there was Sibyl, just ahead of me, walking straight and fast in a fur coat. Now I was close to her. Ten steps. Five. One. "Sibyl!" I grabbed her by the shoulders and turned her around.

An absolutely strange woman was glaring at me. "What do you think you're doing?"

"Ex—excuse me, please. I—I thought you were—"

At that moment the policeman caught up with me. He was out of breath and furious. "This is going to cost you something, sir."

The pain in my leg was excruciating. I couldn't stand up anymore and sat down on the sidewalk.

"What's the matter with you? Are you drunk?"

"My leg," I said.

The policeman looked down. My trousers had shifted up and the leather prosthesis was showing.

"So why do you have to run with a thing like that?" he asked.

It sounded more friendly. People crowded around us. I massaged my leg and apologized and tried to explain the situation. The strange lady shrugged and walked on. The policeman asked for identification and wrote everything down. And I sat on the wet, dirty sidewalk and waited for the policeman to give me back my passport, and thought: How could it have happened?

16

"You made a mistake, Herr Holland. Such things happen."

"But it *was* Sibyl, Robert!"

I was sitting in a corner of Robert's bar and my hand holding the glass was shaking. The bar was almost empty, only two women with their dates were in the booths. Now and then they laughed loudly. They were drinking companions.

"It wasn't Sibyl. You said so yourself. It was a completely strange woman!"

I said stubbornly, "I lived with Sibyl. I knew her for over a year. I often recognized her from great distances. With my eyes closed, in the dark, I knew when she was coming toward me. Don't you know the feeling? Didn't you feel that way about your wife?"

"Yes, yes, of course. But—"

"And I'm telling you, the woman I saw as I came out of the *konditorei* was Sibyl!"

"For God's sake, stop it!" he cried angrily. "You're driving me crazy! It couldn't have been Sibyl or you wouldn't have made an ass of yourself with some strange woman!" He added quietly and with emphasis: "You *thought* you saw Sibyl because you're thinking of her all the time, and talking about her all the time!"

"So why, if it *was* a hallucination, did Sibyl have on a coat I didn't know? Wishful thinking consists of known elements, doesn't it?"

"Please, Herr Holland!"

The women laughed loudly. They looked like middle-class women, only they were heavily made up. "Are they whores?"

"I should say not! They're respectable married women. Their husbands are civil servants who don't earn enough to live decently, so every now and then the women do a little hustling. They have their own apartments and you don't have to be afraid of catching anything."

"And where are their husbands?"

"In a tavern. Drinking beer. The women will go home with their clients when they've drunk enough champagne, then, an hour later, they'll pick up their husbands in the tavern."

"Is that customary?"

"I know a lot of women who do it." He shrugged. "Decent women, all of them."

I told Robert what I had found out in the *konditorei*. "You know so many people in Berlin, Robert! Doormen, boarding house owners. Perhaps you could find out where these Italians were staying. They seem to have been together."

"Hm."

"Sibyl lived in Italy for a long time. These men could have had something to do with her abduction. I have that feeling."

Robert was thinking. "Perhaps they came for a convention," he said slowly. "There are conventions going on here all the time."

He promised to do what he could. I still felt very weak and told him I was going home. "If I find out anything, Herr Holland, I'll call you at once." As I was leaving he gave me a bottle of whiskey.

"But I can't accept that!" I protested.

"You can, you can!" he said, sticking it into my coat pocket. "You can accept anything from me. I'm a friend of Sibyl's."

He called a taxi for me and I drove home to Grunewald. I made myself a cup of tea and sat down with it in the living room beside the bookcase. The critique of Anaximander of Miletus still lay where I had left it on the morning I had flown to Rio, and it fell open again at the same place when I picked it up. I read the marked sentence again: "The origin of all things is boundless. They perish of necessity out of that which formed them because they are penitent and retaliate toward each other for their injustices according to the order of their times."

Had Sibyl marked the sentence? Because she had liked it? One could love a woman for a whole year and still know nothing about her.

The telephone rang.

I went out into the hall. When I picked up the receiver the pleasant voice of a woman asked, "Herr Holland?"

"Yes."

"This is Frau Hansen."

I thought of Robert's warning, but I had had to answer the phone because it might have been Robert, with some news.

"I've tried to reach you several times today, Herr Holland," said Frau Hansen.

"I just got in, *gnädige Frau*."

"I hear you saw Frau Langbein this afternoon."

"Who told you?"

"Never mind who told me." She spoke sternly; any excuses would be lost on her. "Did you see my husband there?"

"Yes."

"Well, then, that's all right." She sounded relieved, then suddenly suspicious. "And no one else."

"I don't understand."

"Herr Langbein wasn't there?"

"No."

"Did Vera mention him?"

"*Gnädige Frau*, I really don't know what all this means."

"Don't let it worry you. I am an old friend of

Sibyl's. You would be doing me a great favor if you would answer my question. It is very important."

"I don't know why. . . ."

"You don't know Herr Langbein!" Now she sounded hysterical. "I have every reason to believe that he still goes to see Vera occasionally. In secret. With my husband knowing."

I asked politely, "You mean that you suspect Herr Langbein is deceiving your husband with Frau Langbein?"

"I am almost positive! What do you think of that? Isn't it monstrous?"

"I should say so."

"My husband and Vera were very happy, you know. And I was so pleased about it. Sometimes they asked me to come over, and we played canasta or we had drinks in front of the fireplace. We were good friends. At last Vera had managed to free herself from her husband and now he's turned up again and wants to destroy everything."

"*Gnädige Frau*," I said. "I don't think you have anything to worry about. I got the impression that Frau Langbein is very happy with your husband."

"Well, that reassures me, Herr Holland. Thank you very much. And what I also wanted to say—I am, of course, terribly sorry about what happened to Sibyl. We were such good friends."

I put down the receiver with the satisfied feeling that I had done a good deed, and would really have liked to know what the despised Herr Langbein looked like. Sibyl had had strange friends. Or was it just Berlin? I decided Berlin was at fault and went back to bed. I was awakened at 3:30 A.M. by the uninterrupted ringing of the front doorbell. I hobbled to the window and tried to see who was standing out there in the park. The fog was too dense, I could see nothing.

There was an intercom in the hall. I pressed the button and asked, "Who's there?"

"Robert Friedmann. Let me in, please. I've found out something."

I pressed the second button and the downstairs door opened. Seconds later the fat little bar owner came panting into the apartment.

He didn't take off his coat but sat down in one of the easy chairs and tried to catch his breath. Then he took a photograph out of his pocket and tossed it triumphantly on the coffee table. It was the picture of five men in front of a plane, standing close together and smiling broadly.

"There you have your Italians," he said, took a piece of paper out of his pocket, and read aloud: "From left to right: Tino Sabbaddini, Emilio Trenti, Mario Turline, Cesare Nuovo, and Carlo Zampa."

The man Robert had designated as Carlo Zampa stood on the extreme right. He was very tall and thin. He had black hair and wore tortoiseshell glasses.

17

"How did you get hold of the picture?"

His pride was touching. "Oh, Herr Holland—old Robert Friedmann is still a man you can depend on. After you had left I got into my car and drove around the city, to one hotel after the other. I began with the big ones. I know most of the doormen. They were all very nice, but not one of them could help me. Either they hadn't had any Italian visitors lately, or too many, or they had been women. I didn't have any luck until I got to the Ritz. And the doorman there knew at once whom I was after. Yes. Five Italians had stayed there not long ago. He showed me their names in the register. The five men had stayed at the Ritz from the second to the tenth of February.

"And on the ninth, Sibyl was kidnapped."

He nodded.

"And on the tenth they left?"

"All together. They flew Air France to Munich."

"What sort of men were they? I mean, what sort of professions did they have?"

"They all did the same thing, Herr Holland. They were dealers in produce."

"In *what*?" I had to laugh.

"They dealt in fruits and vegetables, Herr Holland. Wholesale, of course. And all of them seemed to have been pretty prosperous."

"And what were they doing in Berlin?"

"They were here on business. The doorman said they had already been in Hamburg, Düsseldorf, Hannover, and Frankfurt. They were evidently anxious to do business in Germany."

"And now they're in Munich?"

"I don't know about that. I mean, I don't know if they're still in Munich."

"Do they all come from the same place?"

"Yes. From Rome."

"And the photo? Where did you get that?"

"The hotel sent a car to the airport when they arrived. I found the driver. He remembered that a photographer had taken a picture of the group. At the airport they knew the photographer and I was able to get his name and address. He had extra prints of the picture. His name is Werner Weich and he lives at 34 Olympische Strasse, on the second floor." He looked at me happily.

Later that same morning, at nine, I was at the Grunewald police station, sitting opposite Chief Hellwig. The photo lay on his desk between us. But everything turned out quite differently from what I had expected.

Hellwig was friendly but came straight to the point. "Herr Holland," he said. "I have a report about you.

You caused a minor traffic disturbance yesterday at the Gedächtniskirche."

"Yes," I said. "I know. But please listen to me, sir. The five Italians on this picture—"

"You mistook a strange woman for Frau Loredo—is that right? You thought you had seen Frau Loredo."

"I *did* see her!"

"But the lady you stopped was not Frau Loredo."

"No. But she also wasn't the lady I first saw."

"So why did you run after her?"

"Good God, Chief—can't you see that right now I'm a nervous wreck?"

"That's what I wanted to hear from you," he said amiably.

"What?"

"Your characterization of the state of your nerves. It is indicative, too, of your reaction to these gentlemen from Italy."

"You don't think it's a clue?"

"It's one of the many clues we are pursuing."

"You know about these Italians?"

"Of course, Herr Holland."

"Then why don't you follow up on it?"

"We are following up on it, just as we are following up on various other clues, Herr Holland. During the last forty-eight hours before she disappeared, Frau Loredo saw the jeweler Hähnlein, she went to the Rollenhagen delicatessen, and to the Delphi Cinema. She also went to her hairdresser, Franz Armand, and had her hair set."

"So?"

"So you can imagine, Herr Holland, that in the

course of all these errands, Frau Loredo saw a lot of people. And we are interested in every one of them we can reach. We have our own methods when we work on a case like this. Believe me, Herr Holland, we don't leave a stone upturned."

"But this fellow, Carlo Zampa, asked for Sibyl's name!"

"Herr Holland, have you never tried to find out the name of a pretty woman?"

"Chief Hellwig . . . Frau Loredo lived in Italy for a long time. I am positive that these Italians have something to do with her disappearance."

"I'm afraid you're wrong, Herr Holland," he said coolly.

"What do you mean?"

"Frau Loredo never lived in Italy."

"But that's ridiculous! She told me all about it herself!"

"Our registration bureau knows nothing about it."

"Are you trying to tell me Frau Loredo was lying?"

He shrugged. "A lot of people make up stories, Herr Holland."

"But *why?*"

"To impress. Or because they have vivid imaginations. There are many reasons."

"Frau Loredo *was* in Italy!" I cried.

"I'm afraid that's not so."

I gave up. I realized that I'd have to go ahead on my own if I was to make any progress. "I'm leaving Berlin," I said.

"I suppose you're flying to Munich."

"Yes. I'll be staying at the Vier Jahreszeiten."

"Very well, Herr Holland." He rose and stretched out his hand. "I'm afraid you don't think so much of us."

"Oh, but I do. Certainly," I said, as I made up my mind to trust only my own instincts from here on.

I managed to get a seat on the noon Air France plane. Robert took me to the airport. I gave him the key to Sibyl's apartment and we agreed to keep in touch by phone. We were standing in the lively airport lobby, smoking, and I thought of how I had stood here and waited with Sibyl two weeks ago.

"Attention, please! Air France Flight 769 for Munich is ready to take on passengers at Gate 3. We wish you a pleasant flight."

"So good-bye, Robert."

"Good-bye, Herr Holland. Good luck!"

I walked through the barrier to Gate 3, and Robert Friedmann stood in the lobby and waved. I turned around several times, and each time his sad face lit up with an encouraging smile. I had my typewriter tucked under my arm and proceeded down the stairs to the airfield. The weather was clear and cold. I thought of how I had looked forward to summer. Sibyl and I had decided to go away together somewhere by the sea. We had never been away together, but this summer we had intended to do so. . . .

18

The plane was almost full. I sat on the left aisle, near the front, beside a fat woman who looked worried. Two stewardesses served lunch soon after we started, but I wasn't hungry. I thought about what Chief Hellwig had told me. What did he mean, Sibyl hadn't lived in Italy? She had told me so herself. Had she lied? The question shook me. Or was the registration bureau wrong? The thought that registration bureaus were never wrong disturbed me.

The woman beside me ate, but she was evidently not feeling well, although the flight was smooth. Every now and then she shook her head and sighed. Twice she spoke to herself, but too softly for me to understand what she was saying. She seemed to be about 50. She was wearing a loden suit and had a double chin. After we had left the Elbe behind us, she ordered a cognac. When she opened the little bottle, she spilled half of it. A few drops fell on my trousers. Startled, she apologized.

"It's all right," I said.

"I'm so terribly nervous."

I looked out of the window and said nothing. It was a cloudless day. I could see the snow-covered earth below. The houses were scattered like poppy seeds on the snow. The woman drank the rest of the cognac, shook herself and said, "I needed that. I've lived in the city for twenty-five years. Nobody could say a thing against me. But now they've reported me."

I realized that she was going to go on talking regardless of whether I showed any interest or not, so I said politely, "Reported you?"

"For spreading communist propaganda!" Her double chin shook with indignation. She spoke with a Bavarian accent. "Me! Of all people in Hof—me!"

The copilot came walking toward the rear. He nodded to me.

"I have a radio shop there. In Ludwigstrasse. The biggest one in town. Do you know Hof?"

"It's on the Zone border, isn't it?"

"That's just it!" She looked at me helplessly out of gray, mousy eyes. "Everything was going smoothly until I got the television sets," she went on despondently. "I don't go for these modern inventions, but my sister! She drives me crazy, says we're backward. If we don't have a television set in the window, the other stores will, and that would be dreadful because we have the biggest radio shop in the city. In the end I gave in and ordered three sets."

The four-engine plane droned quietly, evenly; it was 2:30, we were due in Munich at 3:00.

"You see," the nervous radio shop owner went on, "there are seven stations in Bavaria that broadcast the

Munich channel. You can get it everywhere, only not where we are. We're too far north. The mountains lie in between. In Bayreuth and Marktredwitz and Selb and Hof you can't get a Bavarian station. We're in a dead spot for Bavarian programs."

I cleared my throat to indicate my interest.

"We get the Ernst Thälmann station beautifully," said Frau Högl, sounding bitter. "That's on the Katzberg, near Chemnitz, in the East Zone. You never heard anything like it! So clear! Another cognac, please," she called out to the stewardess.

The stewardess brought the second small bottle and Frau Högl went on with her story. "So . . . I put the set in the window and turned it on. Never gave it a thought. On the contrary, I was pleased to see the people stopping in the cold and shoving each other aside to get a better look. Because, as I said, it was the first television set they'd ever seen in Hof."

"What was the Ernst Thälmann station broadcasting?"

"The winter Olympics in Cortina. Beautiful, Herr Holland! You've got to grant them that. Everybody just loved it! I sat down for a while in the back of the store and had a cup of coffee, and my sister said, after all, I had only her to thank for the success of the television set, and about half an hour later we went out on the street to see what they were broadcasting, and there were even more people, and we watched a very interesting documentary film from Taiga. But then they showed a workers' celebration on the Comrade Pieck wharf. That's when I began to get a little worried because the speaker was eulogizing Comrade Pieck and after that they all sang the 'Internationale.' . . ."

"Could you hear it through the window?"

"And how! You see, I had attached the set to the loudspeaker. You never heard such an uproar."

"So what did you do?"

"Dashed back into the store to turn the set off. But just then they finished singing the 'Internationale,' and started a children's hour with 'Hansel and Gretel.' And the children out in the street started to yell, louder than the 'Internationale,' 'Don't turn it off! Don't turn it off!' "

"So what did you do?"

"What did you expect? I'm telling you, Herr Holland, that evening I ran a temperature of a hundred and one. The Reds were smart. You never knew what was coming next! A string quartet and suddenly—a labor speech. A little cabaret, and right after that something cute from the People's Holiday Home for Children. And next day the police came because somebody had reported me as a communist!"

"What did the police do?"

"They were very friendly. I asked them if I should return the sets but they said no, that was out of the question because it would look like interference in personal freedom."

"Well, well, well. . . ."

"Wait a minute, Herr Holland! Then the policeman said I should only let the set play what I could answer for with my political conscience!"

"And that's what you're doing?"

"Yes." Frau Högl drew a deep breath. "My sister

and I—we sit in the shop all day with our hands on the switch. One week she does, the next week I do. Last week it was my turn. When I was through, I took a vacation. Tomorrow the whole misery starts all over again. It'll be my turn. You know, sometimes I think the people at the Ernst Thälmann channel just want to drive us crazy. They never switched programs around that fast before."

She settled down into a moody silence. The cognac had made her drowsy. I fell asleep and woke up after Fulda, just as the plane was passing over the Soviet corridor and entering the West German Bundesrepublik, and fell asleep and woke up again as we were circling over Munich. It was 3:10. I asked why we weren't landing and the stewardess explained, "The Fasching Prince from Cologne just arrived, sir, and people are blocking the runway."

When I finally got off the plane at 3:30, the carnival group from Cologne was still milling around, about 40 people, all of them in uniform, wearing Hungarian shakos, or helmets, and red gold-braided jackets and tight-fitting white pants. The celebration was evidently in honor of the Munich Mardi Gras Prince and Princess, who were facing the visitors from Cologne with a retinue just as colorful. The Munich prince was fat and rosy and looked like the son of a butcher; his princess, standing beside him, was thin and pale.

We couldn't cross the airfield because of the ceremony. Frau Högl stood at my side. "My God . . . my God . . ." she said a few times, helplessly, then she was silent.

When the ceremony was over, the Cologne prince's

bodyguard, knees bent, began slapping their behinds as they roared an obviously ribald verse in incomprehensible Cologne dialect. This was followed by just as ribald laughter. Frau Högl looked at me, then turned away again.

Now the Mardi Gras princesses of both cities kissed and embraced, the princes shook hands. The one from Cologne was wearing gold-rimmed spectacles and his smooth face was marred by dueling scars. The one from Munich had ash-blond hair, cropped close in military style, and he clicked his heels when he bowed.

"Very rich people," the man from airport personnel explained.

A huge beer keg was wheeled on and both parties filled enormous steins, overflowing with Bavarian beer. The princes downed theirs in one go, the foam dripping from their mouths, then shook their empty steins triumphantly at the cameras.

Frau Högl turned to me in disgust. "I'm afraid, Herr Holland," she said.

I looked at her, surprised.

"I go to church on Sunday," she explained, while everyone present was smacking *Funkenmariechen* on the behind, "and last week the priest read a passage from John, and I keep having to think about it."

"What passage was it?"

"If ye do not take heed, ye shall perish," said Frau Högl from Hof in Bavaria.

I walked into the main building of the Munich airport and went over to the Air France counter. They knew me here. I gave the friendly attendant the list of the five Italians and asked her if they had meanwhile left Munich by air, either with Air France or some other company.

"Please wait in the restaurant, Herr Holland. It will take about half an hour. We'll have to go through all the passenger lists of the last few days."

It took an hour, then the loudspeaker called me back to the desk. The stewardess said, "Four of the gentlemen flew back to Rome. We couldn't find the name of the fifth man on our list, nor is he listed with KLM, SAS, PAA, BEA or Sabena. His name is—"

"Carlo Zampa!" I said quickly.

The stewardess looked surprised. "No. Why?"

"Carlo Zampa also flew to Rome?"

"Yes. On February tenth, at 6:30 A.M. PAA Flight 129."

"So what's the name of the man you couldn't find on any of the lists?"

"The name," she said, "is Emilio Trenti."

19

I took a taxi and drove to the hotel. I had reserved a room at the Vier Jahreszeiten, and had also left my new address with the WPA central bureau in Frankfurt. On the way into the city I saw many people in costume, with masks, on their way to the various balls. Munich was celebrating *Fasching*.

My room was on the fourth floor. I took a hot bath, then went down into the lobby, sat in a corner, closed my eyes and started to think things through. Four of the men I was looking for had left Germany, but the fifth, who had not, was not the one who had asked for Sibyl's name at the Wagenseil Konditorei.

Perhaps by this time Emilio Trenti was back in Italy, too. All he would have had to do was travel by train or car. I began to think more kindly of Chief Hellwig. It was really impossible to follow every clue. What should I do now? Go to the police and have them check the hotel registers? That would take days. And I could only be successful if Emilio Trenti had not left Munich. And I realized, suddenly sobered, that even if I succeeded in finding Emilio Trenti, the chances were one in a thousand that he had anything whatsoever to do with Sibyl's disappearance. Suddenly I wished I had stayed in Berlin. There I still had Robert and the apartment. Here I was out of touch.

"Herr Holland?"

"Yes?"

I opened my eyes and looked up. A bellboy was standing in front of me. "A phone call for you, from Frankfurt. Booth three."

"For *me*?"

He nodded and pointed. "Over there, sir."

I walked into the booth, which smelled of disinfectant. The telephone operator from the office was at the other end of the line. "Just a minute, Herr Holland. I'll connect you with Herr Kalmar." Kalmar answered almost immediately. "Paul?"

"Yes. What is it?"

"I'm glad you're in the hotel. I was afraid you'd taken the evening plane. We have news for you. Do you know a man called Emilio Trenti?"

I had to lean against the wall of the booth and my collar suddenly felt too tight. "What about him?"

"He called us. Two hours ago. He said he wanted to see you tomorrow."

I was speechless.

"He said we should try to find you. He wants you to meet him tomorrow afternoon at four."

"Where?"

"In Salzburg."

"*Where*?"

"In Salzburg. His address—"

"Wait a minute." With trembling fingers I found my pencil and wrote down what Kalmar dictated. "Salzburg-Parsch, Akazienallee 3. Got it?"

"Yes."

"He said Parsch was a suburb of Salzburg."

"Telephone number?"

"He doesn't have a phone. And he said there'd be no point in your coming earlier because he won't get there himself until tomorrow afternoon. I hope all this makes sense to you."

"I can't say it does. Did Herr Trenti say what he wanted to see me about?"

"Yes, Paul. He said it concerned Sibyl Loredo."

BOOK TWO

1

I have been living in the Ambassador Hotel for three weeks now—to be precise, for twenty-two days. The weather in Vienna has grown milder, people are sitting outdoors in the cafés, and when the sun shines it is hot. Everybody says summer will come earlier this year.

This morning Dr. Gürtler came to see me for the last time. After he examined me, he put his instruments in his bag and went to the bathroom to wash his hands. I followed him. "A colleague of mine will come to see you tomorrow," he said.

"And you?"

He dried his hands and smiled as he said, "I've given up my practice."

Outside the flower vendors were still crying their wares, "Primroses, narcissus, beautiful violets. Five shillings a bunch!" Dr. Gürtler's lips tightened; he was staring down at the carpet as he said softly, "No man can live without something to believe in."

I looked at him but said nothing.

113

"Sounds ridiculous, doesn't it? When a man of science says something like that."

"No." I was feeling slightly embarrassed. "It doesn't sound ridiculous at all."

"I know how it sounds," he said.

We were alone in the salon of my red, white, and gold suite, but now we looked past each other.

I asked, "And have you found something to believe in, *Herr Doktor?*"

The old man lifted his head as if just awakening. "I'll tell you how it is. You're a journalist, it may interest you. Do you know Floridsdorf, Herr Holland?"

"No."

"Floridsdorf is an industrial district in the north of Vienna. Workers live there. The municipality has just built a new hospital in Floridsdorf, for children."

I sat down opposite him. A gold ray of sunshine slanted into the room, dust motes floating in it.

"The name of the man in charge is Ehrlich. He's much younger than I am. Dr. Walter Ehrlich." Gürtler's voice faded. He was silent.

"And is he the person you picked out to believe in?" I asked softly.

"I admire him," said Dr. Gürtler, sounding as if he were ashamed of his words. "I want to be like him. I want to be doing what he's doing and thinking as he thinks."

I got up and walked over to a wall shelf where my bottle of whiskey was standing. Waiter Franz had also brought up a syphon and an ice bucket. I mixed a drink for myself and thought of Sibyl, and the scar under my heart began to hurt again. Sibyl was dead, I thought, really dead, laid out in a coffin and buried in a deep grave. She would never come back, and my days in Vienna were nearly over. I had to get away. My office had already called twice, wanting to know how long I intended to stay. They wanted me to go to Brazil. They were waiting for me to be declared well enough. But before I left Vienna I had to make a decision.

As I drank, Dr. Gürtler went on speaking. "This man is a surgeon. Like me. As you can imagine, all the children in the hospital are poor children, their parents are laborers, there's no money to be made there." His eyes were bright with excitement. "But you should see the hospital, Herr Holland! It's the most modern hospital for children in the city. Dr. Ehrlich has his own methods. In his hospital the children aren't afraid before an operation. They laugh and are happy. Because a day before a child is operated on, Dr. Ehrlich gives a party, with presents, music, and cake. And the patient is the hero of the hour because he's going to be operated on next day. Everybody admires him. Look how brave he is! He isn't the least afraid! Because he's told the operation is going to make him well."

"And it works?"

"You have no idea how it works, Herr Holland. I saw an eleven-year-old boy who had to lose his leg. At the party he was sitting up in bed, blowing a toy trumpet, and his face was aglow. He was the center of attraction. Only two little boys were crying."

"Why?"

"They wanted to be operated on next day, too, but that wasn't possible. So they had to wait."

We looked at each other silently for a moment, then Dr. Gürtler said, "Dr. Ehrlich keeps an eye on the children even after they've left the hospital. A lot of them live under miserable conditions. They have to sleep in the same room as their parents; they don't have their own beds, they don't have the right nourishment. Every now and then Dr. Ehrlich takes them back to the hospital."

"When they're not sick?"

"Yes. They call it for convalescence. In his hospital there are almost as many healthy children as sick ones."

"Primroses," cried the flower woman. "Narcissus. Violets. . . ."

"And that's where you're going to practice now? With Dr. Ehrlich?"

"Yes, Herr Holland."

"Where are you going to live?"

"At the hospital. With him."

"You're going to give up everything in the city? Your apartment, too?"

He nodded. "I met Dr. Ehrlich a year ago, at a lecture. He said something I couldn't forget."

"What?"

"To do good is more important than to love."

I drank my whiskey and thought of how I had to come to a decision. For three weeks now I had been in Vienna, writing down my experiences with the intention of telling the whole truth. The police had questioned me over and over again. I told them how Sibyl died, but not how her life had really ended. The real truth is what I am writing here. When I have come to the end of my report, it will be clear why I had to go about it this way.

"I'm going to miss you," I told Dr. Gürtler, as we shook hands to say good-bye.

"Perhaps you'll come and see me some day," he said. "The address is Donauuferdamm 324."

Now he has gone. I am alone, seated in front of my desk again, thinking of Sibyl, and I know very well that as a human being she no longer exists, only as an idea, as something to believe in. But can one, may one believe?

I don't know. All I know is that I have to go on writing. I don't have much more time. They're waiting for me in Frankfurt; they want to send me to Brazil. And so I go on, telling the truth about the death of Sibyl Loredo. I shall suppress nothing, not even how she came to such a horrible, insane end.

2

The day after arriving in Munich, I left for Salzburg. I took the 2:30 express. The train was over-heated and almost empty, the countryside lay under a deep blanket of snow. The painfully bright world outside revolved as if on a turntable. The sun was shining in Bavaria. In two hours I would see Emilio Trenti. I wondered how he had heard of me, known how to reach me.

To get my mind off our meeting, I began to leaf through the paper I had bought at the station. According to an American report, the Russians had exploded a hydrogen bomb in the Urals. The Federation of German Industrialists had sent a memorandum to the German Chancellor, to the effect that if the armament industry was to be revitalized, those industrialists who were going to revitalize it should not be exposed to condemnation, as they had been in 1945. In Morocco, the insurgents among the French settlers were responsible for another grisly bloodbath; 45 women and children were dead. The Austrian ski champion, Toni Sailer, was receiving many film offers. A court in Bremen had decided that a victim of National Socialism had no right to compensation of any kind if the persecution had taken place after his seventieth year. At the Twentieth Communist Party Congress in Moscow, the head of the most powerful party in the state, fat little Nikita Khrushchev, had sharply criticized the dead son of a Georgian shoemaker, Iosif Vissarionovich Dzhugashvili, better known as Stalin, and had defended himself and the happenings of the last decade with the explanation, "Many complex and controversial events that took place during the Civil War, between 1918 and 1920, are explained away by some historians as the allegedly treacherous activities of individual party leaders during that time, who were unjustly branded as enemies of the people many years after the described events. Such historic distortions have no place in Marxist history." And the American president, Dwight D. Eisenhower, after his first game of golf since his convalescence, had said, "I'm a little concerned, not only about my golf but also about myself."

I put down the paper and looked out at the glittering winter landscape and thought of Sibyl. She had said once, "Everything has become so confused. Jewish emigrants come back to Germany as nationalists. Communists who have fled from Russia go on the air against the Soviet Union. The French admire the Germans, the Russians get along with the Egyptians, and you have a hard time convincing former concentration camp victims that Hitler was not a great man just because he built the autobahn. . . ."

The wheels pounded out a monotonous rhythm, the train was moving fast. The snow fanned out like silver wings on both sides. I thought how Hitler had done one good thing for us in that he had simplified reactions around the world. The Hitler era had been an easy period, in one respect—it hadn't been difficult to be against Hitler. But now civilization was foundering, misfortune was laying bare roots that had held the world together, creating ever new aspects of revenge, chicanery, sympathy, despair, and trust. The paths through the jungle of our convictions were becoming more obscure all the time. "If only it weren't so difficult to live decently and do the right thing," Sibyl had said. "If only we had nothing to cope with but fascism and anti-fascism! How simple life would be then, and how complicated it is now!"

After Rosenheim the weather grew worse. In the mountainous region around Salzburg, a black icy fog sank down over the land. It grew dark early, and it was eerie to watch the fog descend from the mountaintops like a curtain, obliterating the area. I stood in the corridor and watched it happen. Behind us the sun was still shining over Chiemsee; ahead of us, in the south, it was already night.

When I left the train in Salzburg, a light east wind was blowing. I looked for a taxi but couldn't see one. "I'll phone for one," said the porter, and disappeared. Ten minutes later an old rattletrap of a taxi shows up. "Where to?" asked the driver.

"Akazienallee 3, in Parsch."

"Are you going to want to drive back?"

"I don't know. Why?"

"I'll never get a fare out there," he grumbled.

So that was the Festival City of Salzburg in winter. I only knew Salzburg in the summer when there was so much going on, an invasion of tourists, souvenir booths everywhere, and the morality play, *Jedermann*. Now I drove through the empty streets, along a black, icy river, past closed cafés, bars, hotels. Corrugated metal shutters covered shop windows; the Venetian blinds on hotel windows were down. Only a few street lights were lit. The snow was piled high on the sidewalks.

The taxi drove out of the city and into the suburbs over roughly paved roads. We left the last houses behind us and rattled over the hard-packed snow of a country road toward a mountain that reared up, high and black, directly facing the city. And now the fog closed in around us. The driver cursed loudly and stopped abruptly. "What's the matter?"

"You'll have to get out here. I can't drive into Akazienallee."

"Why not?"

"Because they're still working on it."

I got out and saw that there were only three houses on the street, the rest was dredgers and bulldozers, scattered over a dug-up field. A truck, a crane, and a hut for the construction workers blocked the road.

"Number three's on the left," said the driver. He remained seated behind the wheel and lit a cigarette.

I walked unsteadily out into the snow. It was quite a way to the gate of house number three, and I sank deep into the cold wet slush that covered the pitted field. Water seeped into my shoes, I could feel it icy on my left leg.

The gate to house number three was ajar. It was a low, wooden gate, a type you find frequently in the suburbs, made of split logs. A fence of the same material led from it on either side. Under a brass name plate I discovered a bell. It was very dark here, and because of the fog I could see only a few steps ahead. So I leaned forward to read the name on the plate. Wiegand. I rang, waited, rang again, but there was no answer.

I walked into the garden. Everything here seemed to have been created recently, the garden, too. In the snow I could make out a few newly planted trees. They were at best a meter high, and bare. A little farther away I could see straw-covered flower beds and, floating in the fog, a greenhouse. A long narrow path led to the villa. I decided that the strange name on the gate didn't have to mean anything. Wiegand was probably a friend or relative of Trenti's. It wasn't likely that a man living in Rome would own a villa in Salzburg.

There was a light in one window in the house I had by now almost reached, a two-story house that had evidently been built after the war in a functional, unattractive style. The lighted window worried me a little. If somebody was home, why hadn't he answered the bell?

The path curved, I slipped on an icy spot, and had just regained my balance when I saw the front door open and a man step out of the house. I stopped. He had stepped out quietly and now looked cautiously all around him. All I could see was his silhouette, but he behaved in a way that at once aroused my suspicion. I saw him take a handkerchief out of his pocket and wipe the doorknob. Still using the handkerchief, he tried several times to close the door but was unable to. Leaving it ajar—a little light fell out onto the snow from inside the villa—he ran down the few steps that led to the path and came toward me, walking fast, head lowered, with strangely small steps, his pants flapping in the wind.

He was about 15 meters away when he saw me. Quick as a flash he turned and darted across the flower bed. I was frantic because I realized I have very little chance of catching him, still I ran after him, crying, "Stop! Stop!" He paid no attention but went on running, around the house now. The way I had come was the only way out of the garden and he was evidently trying to reach it by this detour. "Stop!" I yelled, slipping, and constantly on the verge of falling, but I went on running. Then it happened. I tripped over a heavy branch that was suddenly between my feet and fell head-long in the snow. The prosthesis made a horrible cracking sound and I felt an excruciating pain in my thigh.

By this time the man had circled the house and started down the path that led to the gate. When I staggered to my feet, the prosthesis would barely support me. I knew I couldn't run another step, but I also knew I had to catch the man who had run past me on his two healthy legs, this goddamned son of a bitch!

I picked the branch I had tripped over and swung it over my head. Then I let go. The branch whizzed through the air. Let it hit him!

It struck the man between the shoulders. A dull thud, a groan, and he fell onto the snow like a sack of meal. I must have looked grotesque, hopping over to him on one leg. I kept stumbling, but after a few hops I reached him, just as he was trying to get up. I grabbed him by the shoulders and crushed his head into the snow. He groaned. Quite illogically I was sure I had found the man who had taken Sibyl from me, the man whose fault it was. The blood hammered in my temples, throbbed behind my eyes. I knelt beside the creature in the snow, raised him level with me, and turned him around. I wanted to see his face, the face of the goddamned son of a bitch! And saw his face. And it wasn't a man. It was a woman.

3

Her wet hair straggled across her forehead. She couldn't have been more than 35, but her hair was completely white. Her cheeks were smeared with blood and snow, her eyes were light and very large, her lips were parted and I could see her teeth. She was looking at me with an expression of deathly fear. I let her go and she fell onto the snow, on her back, and lay still in her heavy winter coat that was cut like a man's. Her legs were stretched from her at an unusual angle, as if they were broken. She didn't move. She stared at me.

"Who are you?" I asked.

She pressed a fist to her mouth.

"Why did you run away when I called out to you to stop?"

She remained silent and began to shiver. "Answer me," I said softly.

She shook her head.

"If you don't answer me, I'll beat it out of you."

She didn't answer me and I hit her in the face. Her

breath came like a hiss from between her clenched teeth, but she said nothing.

I staggered to my feet. "Get up!" I told her, and this order she obeyed, slowly, trembling. She was a head shorter than I. Mechanically she began to beat the snow off her coat with her small hands. I grasped her arm. "Come on," I said, limping a few steps toward the villa. At last she spoke. "No!" She stopped, tried to free herself. "Not into the house! Please, please, not into the house!"

"But that's where we're going," I said, dragging her along.

"No!" She was whimpering. "Please! Please! I'll do anything you want, anything, but I won't go back into the house. Please!"

I turned her around and slapped her face hard, twice. "Get going," I said, and now she let me lead her without any further resistance. In the distance a locomotive whistled, a long drawn-out whistle that faded slowly into the night. The fog was thicker than ever. I pushed the front door open. "Go in," I told her.

She stood in front of me, her face white, her cheekbones high, ghostly. Under other circumstances, I thought, she must be pretty. I saw that her eyes were a clear light blue. Her white hair didn't go with the rest of her at all. She must be about the same age as Sibyl, I thought, and the thought of Sibyl had a disastrous effect on me. I had to control myself or I would have struck the woman again. I shoved her into the lighted hall and examined the door, which could be locked from the inside.

I leaned against the door and looked at the woman.

She had, meanwhile, dropped into an armchair that stood beside a mirror. There was a closet in the hall, a few old paintings, a fireplace and some pewter ornaments. The floor was carpeted, and there were several doors, all of them closed. The woman sat there and wept—her legs stretched out, her arms dangling over the side of the chair, and the tears running down her dirty white face.

"What's your name?" I asked. "And what were you doing here? I want the truth."

She raised her tear-stained face and tried to speak. Her lips formed words, she gasped and babbled like someone drunk. "I can't understand a word."

She collapsed and began to whisper. I walked over to her. "Can you hear me?"

She nodded.

I saw that the red lacquer on her nails was cracked and caked black with earth. Her hands were trembling so hard they seemed to be jumping up and down on her lap. I said, "My name is Holland. I came here to see Herr Trenti. Do you know Herr Trenti?"

She nodded again.

"Are you here because you wanted to see him, too?"

She nodded a third time. It was absolutely still in the house. A large picture hung over the cold fireplace, an English hunting scene. A lot of dogs and horses. The huntsmen wore red jackets.

"Where is Herr Trenti?"

She gestured with her right hand toward a door beside the fireplace. I could see light under it. I walked over to it. The door opened onto a library with bookshelves along all four walls. Beside a window there stood an armchair and a standing lamp with a green shade.

Herr Trenti lay on the floor in front of the armchair. He was wearing a gray, single-breasted suit with vest, and his face, the eyes upturned, wore an expression of astonishment. His left hand rested on his left thigh; he had lifted his right hand to his throat as if to loosen his tie or open his shirt because he felt hot. But Herr Trenti, produce merchant from Rome, didn't want to open his shirt or loosen his tie; Herr Emilio Trenti didn't want anything anymore, because he was dead. Somebody had shot him. The left side of his vest, the two bottom buttons of which were open, was drenched with blood.

4

When I began to write this book I said that Sibyl Loredo had taken the place in my life in which other people place a political dogma, a god, or a belief in something. Sibyl had meant everything to me. I couldn't believe any more in the Caucasian god whose priests blessed Christian canons and whose Popes had chosen not to break diplomatic relations with the National Socialists but were now excommunicating communists, and I found it just as impossible to believe in the promises of politicians. But since I knew I had to believe in something, I had chosen to love Sibyl Loredo.

Unlike me, Sibyl had been a devout Catholic. It was the constant message and promise of peace in the Christian religion that made her religious. During the hectic weeks following her disappearance, I realized that it had been the last hope of a desperate woman. I found out that the word "peace" had meant to her what the bottle meant to the alcoholic, the lover's body to the nymphomaniac, and the salvation of death to those dying of cancer. Today I know how desperate this hope of hers was, in which I played only a small part, however futile. But on that evening, when I stood beside the dead body of Emilio Trenti, in the library of the house in Parsch, a suburb of Salzburg, I knew nothing at all. I knelt beside the dead man without touching him. I looked at his pale puffy face, with the furrowed brow of a hard-working businessman and the sacks under his wide open astonished eyes. His mouth was wide open, too. He had a lot of gold teeth and altogether impressed me as a once-prosperous man. Then I felt someone move. The young woman with the white hair was standing beside me. "I didn't do it," she said, in a voice that sounded dead.

Her heavy coat was open. I could see the flannel pants she was wearing, and the blue pullover. She had large breasts. She said softly, "He was dead when I got here."

"When did you come?"

"A little while before you did."

"Who opened the door if he was already dead?"

"The door was open."

Her face was caked with dirt. A little blood had seeped out of her mouth where I had struck her. It was drying. We looked at each other for quite a long time and again the house was filled with an eerie stillness. Nothing moved. The silence was stupefying. "Why did you come here?" I asked.

"Why did *you* come here?" Her face was beginning to show signs of life again. She was over the shock and ready to defend herself.

"Herr Trenti wanted to see me."

She looked at the dead man, then at me again, then she asked, "Did you do it?"

I shook my head.

She turned her back on me suddenly and I said, "Answer my question. What were you doing here?"

She answered without looking at me. "He called me. Yesterday afternoon. In Vienna."

"In Vienna?"

"I live in Vienna. He called and said he had to speak to me, it was very important. And he gave me this address."

"Did he say why he wanted to speak to you?"

"No. Did he tell you?"

"Yes. He said it concerned a certain Sibyl Loredo."

I watched her sharply as I said the name, but her dirty face remained expressionless. "Sibyl Loredo?"

"Yes. Does the name mean anything to you?"

She shook her head. She was pretty. As a matter of fact, she was beautiful. But she didn't appeal to me. When I had seen Sibyl for the first time, that evening at the Maison de France in Berlin, from the moment she had entered the room, I hadn't been aware of any other woman. The sight of her had made me feel as heady as wine. This woman had the opposite effect on me. I couldn't see why. Everything about her irritated me: her monotonous, expressionless way of speaking, her little face, her grotesque white hair and limpid blue eyes. The way her body seemed lost in her voluminous coat. Her full breasts. Everything. Meanwhile she asked, and now she sounded exhausted, "Sibyl Loredo? Who is she?"

"A friend," I said. What Sibyl had meant to me was no concern of hers. I asked, "How do you happen to know Herr Trenti?"

She gritted her teeth and shook her head.

"You don't want to talk about it?"

She said angrily, "You struck me!"

"I'm sorry."

"Nobody has ever struck me!"

"I thought you were a man," I said, and thought: if I had known you were a woman, I would have struck you just the same.

"What's your name?" I asked.

"Petra Wend."

"Petra Wend? Your name . . ."

"Perhaps you know it?"

"I think I do, but I can't place you."

"Do you go to the movies often?"

"Yes."

"I'm a costume consultant. I have a fashion salon in Vienna. You've probably seen my name on a lot of film credits."

"Frau Wend, why did you run away when you found the man dead? Why didn't you call the police?"

"Because I didn't want to get involved. I was afraid."

"Of what?"

"I don't know."

I stepped across the dead man and went over to a table with a telephone standing on it. A telephone book lay beside it. "What are you going to do?" she asked.

"Call the police." I found the number and dialed. A deep voice answered. "Police headquarters, Salzburg."

"Paul Holland speaking. Send a car to Akazienallee. A man's been shot."

"Are you drunk?"

"No."

"Then don't try any practical jokes on us."

"I'm telling you—a man has been shot, and I mean it!"

The voice at the other end came to life suddenly. "What's the address?" I repeated it. "We'll be there right away."

5

Six policemen arrived, the blue lights of their cars revolving, their sirens screaming. They brought cameras and lights and fingerprint powder, and they set to work as the police do in every city in the world. They photographed Emilio Trenti, they photographed the room and Petra Wend and me. A medical examiner did his job and declared Emilio Trenti officially dead "since about an hour and a half." An ambulance drew up in front of the house and two men in white came in with a stretcher. They laid the dead produce merchant on it, and Herr Emilio Trenti from Rome left the house in Salzburg, feet first.

"You'll have the results of the autopsy tomorrow," said the medical examiner, a short, bald-headed man, the only one who was obviously irked by the whole procedure. He had been planning to go to *The Countess Maritza*.

Outside, on the snow-covered ground, quite a few curious people were waiting between the bulldozers and cranes. They watched the body being lifted into the ambulance. They stood huddled together in groups, whispering to each other. Their hushed voices sounded like rustling leaves. The siren wailed as the ambulance drove away.

The men from homicide searched the house for clues. They walked around in the garden and examined footprints at the spot where I had struggled with Petra Wend. They talked to the neighbors. In Number 1 they had been celebrating somebody's birthday. That's why there were so many people. The man of the house—his name was Gross—was wearing a paper hat and was slightly drunk. There were traces of lipstick on his shirt. He looked embarrassed as he stood in front of the police officer called Enders, who was conducting the investigation.

They had asked Herr Gross to step into the house where the murder had been committed, and he stood in front of the cold fireplace in the hall and told what he knew. "Did you know Herr Trenti?" asked the officer, a handsome man, graying at the temples and almost too elegantly dressed. He looked like a film star and spoke with a rather refined Austrian accent.

"Only by sight, sir." Herr Gross was short and fat. He burped and quickly raised his rosy hand to his soft lips. "I saw him a few times when he came to see Herr Wiegand."

"The house belongs to Herr Wiegand?"

"Yes, sir." Gross took off his paper cap and burped again. "You must excuse me. I've been drinking champagne."

"What does Herr Wiegand do?"

"He's a produce merchant. Wholesale."

"Where is Herr Wiegand?"

"Away. He travels a lot. Herr Trenti had keys to the house. Whenever Herr Wiegand was in Rome, he stayed with Herr Trenti, and whenever Herr Trenti came to Salzburg, he stayed here."

"You didn't hear anything this afternoon? No shots? No voices?"

"Nothing, sir. I'm afraid we were making such a lot of noise at my house, you couldn't hear anything."

The others hadn't heard anything either. They corroborated what Gross had said—that Wiegand and Trenti had been friends, and they didn't know anything more.

Then I told the chief my story. He listened attentively and took notes. He was wearing a pearl tie-pin and signet ring. There was altogether an old-world elegance in the way he was dressed. He asked, "Do you think the murder of Herr Trenti is connected somehow with the disappearance of Frau Loredo?"

"I'm sure it is."

"Hm."

He turned his back on me and began to interrogate Petra Wend. She had cleaned her face in the meantime and combed her hair. Her lips were too red and she had put too much rouge on her cheeks. In her eyes there still lay an expression of deadly fear.

"And you, madame?" Enders said *madame*. He seemed to like to use French expressions. "Where did you meet Herr Trenti?"

A muscle in her pale, grotesquely made-up face twitched, but her voice was controlled. "In Italy."

"After the war?"

"During the war." The twitch went from the bridge of her noise, across her forehead, to her hairline. It was quite noticeable now.

"When during the war, madame?"

"In 1944. I think. I—I was in Rome at the time, and he was introduced to me at a party."

"What was he doing at the time?"

"He was an official in the Ministry of Food and Agriculture." Petra Wend bit her lip. "I was living in Rome. A lot of people came to my house; he was one of them."

"*J'ai compris*," said Enders. "*Excusez moi* if I have to trouble you, madame. After the war, did you see Herr Trenti any more."

She shook her head.

"And he didn't get in touch with you?"

"No."

"And yet you came here at once when he asked you to?"

"He said it was very important. For him and for me. He said—it sounds melodramatic, I know—but he said it was a matter of life and death—his and mine."

As she spoke I managed at last to get hold of something small and hard that had slipped between the cushion and side of the leather chair I was sitting on. I had felt it when I sat down. Throughout the entire interrogation I had been trying to fish it out without Chief Enders or Petra Wend noticing.

Enders was talking to Petra; his back was turned to me. Inch by inch I moved my hand across my knee, then I looked down. I knew before I saw it what it would be. I had been able to tell by its shape. It was a

gold, oval earring, a clip-on, one of a pair that had
been designed for Sibyl. Two tiny *s*'s were engraved inside the ring. Jeweler Hähnlein in Berlin, Kurfürstendamm 34, had made them, and I had paid 280 West
marks for them.

So there I sat with it in my hand, and it burned like
fire. I stuck my hand in my trouser pocket. When I
drew it out again, I was holding a pack of cigarettes
and the earring was in my pocket. I lit a cigarette and
wondered if Petra Wend had noticed anything. I felt
like a drunkard staggering through the endless tunnel
of his addiction. I couldn't see any way out and it was
growing darker and colder around me all the time.

6

"I must ask both of you not to leave Salzburg,"
said Chief Enders. "I'm sorry to have to inconvenience
you like this, but it's necessary."

"We may not leave the city?"

"No, madame. Not until we have finished our investigation."

"But I must get back to Vienna!" Petra Wend protested. "I'm working on a film that's going into production next week."

"*Deplorable*, madame, but there's nothing I can do about it."

I asked, "Where can we stay?"

"There are a number of good hotels."

"I used to stay at the Pitter," said Petra.

"If you don't mind my coming with you, I'd like to stay there, too," I said, looking at her sharply. Her face remained expressionless. Had she noticed the business with the earring? I thought: this woman was in Italy during the war. She didn't seem to like being reminded of it. Unlike Sibyl, who had talked about her life there all the time. But had she told me the truth? And, startled, I thought: for the first time since I met her, I am doubting Sibyl.

It was because of the earring. How did it get here? Suddenly I felt I had to get out into the fresh air. "Let's go," I said.

Petra nodded. We walked to my taxi through the foggy garden. Two cats were fighting close to the parked car. They ran away as we approached. I limped through the mud beside Petra. "Did you hurt yourself?"

"No. I always walk like this. I have an artificial leg."

"Oh. I'm sorry."

Most people reacted like this. I didn't bother to answer anymore. I sat down beside her in the back and the man drove off. Wisps of amber-colored fog floated past us. We progressed slowly because by now it was very thick. I thought of Sibyl's earring.

"Were you wounded in the war?"

"I beg your pardon." I turned to look at her, but she was looking straight ahead, into the fog.

"Your leg. Did you lose it in the war?"

Very few people asked that. Most of them hastily changed the subject. I said, "No."

"So how did you lose it?" Her voice was as toneless as ever and she was getting on my nerves, as she had done all along.

"I was looking for some schnapps."

"Schnapps?"

"French cognac. Before I was a soldier, I had ten bottles of Hennessey left. In a case. Do you want to hear the rest?"

She nodded.

"I drove to a wooded area near Frankfurt with the case of cognac, and buried it. I wanted to have something decent to drink when I came back."

She was silent. The motor hummed.

"When I came back in 1946, I drove to the place. The case with the cognac was still there. But as I dragged it out, I was unlucky. I stepped on a land mine. And that was the end of the cognac."

"My God!" she said. "How horrible!" She didn't say anything more until we reached the city. The clock in the taxi read 7:30 P.M.

We reached the hotel after driving through an underpass near the station. As I got out I could see the red and green signal lights on the tracks. A train passed by, its lighted windows glowing hazily in the fog, and I could hear the grinding sound of its wheels. I suddenly realized it was possible Sibyl was in Salzburg, somewhere nearby in the dark.

Petra had rented room 312 and when they saw me
with her, they gave me 314. As in many hotels, there
was no 313. We took the elevator to the third floor.
The bellboy stood between us with my luggage. The
elevator smelled of fresh paint and metal. We looked at
each other over the boy's head and I waited for some
sort of expression in her light-blue eyes, a sign of dis-
trust or understanding or hatred. But her face remained expressionless.

In front of her door she held out her hand. "Good
night, Herr Holland."

"Good night, Frau Wend. And please forgive me for
having struck you."

She went into her room without another word and
closed the door, and I was left standing alone in the
passage.

My room had yellow tinted walls, modern lacquer
furniture and a radio. Actually it was a loudspeaker
that played music which was controlled somewhere else
in the house, radio or records. I turned it on and heard
the Marschallin's aria from *Rosenkavalier*. I turned on
all the lights, went into the bathroom and ran a bath. I
undressed, unstrapped my prosthesis, got into the tub,
rested my head on the back and stared at the ceiling.
Now the loudspeaker was broadcasting Wagner. I
shaved and dressed again and stared out the window at
the empty street.

I had put Sibyl's earring down on the table in front
of me. Now I looked at the little piece of metal that
couldn't talk but certainly had a story to tell, then I put
it back in my pocket and began to read my old newspaper. I read the editorials, the theater reviews, and an

account of the rounding up of some cattle. I read my way through the programs of every movie house in Munich, and an installment of a novel by Louis Bromfield, *Early Autumn*. Suddenly, I felt as if the ceiling were coming down on top of me and I couldn't stand it there alone a minute longer. I was so nervous, it took me two minutes to light a cigarette. Finally I walked over to the phone and asked for room 312. It was my intention to ask Petra Wend to have dinner with me. The telephone operator answered, "Frau Wend isn't in her room."

"Did she go out?"

"Just a minute. I'll ask at the desk." Then the desk was on the line. "Frau Wend is in the gaming room."

"Where?"

"She's playing roulette, Herr Holland."

"But the casino used to be—"

"At the bridge. I know. But they moved it. The gaming room is in our hotel now."

I put out all the lights and left the room. "Which floor, sir?" asked the elevator boy.

"To the gaming room."

The elevator began its descent. "Good luck!" said the boy as I got out.

"I beg your pardon?"

"I was wishing you good luck, sir."

"Oh . . . yes. Thank you," I said. "It's very good of you."

7

"Faites vos jeux, mesdames, messieurs!" The croupier's voice was muted by the dimensions of the room. There were two tables, both almost filled. Many of the players were standing. The betting at one table was higher than at the other. The little white ball was just dropping into a compartment.

"*Vingt-sept rouge, impair et passe!*" cried the croupier. There were no chips on the number. Two players had placed on *chevaux*, a few others on simpler bets.

The Salzburg gaming room was not as ostentatious as the one in Baden-Baden—no sparkling chandeliers, no gilded caryatids—but the carpets were good, there were Gobelin tapestries on the walls and massive club-type leather furniture. The staff was in livery, with lace jabots and patent-leather pumps, and the croupiers were dressed elegantly. In Salzburg they also seemed to believe that the gambler preferred to risk his money in luxurious surroundings.

"*Vingt-sept rouge, impair et passe!*"

At table one there were cries of astonishment because the same number had come up twice in succession. An old lady was beside herself. "Dreadful, gentlemen! Simply dreadful! I placed *à cheval* the first time and I wanted to place the same number again and double the *cheval*, but I didn't have the courage." Her voice was trembling. She was almost in tears. One of the croupiers nodded in her direction, the other was already spinning the wheel. *"Faites vos jeux, mesdames, messieurs!"*

There were ladies in cocktail gowns and peasants in loden among the players. The peasants seemed to have the most money. They sat at the table, broad, heavyset men with red chapped hands, and shoved their chips wherever they wanted them. There were a lot more women than men, and most of the women were over 50. Some were accompanied by smart young men who stood behind their ladies and looked bored.

"Trois rouge, impair et manque!"

I thought of the loudspeakers at the airport in Berlin. I closed my eyes and could hear them. "Attention, please! PAA Clipper 754 to Düsseldorf and London, taking on passengers at Gate 3. We wish you a pleasant flight."

I thought of Sibyl and was afraid. Since I had found the earring, I hadn't known a moment's peace. I was certain that at any moment something terrible would happen to me, something I couldn't prevent, something final. To all appearances I was perfectly safe, but it was the calm before the storm, the eye of the hurricane. Emilio Trenti's death hadn't touched me, but finding Sibyl's earring in his house had devastated me.

"Cinq rouge, impair et passe!"

Then I saw Petra. She was sitting at the second table, beside the head croupier, and seemed absorbed in the game. In a silver-gray cocktail gown that left her shoulders bare, her chips in front of her, a cigarette in her hand, she was miles removed from the Petra Wend I had met a few hours ago. I found it hard to believe she had recovered so fast. I wondered why she had come.

She didn't place her chips herself; she pushed them across to the croupier standing beside her and whispered a few words to him. He nodded and placed them for her. I could see that she was playing only 50-schilling chips, each time with at least 8 numbers. Now she was playing the 11, with 4 adjoining numbers, the 35, the last 6 and the last 3.

"Faites vos jeux, mesdames, messieurs!"

Petra flicked the ash off her cigarette absentmindedly. It missed the ashtray and fell on the green felt beside it. She didn't notice. Her light-blue eyes were open very wide, unnaturally wide, as if a doctor had given her atropine. Her cheeks were a hectic red, her lips were moving, she was talking to herself. The croupier looked down at her every now and then, thoughtfully.

The little ball was rolling. *"Rien ne va plus!"*

With that the betting was over, still Petra jumped to her feet and hastily placed on 25, 29, and on the *transversale pleine* 4, 5, and 6, then she sat down with the slow motion of a mechanical doll and stared straight ahead.

"Onze noir, impair et manque!" cried the croupier. Petra had won. Her chips were pushed across to her.

She paid no attention to them but was already giving the croupier new instructions. Then she tossed a 50-schilling chip across the table. *"Pour les employés!"*

"Pour les employés!" the croupier held up the chip before tossing it into the box, and all four croupiers cried in unison, *"Merci, madame, pour les employés!"*

The game went on. Petra won. She played as if in a trance. She doubled the bets and plastered the whole table with her chips. I could see her breasts rising and falling agitatedly under the thin silk of her dress. Now she rose and began to play standing. And she smoked incessantly.

"Seize rouge, impair et manque!"

Nothing on the color, nothing on the number. The croupier cleared the table with his rake. This time Petra had lost, about 1,000 schillings, I figured. She didn't wait for the table to be cleared but put out her cigarette, and shoved a pile of chips across to the croupier with instructions. With the rest of her chips in her evening bag, she walked over to the other table, in the course of which I could see her exquisite figure and beautifully shaped long legs. In her pants I hadn't noticed her legs.

They made room for her at the table, but she didn't sit down. She remained standing and pushed chips over to the croupier and gave him some instructions. He looked up, and when he saw who it was, he nodded and smiled. Meanwhile, the wheel was turning at the first table. Petra went back to it.

"Deux noir, pair et manque!"

Petra had won. She let her winnings lie where the

croupier had put them, he placed for her again and she went back to the other table.

"Trente-trois noir, impair et passe!"

She had won again.

She continued to play at both tables, moving from one to the other, and when she was in danger of missing a game, even running. What was Petra Wend afraid of? I watched her as she continued to hurry back and forth between the two tables, breathless, excited, until about three quarters of an hour later, she collected all her chips and went to the bar, her state of euphoria apparently over. All in all she had lost a few thousand schillings, but she still had chips left. I walked across to the bar and sat down beside her. I still wondered how she had recovered so quickly from the blows I had given her. "Good evening."

"Oh!" She looked startled, then her eyes narrowed. "Have you been here a long time?"

I nodded. The bartender came over to us. "What would you like?"

"A glass of champagne."

"And a whiskey for me," I said.

The bartender left us. In the light, Petra's white hair glistened. She asked, "Were you watching me play?"

"Yes."

She crossed her legs, tapped the tobacco in her cigarette and said softly, "I have been watching you, too, Herr Holland."

In a way I had expected this, and it came as a relief. The bartender brought our drinks and went off again. We could hear the cries of the croupiers from the gaming room next door, and sometimes, the ball rolling.

"Where did you watch me?"

"In the house in Akazienallee."

Her voice was soft. She reminded me of a cat purring. "When you—when you found something in the chair."

I could smell her perfume. She sat there, legs crossed, leaning back, calmly aggressive. Her bag with the chips in it lay in front of her. "I saw you put it in your pocket."

I said nothing.

"You *did* put it in your pocket, didn't you?"

"If you saw me, why didn't you tell the Chief?"

Now she put the cigarette between her lips and I gave her a light. She exhaled the smoke and said, "I decided it was something you wanted to keep secret."

"And that's why you didn't say anything?"

"Yes."

"*Trente-quatre rouge, pair et passe!*" cried the croupier in the gaming room next door.

I realized there was no purpose in hiding anything. "It was an earring. It belonged to Sibyl Loredo. I have no idea how it got into the house on Akazienallee, and I—I don't know what I'm going to do next. I'm very grateful to you for not betraying me," I said, and took a drink from my glass.

"Do you happen to have a picture of Frau Loredo?"

"Yes."

"*Zero!*" Followed by a lot of commotion in the gaming room.

"Of course." I took a picture I always had with me out of my wallet. It showed Sibyl on the Wannsee beach. She was stretched out on the sand in a black bathing suit, and she was laughing. I had always liked the picture. "Here," I said, and handed it to Petra Wend.

"That—that is—" she started to say, then she dropped her glass. It broke and the champagne spread a dark spot on the red carpet.

The bartender came running. "What's the matter?"

"Please help me," I said. "The lady has fainted."

8

Two men were sitting in a corner of the bar. I had noticed them when I came in. I had got the impression that they had lost every schilling they had. They sat there, eyes closed, listening to the croupiers next door. As I walked over to the bar, one of the croupiers had cried, *"Trente-six rouge, pair et passe!"* and one of the men had said, "I put twenty on the *dernière douzaine* and one *transversale pleine* with ten." His companion said, "Damnit! I placed on the twelve again, two left, two right. Idiot!"

The two were still playing. Since they didn't have any money left, they were playing in their heads, placing the chips they didn't have. *"Vingt-neuf noir, impair et passe!"* cried the croupier.

"I played *à cheval* with ten," said the first man, rubbing his hands.

"Nothing," said his companion in this weird game, sounding miserable.

Now, when they saw the bartender and me trying to help Petra Wend, they came rushing over. One of them asked if there was anything he could do, the other picked up Petra's bag, which had fallen on the floor. Two 50-schilling chips fell out of it. The frustrated gambler took advantage of the general confusion and slipped the round discs into his pocket. No one noticed, except me, and I had more important worries.

"I'll give the lady some cognac," said the bartender. The thief said that Fernet Branca was the best thing to give anyone who had fainted, and hurried off to the gaming room.

After the first swallow of Hennessey, Petra opened her eyes. She was still stretched out on the carpet; I was holding her head up. As she came to, her teeth bit against the edge of the glass. It was an ugly sound. As she got up and began to smooth down her dress, she almost fell again.

"What's the matter?" I asked, as I supported her. "What's wrong with you?"

Petra's face was white. She was staring down at the counter. So was I. Both of us were looking at the picture of Sibyl. "Please take me to my room," said Petra. "I have to talk to you."

I paid for our drinks and walked with her through

the gaming room to the hotel. The thief had just placed one of his stolen chips on nineteen. The ball rolled.

"Dix-neuf, rouge, impair et manquel" cried the croupier. The thief had won 700 schillings.

Petra's room was exactly like mine. It also had a loudspeaker that played music—as we came in, Gershwin's *Concerto in F.* Petra turned it off, sat down on the bed and said, "Now I know who murdered Emilio Trenti."

"Who?"

"And who will also kill me," she went on, without interruption.

"Who?" I asked again.

"The woman whose picture you just showed me."

"Sibyl?"

She nodded.

The incomprehensible becomes comprehensible and more bearable, more imaginable, as soon as it leaves the realm of thought and has been expressed in words. A nightmare, recounted in the morning, is no longer dreadful, is in fact sometimes quite comical. We sat facing each other in this light, functional hotel room, Petra Wend on the bed, I in a comfortable chair, and she had just told me that, in her opinion, Sibyl had committed murder. And I was taking the idea into consideration as terrible, yes, but not impossible. I asked, "So you know Sibyl."

"Yes." Her teeth were chattering.

"Perhaps you're mistaking her for someone else. It's not a very good picture, and there are people who look a lot alike."

"Herr Holland, does your friend have a birthmark the size of a schilling under her left armpit?"

"Yes."

"Does she hear poorly with her right ear?"

"Yes."

"Because of an eardrum injury?"

I nodded.

"This injury," Petra went on, in her unnaturally calm, unnaturally clear voice, "was the result of a blow she received as a child."

"Yes," I said slowly. My tongue felt thick, as if I had been drinking. "Sibyl was twelve years old when an old man—"

"An old man on the street struck her."

"Because she was playing with his dog."

We spoke the words simultaneously.

She sighed and said, "I'm sorry for you, Herr Holland. I know it is going to be a terrible blow to you when you hear the truth."

"What truth?"

"The truth about Victoria, the woman in the photograph."

"Her name is Sibyl. Sibyl Loredo," I said softly, almost in a whisper.

She shook her head, seriously, mercilessly, like an angel on Judgment Day. "No, Herr Holland. The name of the woman in the picture is Victoria Brunswick."

9

As I continue this report, I am faced with a difficulty. I have to tell a story, a living experience, to which I was not witness, the story of two women—Petra Wend and the woman I knew as Sibyl Loredo, but whose name actually was Victoria Brunswick.

When Petra Wend told me about herself and Victoria Brunswick in a hotel room in Salzburg, I had no way of checking if she spoke the truth. But as the weeks passed, I found a way and know now that Petra Wend told a true story. I found a witness, and the witness was Sibyl Loredo.

But since using the two names—Sibyl and Victoria—for one person would be confusing to the reader, I shall continue to call the woman who was Victoria Brunswick, Sibyl Loredo. I shall write it as a narrative, in the third person.

The story begins on an evening in April 1944, in the Green Salon of the Italian Embassy in Berlin. The capital of the so-called Greater German Reich has fallen victim to widespread American and British bombing raids. The battle of Stalingrad has been lost, the African campaign has failed. The Allied landing in Normandy is imminent. The people of Berlin —undernourished, fear-ridden, and hopeless, have resigned themselves to a new life-style, punctuated by the howling of sirens, intermittent rain of phosphorus fire, and saturation bombing, endless propaganda by the BBC, rationing and party member spying.

On this evening in April—the Berlin radio had just reported a heavy concentration of bombers over the Bay of Heligoland, heading for the province of Mark Brandenburg—martinis were being served in the Green Salon of the Italian Embassy as the cultural attaché apologized to the ladies that, for obvious reasons, he was not in a position to serve English gin. He was a handsome young man with black hair and passionate eyes. He was especially nice to women and was a homosexual. Many ladies in Berlin and elsewhere had done their best to dissuade him from his deviation, to no avail. The cultural attaché was very happy in Berlin. He loved lanky boys with blond hair and blue eyes, and whenever time permitted, he joined Troop 504 of the Hitler Youth Organization on their cross-country hikes. He was talking in his slightly sing-song voice to a young lady in a black evening dress. "I'm afraid," he said, "that we're soon going to have to move our party to the cellar. It's scandalous!"

The young lady had astonishingly white hair, cut short, her skin was marvelously clear, and her eyes were aquamarine blue. She was 24 years old and her name was Petra Wend. She was in the Italian Embassy for the first time. The ambassador whose attention she

had attracted in a nightclub was old and ugly, but he
was normal, and he liked beautiful women. He was
also very charming. It was said that he understood how
to make a woman happy. Those who knew him inti-
mately were ready to turn their backs on any other
man for him.

"It's horrible in Berlin now," said Petra Wend, bit-
ing hungrily into a smoked salmon sandwich. You
couldn't buy much smoked salmon in Berlin anymore.

"When the final victory comes," said the cultural attaché, "your city will be rebuilt, more modern and
beautiful than ever," and he was pleased with himself
for having been able to say this without a trace of
irony. He spoke excellent German. "You are working
in a film?"

"Yes. In Babelsberg. I'm assistant to the costume
designer."

"That's no profession for a woman as beautiful as
you are, Fräulein," said the homosexual cultural attaché.

He bared his white teeth. Petra really did please
him. She was so exquisitely groomed and was undoubtedly very clean. It occurred to him—and the thought
was depressing—that he really didn't have anything
against women. The only thing that repelled him from
any intimacy was their smell. Women could be very attractive, but who could abide the way they smelled? He
asked, "How would you like to live in Rome for a
while? In a palazzo on the Via Appia?"

Petra had to smile. "Signor Rossi," she said, "the
English will be here any minute. Are you making fun
of me?"

She smells just like all the others, the cultural attaché thought sadly as he said, "No. I'm serious. Could you get out of your professional obligations for—let's say a month?"

"I don't know what you mean."

"Let me explain," said the cultural attaché. "You are young, you are beautiful, you come from a good family. Our ambassador likes to invite pretty young ladies from good families to visit us in Rome. As his guests. They live in small palazzi and may do whatever they like."

"You mean—without any obligations?"

"I mean without any obligations whatsoever, Fräulein. In this way we hope to strengthen the bonds of friendship between our two countries."

"It sounds like a fairy tale. Things like this don't happen!"

"But they do." The cultural attaché was smiling as he thought that it wasn't only the way they smelled but also their lack of intelligence that he found repulsive. Ignorance in men didn't bother him. It bothered him only in women. He thought longingly of a certain idealistic troop leader he knew, Klaus Zschiele, and asked, "So . . . do you accept the invitation?"

"I—I really must think it over."

"Of course, *gnädiges Fräulein*."

"I don't have any money."

"You will be our guest. We will open a bank account for you."

"But I can't accept anything like that!"

"You can, *gnädiges Fräulein*, I assure you. Our ambassador worships beautiful women. They seem to take the place of religion in his life," said the cultural attaché, and the thought that it really was revolting to have to use this same line over and over again. He decided to speak to his boss about it. Why did he want to invite pretty girls all the time? If the Italian department for foreign affairs wanted female German contacts in Rome, then for heaven's sake, it was time they found a different way to get them!

Petra Wend was floored. "I—I think this is the most remarkable invitation I've ever had!"

God bless you, thought the cultural attaché as he smiled and said, "So you'll come?"

"Yes," said Petra Wend.

Outside the sirens began to wail. The heavy concentration of bombers from the Bay of Heligoland had reached Berlin.

10

That night only 526 people lost their lives in the German capital as the attacking squadrons dropped only high explosives and fire bombs. Two days later, Petra Wend, who was getting ready to leave for Rome,

received a postcard asking her to come to see Herr
Jahn in Room 314 on the second floor of the Foreign
Office building in the Wilhelmstrasse. It was important,
wrote Herr Jahn. His first name was Helmut. It was
printed on the door of his office. He was a large man, a
dark, sombre type.

"Fräulein Wend, you have applied for permission to
leave Germany for Italy."

"Yes. But I applied to the police, not to the Foreign
Office." Petra Wend was confused.

"The police passed on your application to us," said
Herr Jahn, concentrating on his long nicotine-stained
fingers.

"I have been invited by the Italian ambassador. . . ."

"We know, Fräulein Wend. We know all about that.
And you are pleased with the invitation?"

"Naturally. Just think, Herr Jahn, in Italy it's already warm. And there are no bombs, none of this
dreadful fear! I'm very happy about it."

"I can imagine you are. Unfortunately you are not
going to Rome."

"And how can I do that?"

"We are not giving you permission to leave the coun-
"I beg your pardon!"
try."

"I don't understand!"

"We won't let you travel, Fräulein Wend, unless—
unless you agree to be of some small help to us."

"Fräulein Wend," said melancholy Herr Jahn, tug-
ging at his upper lip, "you will meet a lot of people in
Rome, above all, a lot of men. Some of these men will

hold important positions in the Italian administration. You will meet economic advisors, politicians . . . I imagine these men will have a lot of interesting things to tell."

Petra was silent.

A one-armed man came in, lifted his one arm in the Hitler salute, and informed Herr Jahn that there might be an air raid warning shortly. Jahn said, "Thank you." To Petra he said, "We know that there is going to be an invasion of Italy before long, but we don't know where. We also know that our brave Italian allies intend to defect. But we don't know when. And we would like to know. If you could be of any assistance to us in this respect, I could get a permit at once for you to leave Germany. We would also express our gratitude financially."

"And if I don't agree?"

Herr Jahn said sadly, "There are so many factories, Fräulein Wend. You are a costume consultant, aren't you? Not exactly war work. I've been told that they need workers on their assembly line at Siemens and Halske. You know the factory?"

"Yes. In North Berlin."

"Exactly, and the working hours at Siemens and Halske begin at six A.M."

Petra said nothing.

"Unless," said Helmut Jahn, and for the first time he smiled, "they put you on the night shift. In that case you would start work at nine P.M. and go home at six A.M."

11

When she had arrived at this point, Petra Wend, 12 years older now, too, looked down and was silent. I thought that in the meantime there was no more Foreign Ministry in the Wilhelmstrasse, there was also no more Wilhelmstrasse, and in all probability Helmut Jahn was gone, too. I asked, "Shall I order something to drink?"

She nodded.

"Champagne again?"

"Yes, please."

I went to the phone and ordered champagne and whiskey, then I sat down and looked at her. "I don't care what you think of me," she said hoarsely.

I said nothing.

"I was so young!" she cried. "And I didn't want to work for Siemens and Halske! I was afraid of the bombs! All my relatives were dead. I didn't have anybody to consider but myself."

"So you accepted Herr Jahn's proposition."

"Yes."

"Please go on," I said. "Please tell about Sibyl."

She pulled up her legs and hugged them. She was shivering. "So I went to Rome," she continued, "at the invitation of the Italians and on behalf of the German Foreign Ministry, with the assignment to keep my ears open. And I was very well paid for it."

Whatever Petra Wend had done was a matter of complete indifference to me. I wanted to hear about Sibyl. That was the only thing I was interested in. She did know Sibyl. She knew about the birthmark under Sibyl's left armpit, she knew about her deaf right ear. I had to go on listening to her.

"The ambassador had reserved a sleeper for me," Petra went on. "Anhalter Station was crowded with women and children, all of them wanting to get out of the city. There had been an air raid alarm. Two policemen made way for me. They pushed the women and children away and escorted me to my compartment. I was alone. The sleeper was in the first-class. The rest of the train was so full, people were even standing in the toilets. You could only get in and out of the train through the windows."

She paused. "Go on," I said impatiently. "So you got to Rome."

"Yes."

"And lived in the house on the Via Appia."

"Yes, Herr Holland."

"Go on."

"The Italian cultural attaché from Berlin came to see me. He introduced me to many people, to Roman society. I was invited to their salons. . . ."

"Go on."

"A man fell in love with me."

"That doesn't interest me."

"But it *will* interest you in a minute," she said. "The name of the man who fell in love with me was Tonio Trenti. He was the son of the man who was murdered in the Akazienallee."

12

There was a knock on the door. "Come in!" I cried.

A smiling young waiter entered with our drinks. He said he hoped the champagne was cold enough; if not, he advised keeping the bottle in the ice bucket a little longer. Then he left us. I poured soda water in my whiskey, Petra sipped her champagne. "Is it cold enough?"

"Thank you—yes."

"Who was Tonio Trenti?"

"He was *chargé d'affaires* at the Foreign Ministry."

"*Chargé d'affaires*? But then he couldn't have been very young!"

"He was very capable, Herr Holland. Everybody

who knew him said he was slated for a sensational career. He was twenty-eight years old, tall, slim, dark . . . He had gray eyes. When he smiled—"

She couldn't go on but threw herself face down on the cushions of the bed and wept. Her dress had hitched up, I could see her lace slip. I sat there, drinking whiskey, and waited for her to stop crying. I waited quite a while. At last she sat up, wiped away her tears with the back of her hand and said, "Excuse me, please."

"You loved this man very much?"

"We loved each other from the moment we met," she went on, sounding lost. "The cultural attaché introduced us and we—and I became his mistress that same night. He came to my house; he didn't leave until morning."

I thought that all this was becoming unreal—this evening, this room, this woman whom I hadn't known a few hours ago and who was revealing an intimate chapter of her life to me.

Petra Wend went on, "It was Tonio Trenti who made it clear to me that the ambassador's invitation hadn't been so entirely altruistic as it had seemed at first."

"He expected you to work for the Italian Foreign Ministry."

"Yes. How did you know?"

"It wasn't hard to guess. It's common procedure."

"Common procedure?" She looked at me suspiciously, then she shrugged. "Oh well . . . then . . . Tonio said that I would be meeting frequently with members of the German embassy. He wanted news, plans. He confided in me. He told me that a group of Italian diplomats, to which he belonged, was already in touch with the Americans, trying to negotiate a separate peace."

"That would have been a nice piece of news for Herr Jahn," I said.

"Yes," she said dully, "and it reached him."

"You—"

"Not I, Herr Holland."

"Who betrayed your love?"

"Another woman."

I took a drink. I had to hold the glass with both hands because my fingers were trembling. Still I spilled some of it. This was it, I thought.

"The woman who betrayed Tonio was Victoria Brunswick," said Petra Wend.

Was Sibyl. Was my Sibyl. . . .

13

German Foreign Minister Joachim Von Ribbentrop lacked imagination, especially when it came to understanding women. Only when taking this into consideration can one understand what he called his "favorite plan." Ribbentrop had the *idée fixe* that beautiful women of good family could be useful in politics. According to him, they could easily find entry into high society, and there wasn't a secret that wouldn't eventually be revealed to them.

Up to a point, Ribbentrop's theory had validity, but it was ridiculous for the Foreign Minister to believe that these beautiful women would immediately, like dutiful Germans, report to the Foreign Office everything they found out from their lovers. The fact that a woman in love usually belongs first and foremost to the object of her passion was beyond the comprehension of this former traveling salesman for a famous champagne company.

It is a fact that approximately 300 beautiful young ladies from good families were sent out of Germany to those foreign countries that were accessible to the German Foreign Office from 1939 to 1945. That spring there were two ladies in Rome with this kind of mission, and Roman society met in their salons. One of them was Petra Wend, and Sibyl was the other, but Sibyl's position was more important. Petra Wend had been Tonio Trenti's mistress for one week when she received an invitation from Sibyl.

Sibyl Loredo—or Victoria Brunswick, as she called herself then—lived in a house halfway up the Piazza de Spagna, on the left side of the famous Spanish Stairs. In the garden there were pines, amorini, and a stone Roman god who had lost his head. There was also an aviary with many colorful birds. Sibyl received her guest on the roof terrace. She was wearing a green silk dress with a design in gold thread, her black hair was combed high, and her lips parted in a big smile as she greeted Petra.

"I'm so glad we meet at last," she said. "I know we're going to have a lot to tell each other because we have so many mutual friends."

A servant brought tea. The ladies were sitting on wicker chairs under an awning. The cries and laughter of children playing rang into the still air from the direction of the Spanish Stairs. Sibyl poured tea. Still smiling, she asked, "Sugar?"

"Two, please."

Sibyl dropped two pieces of sugar into Petra's cup, crossed her legs and said amiably, "So that's what the little whore looks like with whom he's deceiving me."

Petra put her cup down gently on the low table in front of her. "I presume this is a joke," she said, "but I don't understand it."

"I am not joking," said Sibyl. "I am serious. He is deceiving me with you, and I have no intention of putting up with it. It isn't difficult to seduce Tonio. After all, I did and I know. He is weak and sentimental. That's why I wanted to speak to you."

"Just a minute," Petra said shakily. "Are you talking about Tonio Trenti?"

"Stop putting on an act," Sibyl said softly. Her tone was icy and her cat's eyes were half closed. "Don't try to tell me you didn't know Tonio was my lover when you took him into your bed!"

"I *didn't* know!"

"You didn't know what all Rome knows?" Sibyl asked scornfully.

"I swear I didn't know."

Sibyl's mouth was twisted. "All right," she said. "But you know now. Tonio Trenti has been my lover for over a year. And you will please leave him alone from now on."

"Leave him alone?" cried Petra. "But I love him! And he loves me! He has told me so over and over again!"

"And that's why he sleeps with me?" They were talking about their lover as if he were a wild naughty boy.

"I—I must talk to him," Petra cried, and jumped to her feet. "I'll listen to him, not to you." But Sibyl was standing in her way. "Sit down!" she said.

"Let me go!"

With one hand Sibyl struck Petra on the shoulder so hard that she fell back in her chair.

"How dare you!"

"Be quiet! I'm not through with you yet." Sibyl lit a cigarette and said, "It's all the same to me whether Tonio has told you he loves you or whether you love him. You don't interest me in the slightest, and Tonio doesn't know whom he loves. He is stupid. One has to think for him. It won't be difficult for me to make him realize that I am the woman he loves."

"I can see that you are mad. Quite mad," said Petra, said it honestly and with relief over the sudden revelation. "You are out of your mind or you couldn't talk like this!"

Sibyl had nothing to say to that but went on, "I therefore forbid you to talk to Tonio about this. You are simply to throw him out."

"I am *what*?"

"You will tell him that you're through with him, that you've had enough, that you can't stand him anymore."

"You're crazy!"

"That he's to get out of your life, at once and forever!"

"Mad! Absolutely mad!"

"That's what you're to say to him. When are you going to see him?"

"Tonight."

"Then you'll tell him tonight."

"I'll do nothing of the sort."

"No?" Sibyl was smiling again. "Listen to me, you little whore. In one respect you and I are alike. We both work for the German Foreign Office."

"But—"

"Shut up! You are supposed to report to Helmut Jahn, right? So am I. Only I haven't reported anything important yet. Neither have you, as I happen to know. They're not very satisfied with either of us."

"I—"

"Be quiet! If we don't come up with something soon, they'll recall us. Did he tell you about the job with Siemens and Halske? Well . . . there you are."

"I don't know what you're talking about."

"Oh, yes, you do! And now you're scared, aren't you? Now you're afraid for him. I was expecting that. If you could see yourself—you look green with fear. I don't think you could walk three steps right now without falling flat on your face. Tonio talks, doesn't he? Especially in bed. That's when you can't shut him up. What do you think would happen if our mutual friend,

Herr Jahn, were to find out about Tonio's involvement in the efforts toward a separate peace?"

Petra stared at Sibyl with wide, unblinking eyes. "Not only Tonio's efforts but also those of his friends would interest Herr Jahn very much. Just consider the people involved: Cesare Frank, Professor Solti, Elia Carniel . . . ."

"You would do *that*?" Petra's voice was a hoarse whisper. "You would betray the man you love? Do you realize what would happen to him?"

"They would kill him," said Sibyl. "Him and his friends, probably also friends of his friends. They kill a lot of people. It doesn't seem to trouble them."

A sound made her look up. The servant who had served tea was standing behind her. "What is it, Angelo? Why are you disturbing us?"

"Excuse me, signora," said the servant. "I just wanted to report that Signor Tonio Trenti has arrived."

14

Well, that fits in perfectly," said Sibyl. "Please tell Signor Trenti to come up here."

A few seconds later Trenti appeared. The servant

must have told him of Petra's presence because he showed no sign of surprise. "It's a good thing," he said, after having kissed the hands of both ladies, "that the three of us meet here. I must ask you to forgive me, Victoria, and you, Petra. I've behaved very badly."

The two women looked at him silently. The pretty young man with the broad shoulders and narrow hips looked more feminine than the two women he had deceived. "Petra," he said, "you know now that I have had an affair with Victoria for a long time. I loved her, but I don't love her anymore. I love you, Petra. I regret that I've had to say this, but it's the truth." He turned to Sibyl. "Forgive me, But I would have told you this afternoon anyway, even if we had been alone."

"Darling," said Sibyl—her voice was patient—"you don't know what you're talking about."

"Oh, but I do, Victoria. I intend to marry Petra."

His words were followed by a long silence. Then Petra, who until now hadn't spoken a word, said, "She is going to betray you to the Germans, Tonio. You and your friends. She's going to tell them everything she knows if you don't stay with her."

"You're not going to do that?" Now he was addressing Sibyl, and little beads of perspiration had formed on his pretty forehead.

"The situation is comical," said Sibyl. "Don't you agree? Two hens and one handsome cock. Yes, little cock. I intend to tell the Germans everything I know. Everything!" Her voice was soft, gentle, friendly. "I'm sorry, but I have to threaten you with it so that you realize what a mistake you are making. You really have behaved badly, Tonio."

"So why threaten me?" he asked bitterly. "Why persecute me? Why don't you leave me in peace?"

"Because you're so marvelous in bed," said Sibyl.

Tonio Trenti took Petra's hand. "Come," he said, and Petra got up. Together they walked across the terrace to the door.

"Stay!" Sibyl said softly. "Stay! Please, Tonio, stay! Don't go away! Please!" But he wasn't listening. Hand in hand, he walked out onto the Spanish Stairs with Petra just as the late afternoon sun was shining on it.

The German Secret Police arrested Chargé d'Affairs Tonio Trenti that same evening at approximately eight P.M. They found Trenti in the garage of his house, about to leave Rome. He shot at one of the two officers, but missed; the other man knocked him down. He was taken at once to the Minerva Hotel, headquarters of the Gestapo in Rome. Trenti's friends were arrested at the same time.

By next morning, Sibyl had disappeared. Her servant, Angelo, explained that she had gone away. "I am not in a position to say when she will be back."

Actually, Sibyl never returned to Rome. She vanished. A month after her departure, the German consulate took over the villa on the Spanish Stairs, and a certain Freiherr von Weidebreck moved in. He was an old gentleman and suffered from asthma.

Tonio Trenti and his friends were taken to Berlin. Petra heard nothing more from them. All her efforts to get in touch with her lover remained futile. During the time of her desperate efforts to save Tonio, she met his father, Emilio Trenti. The latter came to Berlin and managed to get to see Ribbentrop, but he was also able to do nothing. On May 28, 1944, between seven and eight-thirty A.M. Tonio Trenti and his friends were hanged in the courtyard of the Moabit jail.

15

Petra Wend was still sitting on her bed, but she wasn't crying anymore. She said, "I know this must be dreadful for you, Herr Holland."

At the moment I was actually in no position to grasp the incredible story she had told me. When I stepped on the land mine in the woods near Cologne, I hadn't felt any pain at first either. The pain, and the realization that one of my legs was missing, came later. I drank whiskey and asked, "And you never heard anything from Sibyl again?"

"Never."

"You stayed in Rome?"

"No. My Italian friends warned me that I was to be recalled. They were afraid I would be punished, too."

"So what did you do?"

"The Italian cultural attaché from Berlin had friends in Vienna, a couple. The husband was a dentist. He had a house outside the city, in the wine district. He and his wife hid me there until the war was over. For a while it looked as if the Austrians would deport me because I wasn't working, but then I got a job with a film company and was able to stay in Vienna."

"Did you ever denounce Sibyl?"

"Of course I did. In April 1945."

"And what happened?"

"They wanted more information. A prosecutor in Vienna interrogated me, at the request of the Munich prosecutor."

"Why the Munich prosecutor?"

"Your friend came from Munich, Herr Holland."

Of course. And that was why she had moved to Berlin, that was when she received false papers under the name of Loredo. I wouldn't have stayed in Munich either. Much too risky.

"And what did the court find out?"

"They found an entry in the death register of Munich-West. It reported that Victoria Brunswick had died on the street of a heart attack on August 11, 1944."

"And you think the entry was forged?"

"I'm sure it was." Now the dreadful fear was in her eyes again. That was what she had looked like in the house on Akazienallee. "Victoria got false papers and moved to Berlin and lived there peacefully for ten years until Tonio's father saw her."

I nodded. What she had just said made sense. Terrible, but it made sense. It could have happened just like that.

"She rigged up a phony kidnapping, followed him to

Salzburg and shot him. And now—and now—" Petra stopped talking and stared wide-eyed at me. "What will happen now?" she whispered. "She is in the city. She's nearby. I can feel her! I'm terrified, Herr Holland. Tell me what to do! Go to the police and tell them everything? Don't leave me alone!" She got up and threw her arms around me, but it was no embrace.

I moved her arms gently from my shoulders. "Good night, Frau Wend. Lock your door and take something to sleep."

She fell back on her bed, and sat moving her hands helplessly.

I got my coat and took the elevator down to the lobby. At this time—after ten P.M.—it was empty, only the night clerk was on duty. He was standing behind the desk, sorting mail. "Are you going out again, Herr Holland?"

"Yes."

"Drive carefully. It's very foggy."

"I'm going to walk."

You could barely see ten steps ahead. The fog was amber colored and smelled like smoke. I walked through the dark underpass to the station and from there to the river. I thought of Sibyl. It was, of course, out of the question that the woman I loved and the woman Petra Wend had described were really one and the same person. I knew Sibyl. It had to be a colossal misunderstanding, a mixup due to resemblance. It couldn't be anything else.

"Please could you tell me how to get to the Hotel zum Goldenen Hirschen?"

He was little and he looked lost. He stood at a dimly

lit street crossing, swaying, and he stank of schnapps. He was very drunk and spoke with a Swiss accent.

"Come along with me."

"Do you live in the Goldenen Hirschen?"

"No. But I'll get you there."

"But I can't accept that!"

"Come on. I'm only taking a walk."

He began to walk beside me. It was an effort for him, and every now and then he stumbled.

"Damn' city!" he said bitterly. "No police! No taxis!"

Perhaps the whole thing was a nightmare. I was dreaming. Or Petra was crazy.

"In the summer it's supposed to be very beautiful here," said the little man. "Mozart and all that. I like Mozart. Do you?"

"What?"

"Do you like Mozart?"

"No." Now I was sorry I'd taken him along. He said, "By the way, my name is Wälterli."

"Holland."

"My pleasure, Herr Holland. You don't happen to want a church."

"A *church*?"

"A church. To pray in. I have one too many. You could have it cheap. At cost."

"What sort of nonsense is this?"

We were passing a theater. Until now we hadn't met a soul. All windows were dark and our steps made a hollow sound.

"It's not nonsense," he said sadly. "I build churches.

I've built churches all my life. Wälterli churches. Haven't you heard of them?"

"No." And I was thinking: what if Petra murdered Emilio Trenti and she's lying. . . .

Meanwhile the church architect was saying, "Prefabricated." He said the word in English. "Do you know what that is—prefabricated?"

"What is it?"

"That's how we build today. An American system, Herr Holland. Just imagine—the Swiss government gives me an order: forty-six churches, for some of their more isolated villages. Not big churches, just big enough for a congregation of eighty, all the same—a tremendous order. All prefabricated. The doors, the walls, the benches, the crosses for the entrances, the altars—all made in a factory. The pulpits, the statues, the confessionals . . . down to the last nail. But separate pieces, you understand? Numbered. With instructions on how to assemble them. Any child can assemble my churches. In the end all of them were packed and shipped, by freight. And, can you imagine this, Herr Holland? We discovered that we had built forty-seven, not forty-six. What do you think of that, Herr Holland?"

"It must have been very annoying," I said.

"Annoying!?" He cast his eyes heavenward. "I nearly fainted. Just imagine—one complete church left over. And nobody wants it. What do you think? Will I ever sell it?"

"I feel for you, Herr Wälterli," I said. We were passing the Café Bazar. I had often sat outside it, now it was closed. The little garden looked desolate. The bridge across the Salzach loomed suddenly out of the fog.

"There's nothing as difficult to unload as a church. And you can't just dump it. It's too big. Too many parts. Prefabricated. That was all I needed. My father would have caned me if I'd suggested any of this modern nonsense to him. But I? I have to try everything, and now I'm stuck with the mess." He looked around. "I think I know my way from here."

"Through that gate, turn right and you can't miss it."

We had stopped on the bridge. The black water was rushing underneath us. Every now and then a chunk of ice floated by. Herr Wälterli shook my hand and thanked me for having shown him the way. Then he walked on unsteadily into the fog. I could hear him muttering angrily to himself: "Prefabricated . . . that's all I needed!" Then his voice was lost.

It was quiet, as quiet as if I had been the only person on earth. I leaned my arms on the wet balustrade and looked down at the rushing river. It made me feel dizzy. This crazy church architect had been the bloody end. I felt drunk myself. I couldn't think straight, not a single sensible thought. The water gurgled against the bridge piles, and suddenly I could hear steps. They grew louder, came closer . . . I didn't move. The steps stopped beside me. The steps of a woman. I turned slowly. She was standing close to me; I could have touched her with my hand if I'd wanted to. It wasn't a dream, it wasn't imagination, I had not gone mad. She stood there, breathing, alive; her cat-eyes were glittering, her face was white, and her red lips were parted. "Good evening," said Sibyl Loredo.

She had on a nutria coat, brown fur boots, and a dark scarf tied around her head. She came up to me and pressed her lips against mine. Her lips were cold and I could feel her tongue against my teeth.

I pushed her away. "What have you done?"

"Don't you know yet?" she asked, and her voice was low and hoarse, as it always had been. "Hasn't Petra Wend told you?"

"She told me a lot of things," I said, and tried to draw a deep breath. Suddenly it had become difficult to breathe deeply. "You shot Emilio Trenti."

"Yes."

Down below, a large piece of ice smashed against one of the bridge supports. It sounded steely and hard, but the fog soon drowned out the sound. There was an echo. "I lost an earring in the house," she said. "You were there before the police. Did you happen to find it?"

"Yes, Sibyl," I replied obediently. "It had slipped between the cushion of a chair."

"Do you have it with you?"

"Yes."

"Give it to me."

I took the earring out of my pocket and gave it to her. She put it in her pocket and said, "Thank you." Then she took my hand—hers was cold and lifeless—and said, "Come."

"Where to?"

"Away from here. Nobody must see us," and she pulled me away, into the fog, and I went with her as if in a mad dream from which there would be no awakening.

16

At the end of the bridge, a cement staircase led down to the water. The stones were slippery, and I held onto the railing as I followed Sibyl. She took the stairs fast. Halfway down I saw two dark openings in the bridge wall, like entrances to a bunker. They led to toilets. On the stone wall between them somebody had scrawled the words *Ami Go Home!* We reached the bottom of the stairs and stepped onto the river bank, which was narrow here, and uneven. Tin cans and piles of garbage stuck out of the snow.

"Don't stop here!" said Sibyl, pulling me along until we were under the bridge, standing beside one of the piles. She was breathing hard, her eyes were open wide, and her face glowed as if she had a fever. Chunks of ice hit the shore, the piles, and smashed against each other with monotonous regularity. The water made a lot of noise here, and the fog acted as a shroud. I saw only Sibyl, nothing else. I wanted to get closer to her, but slipped on a piece of debris. She grasped me and prevented me from falling. I could feel her breath on my cheek. She whispered, "Kiss me."

I shook my head.

"I love you!"

"You have murdered two people."

"You are all I have. I don't have anyone else in the world. Forgive me."

"You must be mad!" I said. "How can I possibly forgive you? You have killed, Sibyl! You have committed murder!"

"I love you," she said stubbornly, like a child.

I sat down on a cement block at the foot of one of the piles, she sat down beside me. We looked at the snow and filth under the bridge, the ice cracked and the water made a rushing sound.

"Trenti recognized you in the Wagenseil Konditorei, didn't he?" It was the best I could do. I found it difficult to say anything.

She nodded. She looked small and frail, this woman sitting beside me, this woman I loved, this woman who had killed two human beings.

"Do you have a cigarette?"

"You shouldn't smoke now," I said.

"But I must. Please. My heart—"

She had a weak heart. She was a murderess with a weak heart. I gave her a cigarette. By the light of the match I saw her face and was overwhelmed with a desire to kiss her. I threw the match away. It fell on the grimy snow and went out.

Sibyl smoked in hasty puffs. "I had to get away before he found me," she said. "So I staged the kidnapping. I flew to Munich the same day."

"So why wasn't your name on the passenger list?"

"I didn't give my right name. Inside Germany they don't ask for identification." Her cigarette glowed. She exhaled the smoke through her nose. "Next day I read in the paper that the police had decided I'd been kidnapped. I had to get out of Germany."

"Why?"

"Because they were looking for me. It doesn't take long to put out a pick-up order."

She was right.

"I was lucky." (She said "lucky"!) "I showed my passport at the bridge and they gave it back to me without noticing anything. When I got to Salzburg, I called Emilio Trenti in Munich. When he heard my voice, he couldn't speak. I realized at once: he was afraid. Terribly afraid. And I also knew that he hadn't gone to the police—yet."

"What was he afraid of?"

"Of me, Paul. Of me!" She laughed. It sounded eerie. "He was afraid I would kill him."

"As you killed his son."

"That was during the war," she said. "And besides, I didn't kill him."

"You reported him to the police."

"I didn't know the Germans would kill him."

"Yes, you did."

"No!"

"Don't lie!"

She said in a low voice, "I don't want to lie. I knew it."

The chunks of ice in the black water knocked against each other with a brittle sound and hit against the banks of the river. "I love you," she said.

17

Once, during the war, I threw a hand grenade into a trench opposite us. There were five Russians in it. Later, when we reached the trench, I saw that all of them were dead. A few other hand grenades, besides mine, had hit the trench. Perhaps they had killed the five men. Or maybe I had. There was no way of telling. I was given a medal for taking the trench; I received it for murdering five men. A piece of metal attached to a ribbon. And I hadn't even known them.

I thought: Sibyl had known Tonio Trenti. He had been her lover and left her for Petra Wend. She had had greater reason to commit murder than I.

I thought: with Emilio Trenti, Sibyl had a motive. That was the fatal thing about it. But what decent person commits murder without a motive?

I thought I had lost Sibyl, but here she is, sitting beside me, living and breathing. But they're looking for her. They'll find her and make her pay the penalty for what she has done. Why did all this have to happen? We were so happy.

"I love you," she said.

I thought: I've got to face it. I must report her. Any other course of action would be criminal.

"Go on," I said.

"Emilio Trenti didn't think much of the police; he didn't think they would find me. . . ."

"Go on." I was beginning to feel terribly cold.

"I told him to come to Salzburg. I told him his son hadn't died because of me. In Salzburg, I said I would tell him who it was. I told him about you, too. I said I could talk more freely if you were there."

"And he believed you?"

"He was an old man, Paul. And he was afraid. And when a man is afraid, he can't think clearly. He said he would come to Salzburg at once. I was to be at the house in Akazienallee at four o'clock."

"That's when he told me to come."

"That's what I thought," she said. "I thought it might be a trap. That's why I came at three. He led me into the library. I apologized for having come an hour early and shot him just as he was lifting the receiver."

"Whom was he going to call?"

"The police. He was dead immediately. Half an hour later, Petra arrived. And then you came."

"You saw us?"

"Yes. I was standing in the garden, behind the greenhouse. I saw you both. I saw you strike Petra. Then I left."

"Where did you go?"

"To my hotel."

"You're staying in a hotel? Here?"

"I've got to stay somewhere. I'm at the Excelsior."

"Under the name of Sibyl Loredo?"

"It's not a bad name," she said softly, "as long as they think Sibyl Loredo was abducted to East Berlin, as long as they don't know it's not my real name."

"I showed Petra Wend a picture of you and she recognized you."

"And went to the police?"

"Not yet."

"Why not?"

"She's afraid, too."

"Did she ask you what she should do?"

"Yes."

"And what did you tell her?"

"I told her I had to give it some thought. How did you find me, Sibyl?"

"I called every hotel in Salzburg and asked if you were staying there, until I found out you were at the Pitter. So I went there and waited. When you came out, I followed you, you and your strange companion."

"He was a church architect."

"Whatever happens to me now," she said, "depends on you. I am a prisoner in this little country. I can't cross any borders again. If you expose me, they'll arrest me."

"Petra Wend may report you."

"She doesn't know where I'm staying."

"That wouldn't be difficult to find out."

"I know," she said.

"Why did you follow me? Why did you drag me down here? Why couldn't you leave me in peace?"

"Because I need help," she answered softly, "and because I love you."

"Not because you love me," I said, "but because you need help."

"Because I love you," she persisted. "If I didn't love you, I wouldn't be here. I would be far away by now, so far away that they could never get me. I only stayed because I hoped to find you."

18

She said it once too often. I left her and walked toward the stairs that led up to the bridge. She remained seated where she was and said in that low, hoarse voice, "Are you going to report me?"

I didn't answer.

"You can, if you like," she said. "I'm not going to run away anymore. I'm not going to hide anymore. I'm going to stay in my hotel. You can go to the police and tell them where I am. I'll be waiting for them."

She sat on the gray cement block and didn't move. She is stronger than I, I thought, and she knows it. With her love she puts me in an untenable position. She sits there and watches me go and tells me she isn't going to run anymore. She is the stronger, and she knows it.

"Report me," she said, and in the fog her voice sounded even deeper and hoarser. "Don't forget the address. Excelsior Hotel. Farburggasse 12. Room 307. On the third floor."

I limped up the stairs to the bridge. "Go to the police, Paul," she said. "They work day and night. There's a newspaperman here; you can tell him everything."

I was passing the men's toilet. I could read the word *Ami.* . . . Her voice reached me from down below. "I'll stay here another fifteen minutes. They can come and get me. You can come with them, Paul."

". . . *Go Home*," I read, as I limped past the women's toilet.

"If nobody comes in fifteen minutes," she said, "I'll go back to my hotel, and they can arrest me there."

Ice floes hit the piles. They scraped and clawed at the bridge, icy, metallic, with no echo. And they were followed by others. The swiftly flowing current was full of them.

19

According to the paper I had read on my way to Salzburg, fat, bald-headed Nikita Khrushchev had burst into tears in the course of his long speech before the Congress of the Communist Party, and had fainted. Three members of the congress who had been in the audience had fainted, too, and had had to be carried out of the hall. It had been too much for them when the new party boss had called the dead son of a shoemaker—Iosif Vissarionovich Dzchugashvili, better know as Stalin—a traitor, a despot, a monster, and a murderer. At his reception in honor of foreign plenipotentiaries, Khrushchev had explained, weeping, that Stalin had cried out to him, "Dance!" and he, Khrushchev, in fear of his life, had danced. A god had failed.

It wasn't opportune any longer to believe in Stalin, Father of the Proletariat, hero of the war against Hitler fascism, the first and greatest son of the Soviet Union. Schoolchildren were writing "spontaneous" letters to Stalin's daughter and asking if she didn't think it would be right to remove the remains of her father from the Lenin mausoleum and bury him somewhere privately.

Details of Khrushchev's epoch-shattering speech had already reached the outside world when I arrived in Munich. The taxi driver taking me from the airport to the Hotel Vier Jahreszeiten, was talking about it. With the eternal inferiority complex of the European, I said, "It can't be just a propaganda maneuver to regain the confidence of those communist sympathizers who feel the Bolsheviks let them down. The whole thing may be a brilliant ploy to catch all those homeless leftists—I mean, the fallen red angels." But my taxi driver didn't agree with me. "That's possible," he said. "But whom are they going to catch with that sort of propaganda? Who's going to be happy about it? The intellectuals? You can't get anywhere with them. They're cowards, they have character. The first chance they get, they give up. You can't start a world revolution with the intellectuals." A skeptic, my taxi driver.

"I had a friend who was a dedicated communist," he went on. "He fought in Spain, the Nazis locked him up, he was always in trouble with the authorities. He was no intellectual. He was a decent, brave man. Only a week ago he told me he believed in Stalin like other people believed in God. They'd been indoctrinating him for years to believe in Stalin."

"So what does he believe in now?" I asked.

"Now," said the driver, "he believes in nothing. Yesterday he hanged himself. He wrote me a letter before he did it. In the letter he said you can't believe in someone as if he were a god for ten years and suddenly find out you've been believing in a murderer, a mon-

ster, a criminal, and go on living. Anyway, he couldn't.
You see, those are the people who didn't like Herr
Khrushchev's speech; those are the people the communists are going to lose now. Your intellectuals can believe in something different every week. It's the simple
little man who's in trouble." He shifted into second
gear and slowed down to let a group of carnival people
cross the street, then he finished with the words,
"You'll see what will happen next. In a few years
they'll forbid the Communist Party in Russia."

I walked back to the Pitter through the empty streets
and thought of Sibyl. She was sitting down there by the
river, waiting for the police to come and get her. She
had murdered two people. I couldn't imagine that the
taxi driver's friend had believed in Stalin more fer-
vently than I had believed in Sibyl. True, he may have
believed in him longer, but not more. Anyway, one
couldn't believe more or less. One believed, and that
was that!

What was I to do? Should I hang myself, too? Or
should I go to the police? I didn't have the courage to
hang myself.

I had to go to the police. It was my duty. Two
people had died, I knew their murderer. She had
confessed. It was my duty to report her.

I walked on. It would be cowardly to report Sibyl.
Was she aware of that? Was she really afraid of me? "I
love you," she had said.

When I reached the hotel, I found the front door
locked. I rang. The night clerk opened the door
sleepily. "You've been for a long walk, Herr Holland,"
he said, then he looked startled. "Are you all right?"

"No, I'm not," I said. "Do you have any sleeping pills?"

He gave me two. When I got to my room, I took them both. But they didn't work: I didn't sleep all night. I lay there, staring into the dark, and thought of Sibyl and the man who had hanged himself. Once, around four, the phone rang, but when I picked up the receiver, nobody answered. All I could hear was the hum on the line. I pressed the fork up and down several times, and finally the night clerk answered. "Yes, Herr Holland?"

"My phone rang."

"Yes. It was somebody asking for you."

"Who?"

"I don't know, Herr Holland. The lady didn't give her name."

"Thank you."

The lady didn't give her name. Perhaps the lady just wanted to know if I was in my room. As soon as she had found out I was, she had hung up. Suddenly I was startled to realize that I didn't love Sibyl anymore. . . . I hated her! Hate and love seemed to subsist pretty close together. But one can only hate or love something in which one believes. Even hatred demanded faith first. And I realized with horror that I had not stopped believing in Sibyl.

I got up and sat by the window. The street was empty, the street lanterns were still burning. Above the roofs of the houses the sky was turning gray. A milk cart rattled by. And then the day dawned.

I shaved and ordered my breakfast. After I had drunk some hot coffee, I felt better. I ordered a taxi.

At 8:30 A.M. I stepped out into the sunny street. The taxi driver opened the door of the car for me. "To the police station," I said.

The taxi drove off. The sun shone down on the dirty snow, and I saw a lot of people on their way to work. It was a beautiful winter day, with a blue sky and a light east wind, and I was on my way to the police station to report Sibyl Loredo.

20

The mistake was that she kept telling me over and over again that she loved me. Actually, she didn't love me at all. She never had. I loved her. And she knew it. And she thought she could do anything she wanted with me. "I love you," and I promptly did everything. It was that simple.

But she was wrong. It wasn't that simple. As I drove through the snowy streets of Salzburg I thought: she's had her chance. I've given her the whole night to get away. If she's so sure of me that she stays in her hotel, then she deserves everything that's coming to her.

"Sir?"

"What is it?"

The car had stopped. The driver was looking at me suspiciously. "This is the police station. I can't park here." I paid him. "Do you want me to wait?"

"No. I don't know how long I'll be."

Salzburg police headquarters were in an old building with high walls and an arched entryway. A policeman was standing in it and he saluted as I walked up to him. "Chief Enders, please."

"Second floor. Room 134."

"Thanks."

"First staircase on your left!" he called out after me as I crossed the courtyard.

It was a square yard with one chestnut tree standing black and bare in the snow. Bicycles were leaning against a wall, surprisingly many. I climbed up a narrow, worn spiral staircase to the second floor. The house smelled of Lysol. I came to a long high corridor with many doors, large windows opposite them. People were sitting on the broad sills, waiting and talking softly. Nobody was waiting in front of door 134. I knocked.

"*Entrez!*" said Chief Enders, in his soft voice.

I walked in. "I'm sorry," I said. "I thought you were alone."

"Come on in," said the elegant, meticulously groomed chief of police, looking from me to his other visitor, sitting opposite his desk. "Frau Wend doesn't have any secrets from you."

21

I had forgotten her completely—the woman with the white hair and clear blue eyes. There she sat, staring at me. She was pale, she was wearing no makeup, she looked as if she, too, had spent a sleepless night. I nodded. She lowered her head. She was wearing a blue suit and a white blouse. The chief had on an Austrian loden suit, gray and green. We shook hands, then both of us sat down.

"We've been looking for you, Herr Holland," said Enders.

"Yes? When?" A huge wheel was revolving in my head. I looked at Petra and looked away again; I looked at Chief Enders, he was looking down at his desk. Both of them were trying not to look at me.

"Last night, Herr Holland, around eleven." Enders was toying with a letter opener. Now he cleared his throat. "You weren't at the hotel."

"I went for a walk."

"It was very foggy last night, wasn't it?"

"Yes. Why?"

"I was just thinking." And I was thinking: both of them mistrust me. I must tell what I know. I must report Sibyl. But I said nothing.

"Our interrogation brought in some results," said Chief Enders. "I wanted to pass on the information to you. We were successful. The Vienna Registration Bureau is *excellent.*"

"What did you find out?"

"We found out, Herr Holland—I'm sorry, but this is bad news for you—that your friend who has disappeared is being sought under the name of Victoria Brunswick."

I said nothing.

"That's why I asked Frau Wend to come to see me this morning. Because she knows Frau Brunswick. In 1945 she filed a report—"

"You don't have to say anything more, Chief. I told Herr Holland the whole story last night."

"J'ai compris," said Enders, and turning to me, "Frau Wend told me all about it an hour ago." He looked at me sharply. "Did you go for a walk in the fog before or after Frau Wend told you the story?"

"Afterwards." I raised my head. "Why do you ask? Do you think I am an accomplice of Frau Loredo? That I met her last night and helped her to get away?"

"If you *had* met her last night, *would* you have helped her to get away?" He was pointing the letter opener at me, and he was smiling.

"What sort of a question is that?"

"Pardon, Herr Holland. You love Frau Loredo, don't you?"

"Yes."

"It would be very natural for you to want to help her."

"Do you believe she committed the murder?"

"But of course," he said, amiably. "*Naturellement*, Herr Holland!"

Suddenly I felt unbearably hot. I closed my eyes and a sigh, more like a groan, escaped my lips.

"It is a great *malheur* for you, Herr Holland," said Chief Enders. "You have my *sympathie*. Why did you come here?"

I managed to say in a normal voice, "I wanted to find out if your investigation had made any headway, and if I could leave the city."

He gave me a curious look and said, "Frau Loredo won't escape us. You may leave whenever you like."

"Thank you."

"Where will you go, Herr Holland?"

"I don't know yet."

"When you do, please inform us at once."

"Certainly, Chief Enders."

Oh, Sibyl, Sibyl, Sibyl. . . .

I noticed that Petra was still looking at me earnestly. "What's the matter?" I asked her. "Why are you staring at me?"

Petra replied, "Because I feel sorry for you, Herr Holland."

And I felt sorry for myself. My God had forsaken me and I was refusing to take the consequences. The taxi driver in Munich had been right.

"Thank you for your compassion," I said to Petra. It was 9:45. I limped out of the room. I hopped down the stairs on one leg because it was faster. The policeman at the entrance saluted again. I walked as fast as I could to the Residenzplatz. At the Café Tomaselli corner I turned around quickly to see if anyone was following me.

The café was as empty as the street. A sleepy waiter came shuffling up to me. "Good morning, sir. What do you want?"

"Coffee," I said. "Where is the telephone?"

He gestured with his head. "Over there."

I hurried into the little padded booth, leafed through the dog-eared telephone book, dropped in my coin and dialed.

"Excelsior Hotel. Good morning."

"Frau Loredo, please."

"Just a minute." Then I heard her voice. "Hello?"

"This is Paul. You must leave the hotel at once."

"Yes, Paul."

"They're looking for you."

"Yes, Paul."

"I've got to see you."

"Where?"

I had already decided where. "Go to the Newsreel Cinema, near the bridge. Leave your suitcase in the checkroom. I'll be sitting in the twentieth row. In a quarter of an hour. Got that?"

"Yes, Paul."

I put down the receiver and went back to my small table. The coffee was there but I spilled half of it as I tried to drink it. My hand was shaking as if I had the ague.

22

I put in an emergency call to Frankfurt. Now everything had to happen fast. Three minutes later I had the office. I asked for Kalmar. He was a friend. I asked him, "What do we know about coffee smuggling between Salzburg and Germany?"

"You mean what we haven't printed yet?"

"Yes. On whom do we have the most material? Whom can we hurt most?"

He thought for a moment, then he said, "Alice Totenkopf. She's in up to her neck."

"Is she still operating?"

"And how! What's the matter? What do you need her for?"

"I haven't time to go into that. Give me her address."

I waited. In a few minutes Kalmar was back. "Burggasse 24. Telephone—"

"I don't need it. I'm going straight there or she'll get away."

"What's happened, Paul?"

"Good-bye," I said, and hung up. I had to wait a few minutes for the charges, then I left the café, with its quaint balcony over the entrance. I took a taxi and drove to the Newsreel Cinema. I looked back once or twice but nobody was following me. When we got there, I told the driver to wait.

At this hour of the day the movie house was almost empty. Children playing hooky were occupying the front row. I sat down in the twentieth row. Sibyl hadn't arrived yet. I saw the end of a newsreel; it was followed by an American cartoon, *The Missing Mouse.* The story was simple. A poor gray mouse was being tortured mercilessly by a powerful tomcat. The cat chased it through the house, caught it, put it through the meat grinder, squeezed it on the lemon squeezer, and hurled it through the air so that the wretched animal fell into a can of white paint. Now the mouse was white.

The cat, sure that the mouse was dead, settled down beside the radio and listened to some popular music. Suddenly the program was interrupted by an announcement that a white mouse had disappeared from a research lab. This mouse had swallowed enough dynamite to blow up a whole city if handled too roughly. There was an alert out for the white mouse.

Now the big moment of the mishandled mouse had arrived. All in white, it danced by the horrified cat, who was sure it was the loaded mouse that had escaped. The dramatic situation was suddenly reversed 180 degrees. The cat hovered over the mouse like a mother over her baby while the mouse did one crazy thing after the other and finally jumped out of the window. But the cat jumped faster and managed to catch the mouse, in the course of which the cat lost its tail. The mouse bit through the prop of the open grand piano so that the lid might fall on its own head, but the cat stuck its head in between instead. The children in the front row shrieked with delight.

"Paul?"

Sibyl was standing at the end of the row. I motioned, and she came and sat down beside me. The children were making so much noise, we could talk without being heard. In its bravado, the mouse had fallen into a tub full of water and was gray again. The furious tomcat realized he had been fooled, but the mouse, who didn't know she wasn't white anymore, went on prancing in front of the cat.

"What happened?"

I told Sibyl everything.

"How do I get out of the city?"

The cat kicked the mouse so hard, it flew through the wall into freedom. At the same time the real white mouse appeared in the open doorway. The children screeched with joy.

"I'll get you across the border."

The cat saw the new visitor, took it to be its old enemy, jumped on it, smacked it with its paw, and went up in smoke with the whole city. Chaos on the screen and in the front row!

"Come," I said.

We retrieved Sibyl's suitcase and hurried outside. "You're going already?" The cashier looked astonished. I had hoped she wouldn't see us. I said hastily, "We have to make a train." She looked at us curiously.

"Burgstrasse 24."

The taxi took off. Sibyl was sitting beside me in the back. She looked more beautiful than ever, an unearthly beauty. Suddenly she said, "Thank you, Paul." I said nothing. The sun was blinding, and I wished it would get dark.

Burgstrasse 24 was an old house with damp stone archways. The electric light bulbs on the stairs were dim. They hung down from the mildewed ceiling, attached by wires. There was a smell of cabbage and fat. The water faucets were in the hallways, so were the toilets. The kitchen windows were beside the apartment doors. In one kitchen a man was quarreling with his wife. "Don't lie!" she screamed. "I saw you kiss the bitch!" The man replied, "Shut up, and give me my money!"

Alice Totenkopf lived on the second floor. Her name was on the door. Under the white enamel name plate was the word *Trucking*. I knocked. A shrill woman's voice cried out, "Who's there?"

I gave Sibyl a sign to be silent, I said nothing, too. Heavy, dragging steps came closer. "Can't you speak? Who's there?"

The door opened a crack and I kicked it open wide, shoved Sibyl ahead of me and walked into the dark, dirty kitchen. It all happened very fast.

"What do you think you're doing?"

Alice Totenkopf was the fattest woman I had ever seen. She had no neck, nothing but row upon row of chins. Her enormous breasts rested on her high stomach which she pushed ahead of her, big and round, when she walked. The fingers of the hand she was holding out in front of her, as if in defense, looked like little sausages filled to bursting. She must have been over sixty, and her breath whistled. She had asthma. "Get out of here!" she croaked, "or I'll call the police!"

I was already walking into the living room, which was hideously furnished in turn-of-the-century style. I saw a lot of plush, ornately turned wood, an enormous buffet, and a leather sofa with a Pomeranian sitting on it. The dog began to whimper. Alice Totenkopf caught up with me just as I was putting down Sibyl's suitcase. She grabbed me by the arm and yelled, "For the last time—who are you?"

"Names aren't interesting, Frau Totenkopf," I said. "You've got to help us."

"Be quiet, Fifi! How am I supposed to help you?" Her sly eyes flitted back and forth between Sibyl and me, and I could sense that she was afraid. And if she was afraid, all was well.

"We've got to get across the border, Frau Totenkopf, but we don't have any papers."

"So? What am I supposed to do?"

Now that she knew we were planning something illegal, she was calmer. She sank down on the sofa. Mechanically the dog crept onto her lap. She sat with her legs spread wide—the only way she could sit—and said with her whistling breath, "Why have you come to me?"

"Frau Totenkopf," I said, stepping closer to her, which started the dog whimpering again, "I know that

your trucks are smuggling coffee as through freight.
You switch cargoes in the Reichenhaller Zipfel."

"That's a lie! A vicious lie!"

"You have a previous conviction. However, the police don't know anything about this new project of
yours," I said firmly. "If you don't help us, I shall go
to the police and tell them everything."

"You're bluffing," cried Alice Totenkopf. "I'm going
to call my lawyer."

She tried to get up but I pushed her back. I thought
of another name Kalmar had mentioned. "Your partner in Trauenstein is Julius Obermaier," I said, and
now she was silent.

"I am prepared to pay," I told her. "Three thousand
schillings for the two of us."

I could hear Sibyl behind me, sitting down, but I
didn't turn around. I held the money out to Alice Totenkopf.

"Are the police after you?"

"Yes."

"And if they find you?"

"If they find us, they'll also find the coffee. Then it's
all over for all of us."

She got the message.

"That's why I'm paying now."

She had herself in control again. "Five thousand,"
she said. We settled for four, after which Alice Totenkopf dragged her hulk over to a wall telephone and
dialed.

"This is Alice," she said. "Let me speak to Otto.
Don't be an ass! What do you mean, he's still asleep?
So wake him up!"

I walked over to Sibyl. She was sitting in the middle of the room, on her suitcase. "Why do I have to go back to Germany?" she whispered.

"They're looking for you in Austria," I said softly, while Alice Totenkopf explained to Otto, whom they had evidently managed to rouse, that he had to take on some more freight. "You can't cross any border anymore with your passport. We've got to get new papers for you. That will take a few days. In the meantime, no one must see you."

"But—"

"I know a hotel in the mountains. I'll take you there."

Meanwhile Alice Totenkopf was screaming into the phone, "It's for two friends of mine, and I can't say no! And it's got to be today! Wait . . . I'll ask." She turned to me. "In an hour. Is that all right?"

"Now? In daylight?"

"We only drive by day."

"But isn't it much safer to change cargoes at night?"

"At night there are more troopers. So . . . do you want to go or don't you?"

"Six thousand if you'll travel by night."

"No," she said, and her tone was final. "By daylight or nothing."

"Very well."

"My friends say it's all right," she told Otto. "Send Frankie over to get them. When? Yes, in fifteen minutes." She came waddling over to us. "You'll be picked up in fifteen minutes."

"Thank you."

"And—and what happens then?" Sibyl asked hesitantly.

Alice Totenkopf looked at her with curiosity. "You're a strange pair," she said. "What have you done?"

"What do you think we've done?"

She thought if over, a serious expression on her face, which gave her another chin. "Played with false chips!"

"Good guess!"

She shook her head. "How childish.! You can't win that way. Forged them yourself?" I nodded. "Out of amber?" I nodded again. "Crazy! Didn't you know that all chips over a thousand schillings are marked?"

"We marked ours, too."

"Idiotic! You look too intelligent for that."

I shrugged. Sibyl asked weakly, "What happens when they come for us?"

"I'll explain it to you," I said. "There's a piece of German territory that juts into Austria near Salzburg. It's called the Reichenhaller Zipfel. There's an Austrian highway for passenger cars that runs around the Zipfel, from Salzburg to Lofer, about a hundred and fifty kilometers."

"A hundred and twenty-five," said Alice Totenkopf pedantically.

"A hundred and twenty-five," I repeated dutifully. "But there's a second road that runs through the Zipfel, that is to say—through German territory. Of course it's much shorter. How much shorter?" I asked Alice Totenkopf.

"Forty kilometers," she said, and sat down next to the buffet. A monstous clock stood on it with a thoughtful Walter von der Vogelweide perched on top. The clock must have weighed at least fifty pounds.

"This second road," I said, "is for through freight. The trucks are sealed at customs in Salzburg. A customs officer phones the office at Lofer. If the truck arrives in Lofer at a reasonable time, they let it pass through into Austria without inspection, because the truck can't possibly have stopped to switch cargoes."

"But then how do they do it?" asked Sibyl.

"Why don't you tell her?" I asked Alice Totenkopf.

"No, you tell her." She was looking at me with undisguised admiration. "I'd like to know how you found out about me."

"I know a lot about a lot of people," I said.

The Western Press Agency had sent my friend Kalmar into the Reichenhaller Zipfel about six months ago. At the time the smuggling had been in uranium. While there he had also become interested in other aspects of smuggling. Today I was grateful to him for his curiosity.

I said, "Frau Totenkopf smuggles coffee. Coffee costs more in Germany than in Austria, which makes it very worthwhile."

"Not as much as it used to be," she said.

"But still nothing to be sneezed at, am I right?" I turned to Sibyl again. "Frau Totenkopf sends out a truck filled with sacks of coffee. At the Austrian border she declares it honestly as coffee. The truck is sealed; the driver takes the through-freight road. In a quiet corner in the woods, an empty truck draws even with him. Neither truck stops. The codriver of the coffee truck tears off the seal and throws the sacks of coffee into the empty truck driving alongside him. If they meet a car they stop the operation temporarily. . . ."

"You're from customs!" cried Frau Totenkopf, momentarily panic-stricken.

"No," I said. "When the first truck is empty, a third truck appears with a cargo of cement sacks. A few sacks of coffee remain in the original truck, so that the truck still smells of coffee, just in case the officer in Lofer decides to spot-check. The seal is put back. And that's it. Frau Totenkopf's truck arrives in Lofer on time, only the coffee stayed in Germany. Am I right, Frau Totenkopf?"

She nodded, obviously shaken. "And a man like you gets caught passing false chips?"

23

I don't know if you have ever really smelled coffee, not coffee in cans or chips, but coffee in sacks, many, many kilograms of it. It is a bitter smell. The driver, Otto (his last name was Frühbeiss), had given Sibyl and me damp cloths before locking us in behind the sacks. He had also torn a small hole in the tarpaulin covering the truck so that we could get some fresh air; still the acrid smell of the coffee beans was suffocating.

We drove to the border on the autobahn. Sibyl didn't say a word. She sat crouched beside me, holding the damp cloth to her nose. The driver had told us to breathe as shallowly as possible. He was a pale little fellow with the face of a ferret. His codriver's name was Lohschmidt. He was a red-faced giant. He had to be strong because he was the one who handled the sacks.

The worst time was while the truck was parked at customs. Frühbeiss had promised to be as quick as possible, still the whole procedure seemed to last an eternity. Sibyl grew restless. Once she moaned. "Be quiet," I whispered.

The smell was unbearable. The sweat broke out on my forehead. Outside I could hear the customs men walking around the truck, talking to Frühbeiss. Sibyl squirmed. "Oh God," she groaned, and I covered her mouth with my hand. "Open up at the back," a voice said.

"Yes, sir."

The truck shook a little when Frühbeiss dropped the tailgate. We were sitting behind the sacks, out of the light. A tremor ran through Sibyl's body, then she was still, leaning heavily against me. She had fainted.

"You may drive on," said the voice. "It's exactly 12:34."

A moment later we began to move. I pressed my mouth against the hole in the tarpaulin and tried to breathe the fresh air. It cut like a knife. After drawing a few breaths, I pressed my back against the wall of the truck and dragged Sibyl up so that she might get some air, too. After a while she regained consciousness. She was wheezing, her breath came fast, and she was trembling all over. Suddenly the truck stopped, I could hear steps, then a voice—codriver Lohschmidt. "We're going to start unloading now. Are you all right?"

"Yes!" I yelled.

The truck started to move again. "Not much longer," I whispered. "Only a few minutes more!"

Sibyl groaned.

"Breathe! Put your mouth to the slit and breathe! Are you getting any air?"

She groaned again. Now I could hear the motor of another car, driving beside us. A voice cried, "Let's go!"

We couldn't see him, we were separated by a wall of coffee sacks, but Lohschmidt had started throwing the sacks onto the truck beside ours. He worked fast and with the precision of a machine. In a very short time it grew lighter around us, fresh air streamed in on us, Sibyl opened her mouth wide and breathed deep, like someone recovering from drowning. The smell subsided. Then we could see Lohschmidt. He was standing upright, tossing one sack after another into the second truck. There he stood, in the weak sunlight of a winter's day, like a sweating, snorting giant out of a Germanic saga. We crept past him. Three sacks were still in the truck. Lohschmidt whistled, Otto Frühbeiss stepped on the brake, the truck slowed down. "Hurry!" yelled Lohschmidt.

The truck stopped. Lohschmidt tossed Sibyl's suitcase into a ditch, my small bag followed. "Jump!" he yelled. Sibyl jumped and stumbled in her high heels. She fell into the ditch and didn't get up. I twisted sideways until my legs were dangling over the side of the truck, then I let myself drop. I landed on my healthy leg and had just let go when Frühbeiss stepped on the gas again. I limped across to where Sibyl was lying, on her back, looking at me, her eyes wide open. Her lips were parted, her black hair was spread out in the snow.

She stretched out her arms to me and I wanted to help her to get up, but I slipped and fell on her. She kissed me. This time her lips were hot and wet. Her teeth sank into my lips, blood ran across my tongue. Another truck tore past us in the direction of Lofer. It was the truck with the sacks of cement which now had to be reloaded. Alice Totenkopf had developed a foolproof system.

24

Ten minutes later a taxi drove up. Alice Totenkopf had contacted the driver from Salzburg. She had told him to be at kilometer marker 17 on the through-freight road at 1:00 P.M. It was 1:05 when he got out of his Mercedes, removed his cap and said to Sibyl, "I'm sorry I'm late, *gnädige Frau*." He opened the door to the car and Sibyl slipped into the back. I was about to follow her when he held out his hand. "Two hundred marks."

"I know," I said. "You'll get your money."

"But I must have it now," he said, not unfriendly. "There are just too many police around. If we are stopped you may not have a chance to pay me."

But nobody stopped us. We drove to Munich on the autobahn. The car didn't have a dividing window between front and back, so Sibyl and I didn't speak. She sat beside me, looking out at the snow and avoided looking at me. After Trauenstein the sun went down; at Chiemsee it began to snow heavily. A gusty east wind was blowing; the sky over Munich was black. "We're going to have a storm," said the driver.

His car skidded frequently, he was having difficulty keeping it in the right lane. Suddenly Sibyl sat up. "What's that?"

"Where?"

She pointed to a bloody mess in front of me. An animal, run over. Parts of the body were scattered over the highway. A huge blackbird was perched on the particularly large piece. He was hacking at the cadaver with his yellow beak. "Only a cat, *gnädige Frau*," said the driver.

The bird heard the car and flew up, taking a piece of the carcass with him. The Mercedes drove fast over the bloody mess. I looked back. The bird had flown down onto the carcass again.

At Rosenheim we left the autobahn and drove inland. The snow grew heavier. The windshield froze up, the wipers were stuck on the icy surface. Every now and then the driver stopped, got out cursing, and scraped off the ice. The wind grew stronger, the light failed, it grew darker and darker. We drove through villages with low houses and little churches. The Bavarian Alps were in the clouds.

"How did you find out about the hotel?" Sibyl asked.

"I've stayed there a few times. I called. They're expecting us." The driver heard every word.

The Hotel am Himmel was situated on the plateau of a mountain called Am Himmel. It lay about 800 meters above sea level and could be reached only by cable railway. There was no other way up; the mountain was too steep. The car ran over several deep gorges. The hotel had 30 modern rooms, a bar, excellent food, a sauna, and a solarium. A Rhinelander had had the left wing rebuilt as private quarters for himself and his friends, but he had never got around to living in his home above the clouds because he had died just when it was finished. The excitement connected with the dissolution of the Krupp empire had caused an old myocardiac condition to become acute.

His heirs built on a second wing and turned the whole building into a hotel, hoping to make a profit on it, but this hope had not been fulfilled. The hotel, never full, was operating at a loss. Film companies and publishers like to quarter their authors at Am Himmel, when they were running short on time. My agency had sent me to the hotel three times, to finish an assignment. Once I had taken a girl along, but after a while she had declared she couldn't stand it another minute and had left me. It was lonely at Am Himmel, just the sort of loneliness I was looking for to hide Sibyl.

We reached the valley station of the cable railway at 3:30 P.M. A toothless old man, who was almost stone deaf, carried our bags from the taxi to the little wooden station. Our driver meanwhile left us without a word of farewell. Sibyl's stockings got wet and she kept twisting over on her ankles in her light, high-heeled shoes. "Call them up at the top," I told the old man as I helped Sibyl into the lightly swaying car.

"I'm sorry. I don't hear very well. What did you say?"

"Call them up at the top!" I shouted. "We're house guests. Herr and Frau Holland."

"Yes," he said forlornly, wiping a drop off his nose, "you're right, sir. The weather's awful." He shut the car door. The glass window was down.

"My name is Holland!" I shrieked. "Don't you understand the name?"

"Holland. Yes, yes, Holland."

"Call them at the hotel!"

"Don't move around too much as you go up, and don't lean out." I gave up and handed him a mark. "Yes, yes. And the snow," he said. "The snow isn't right either, but the worst thing is the storm. I can feel it coming. You'll see." He stepped up to a loudspeaker on the wall, pressed a button and said in his croaking voice, "Ready, Seppl."

The car began to ascend. We were gliding up to "heaven." The little valley station disappeared fast; in two minutes we were in the clouds. Gray fog surrounded us. The car creaked and groaned. As we passed over the trestles it jerked and swayed harder. It was cold in the little car. For the first time since I had met Sibyl again, we were alone. She sat opposite me, hunched in a corner of the car, shivering with cold.

I said, "I shall introduce you as my wife. The hotelier's name is Ohlsen. He's a very nice fellow. I'll go straight back to Salzburg."

"That's what I thought," she said.

The car began to sway wildly as gusts of wind hit it. I said, "I went to the police station this morning. I was going to report you."

"But you didn't," she said, without a trace of triumph in her voice.

"No. I couldn't. I shall help you, Sibyl. I'll get new

papers for you. But we must part. I can't live with you anymore."

She said nothing, only nodded. "I can't do it," I went on. "You committed murder, you have killed two people, with the lowest motives. There's no excuse for it."

"You say you love me. How can you leave me if you love me?"

"I don't love you anymore."

The car stopped in front of one of the trestles. I said quickly, "Don't be afraid. They do that because of the storm. We'll move on right away," and with that the car did pass across the trestle, very slowly, then went on up again, faster. A black shape glided over the snow below us—the second car. We had passed the halfway mark.

"I'm afraid of you," I said. "I realize that I don't know you at all. I love your face, your voice, your hands, but your hands have killed and your voice has lied to me and your face has deceived me. I'm still utterly confused, but I know one thing—I don't want to have anything to do with you, not anymore."

"How self-righteous you are!" she said bitterly. "How respectable and pompous! What wonderful words! They sound so noble."

"What would you do in my place? What else can I do?"

Suddenly she began to cry. "I didn't mean it. I'm a nervous wreck, Paul. You are absolutely right, but please, please stay with me! Don't go away. I can explain everything."

"There's nothing to explain."

"But there is! You don't know everything." Now she was talking fast. "Petra didn't tell you everything. She couldn't have. I'll tell you how it really was."

The little car continued its slow ascent, the cables made a grinding sound, by now it was quite dark. "We'll be there in a minute," I said. "Wipe your face, Sibyl."

She passed a trembling hand across her eyes and said, "I'll do anything. I'll go to the police and give myself up, if only you'll stay with me."

"You didn't go to the police before."

"Because I hoped they'd never find me; and they didn't. Not in all these ten years." She sounded like an unhappy child. "I prayed to God. . . ."

"You prayed to Him for *that*?"

"Yes," she said. "Because He forgives all sins."

"I don't want to talk about your God."

The car slid into the little mountain station. The electric light was on. Seppl, a huge Bavarian in knee pants, opened the car door and greeted us. The hotelier was with him. "Hello, Herr Ohlsen," I said. "May I introduce my wife?"

Ohlsen kissed Sibyl's hand. He was a handsome fellow and he blushed when he was embarrassed. "I'm so glad to see you here again, Herr Holland. Unfortunately the weather's bad."

We walked the short distance to the hotel across the snow, through the clouds, over a path that had been cleared. Night had already fallen up here. "Are we the only guests?"

"Practically, Herr Holland. There are two

ladies. . . ." He went on bitterly, "You can choose
your room. We have a lot vacant."

"Unfortunately I have to leave again tonight."

"Oh." He sounded resigned.

"But my wife will stay a few days. I'll come back for
her."

Suddenly Sibyl stopped and stood still, her body
racked by sobs. "Oh dear," said Ohlsen, looking upset.

"Please excuse her," I said. "She needs rest."

25

The exterior of the house had been built in Bavarian style, a lot of wood, narrow balconies and a
broad, overlapping roof. The interior was quite elegant—old prints, good carpets and antique furniture. A
few wood-carved saints in the hall. It was warm and
very still in the house. The staff was friendly.

Ohlsen took us up to the second floor and gave us a
room in which I had stayed a long time ago. It had a
small living room and bath. The heads of two angels
were attached to the wall. The massive bed faced a
window that took up the entire opposite wall. As he

drew the curtains, Ohlsen said sadly, "When the weather is good you can see the Bavarian Alps from this window, all the way to Austria."

Sibyl was in control of herself again. "The weather doesn't bother me, Herr Ohlsen." Suddenly there was a strange sound, like a moaning. "What's that?"

"It's the wind," said Ohlsen. "There's a storm coming up." He added, "I'm not very lucky. My wife is expecting a child."

"How very nice for you. You must be very happy."

"We were, Herr Holland. But now it looks as if the owners are going to close the place, and what will we do then? I've put quite a bit of money in it already."

Again the strange moaning sound, thin, forlorn. A wooden beam creaked. The curtains opened. I had to get away.

"Try not to worry about it, Herr Ohlsen," I said. "The owners are rich," which was true. I had heard that they owned a lot of race horses in the Rhineland. As an experiment they had once sent some hay from the southern slope of Am Himmel to the Rhineland horses, which had preferred the Bavarian hay to what they were fed at home. After that, grass mown on the south slope was sent regularly by air express to Düsseldorf.

Ohlsen said, "The rich are cautious with their money, Herr Holland." He bowed to Sibyl and withdrew after saying to me, "I'll send up the registration form."

"That won't be necessary," I replied hastily. "I'm going down with you."

I didn't look at Sibyl as I left the room. I could feel

her looking after me, as if trying to make me turn around, but I walked down the passage to the stairs with Ohlsen without looking back. Our steps and the rushing noise of the impending storm were the only sounds in the eerie stillness.

At the desk I filled out the registration form. I stood there in my coat, my suitcase beside me. I filled out the form with wrong data. "Do you want to see my passport?"

"If you please, Herr Holland," said the desk clerk.

"I've only been married a month," I said. "My wife isn't on my passport yet."

"That's perfectly all right, Herr Holland." He wrote down the number of my passport and gave it back to me. "Thank you. That's all."

"I want to go down right away, before the storm gets worse."

"Yes, Herr Holland. Do you want me to—"

"I've already said good-bye to my wife," I told him. I didn't want to see Sibyl again. I would call her from Salzburg.

"Good-bye, Herr Holland. We hope you'll visit us again soon."

Outside the house I was hit hard by the wind. I walked down the path toward the lights of the cable railway station. The sliding door was closed, the little cabin was empty. "Hello!" I cried.

The window of a small room above the station was flung open and Seppl stuck his head out. Apparently he lived up there. "Yes, Herr Holland? What can I do for you?" The wind howled and wispy clouds flew past me up to him.

"I want to go down."

"You can't go down now, Herr Holland. We're reading a wind velocity of eleven. We're only allowed to operate up to ten."

"But I have to go down!"

"Sorry, Herr Holland, but that's impossible. You wouldn't make it."

"And if I tried it on foot?"

"But Herr Holland! You can't even do that in summer!"

"When will you be operating again?"

"As soon as the wind dies down," he said, grinning at me.

26

It was dark in the bar. I sat down in a corner and listened to the wind growing stronger. Somewhere below, probably in the kitchen, a girl was laughing. I sat in the dark, smoking, feeling angry and bitter against Sibyl. I hated her.

Steps coming toward the door. It opened and a waiter stuck his head in. I knew the man. "Anybody here?" he cried, as he turned on the light. "Oh, Herr Holland. We've been looking for you everywhere. Your wife has been asking for you."

"Tell her I'll come upstairs in a few minutes."

"Yes, Herr Holland."

"And Hugo?"

"Yes."

"I want something to drink. Bring me a Johnny Walker."

"With soda?"

"No."

He came back with ice and a glass, and poured me a drink. I said, "Put it on the bill. And leave me the bottle."

He nodded and left. I tossed two ice cubes into the glass and drank it down. The whiskey tasted oily, different from what I was used to. I filled the glass again and stirred the ice around for a while. The second drink tasted better and the third one was just right.

I was drunk fast because I hadn't had anything to eat. The wind seemed to grow more persistent by the minute. A console radio stood within reach. I turned it on and had to laugh when I heard what it was playing—the last movement of the Rachmaninoff Piano Concert II I had heard most recently in Sibyl's empty apartment in Berlin. I filled my glass again and listened to the music I loved. After that a man spoke. He said at the sound of the gong it would be five P.M. Radio Munich was broadcasting the news. First the weather: cloudy and cool. New snow in the Alpine regions. High winds in the northeast. . . .

I finished the whiskey in my glass and left the bar.

On the stairs I slipped and almost fell. By now I was very drunk. I walked down the long passage to Sibyl's room, the wooden floor planks creaking under my feet, and I could hear the wind rattling the windowpanes. The whole house was suddenly restless and filled with whispering sounds, wood creaking, air rushing, a rattling and a groaning everywhere. . . .

I walked in without knocking. Sibyl was stretched out on the bed. She looked at me, her eyes wide. "The car isn't running?"

"No." I sat down beside her.

"And that's why you've come back?"

"Yes."

I began to unbutton the jacket of her suit. She lay on her back, very still, looking at me. Her lips were parted and her breathing was fast. I took off her jacket and her skirt and went on undressing her—her shoes, her stockings, her slip. She turned from side to side to make it easy for me, never ceasing to watch me, moving slowly, very slowly. Her eyes were slits and her breath made a hissing sound as it came from between her clenched teeth. And then she was lying before me, naked.

I undressed and could feel myself getting drunker all the time. The whiskey warmed my blood and the blood was pulsating, hot and heavy, in my temples. She sat up and unstrapped my prosthesis. It fell heavily to the floor.

God protects lovers, I thought, and was filled with hatred as she took me in her arms. And I was to discover that the intimacies of hatred were even more sensational than the intimacies of love. We spoke, words that came without volition, words of passion and greed, always the same words. And I could hear the noise the wind was making, louder, louder, until it became dominant and turned into the roar of a plane flying over the mountain toward Munich. The windows shuddered as it flew low over the hotel, like the planes in Berlin over the Grunewald villa in the nights I had spent there. Sibyl moaned, "Now. . . ."

27

I slept badly that night. I had an endless nightmare and kept waking, then going back to it. At about three I woke up thirsty. My lips were dry, my tongue felt swollen and hot. There was water in the bathroom, but to get to it I would have to turn on the light, and strap on my prosthesis, without waking Sibyl. She was fast asleep beside me, breathing deeply and regularly. When I couldn't stand it any longer, I decided to slide on the floor to the bathroom in the dark. I had taken note of where the furniture stood and everything went all right. In the bathroom I switched on the light, turned on the cold water and held my mouth under the tap. I swallowed a lot but it didn't quench my thirst. It was always like that when I had drunk too much whiskey.

On the return trip, after I had turned out the light in the bathroom, I got lost. I couldn't find the bed, and it was so dark in the room, nothing was visible. For a while I tried to find the direction by listening to Sibyl's breathing, but it didn't help. Gradually I became angry. I felt my way along the carpet, determined to find where it ended, but it didn't end.

My anger turned into despair. Where was the goddamned bed? I made a quick move with my arm and struck the table. Suddenly feeling dizzy and sick, I gave up and pulled the heavy cloth off the table and covered myself with it. I pulled my good leg up to my chest, cradled my head in my arm, and remained lying on the carpet. It was warm in the room and I wasn't cold. I felt less dizzy and was quite content lying there, thinking of what Sibyl had told me before falling asleep.

Sibyl's earliest memories of her childhood were of a weeping mother and a father playing the piano in an apartment void of any furniture except for the piano, two beds and a table. It was a hot day in August, and she had been playing in the park. When she got home, she found the apartment empty except for the aforementioned articles of furniture, and books, clothing and china, all lying on the floor. Her father was sitting on a wooden crate, playing a Chopin waltz. Her mother was standing in front of the stove in the kitchen, crying. The mascara on her lashes had run and made black stains under her eyes. At 35, Sibyl's mother was still a beautiful woman.

"What's happened, Mother?" Sibyl asked. "Why is all the furniture gone?"

Her mother wiped away her tears and put her arm around her five-year-old daughter. "We sold it, darling."

"But why?"

"Because we didn't like it. And it *was* ugly, don't you think so?"

"I don't know. I liked my bed."

"Your bed wasn't pretty, either," said her mother. "That's why we sold it, too. We're going to get new furniture, beautiful furniture."

"When?"

"It will take a few weeks. Right now the furniture dealers are very busy. But in the autumn, wait and see—you won't recognize our apartment."

"Why not?"

"Because it will be so beautiful."

"And where am I going to sleep until then?"

"I have a big surprise for you," said her mother. "You like to sleep on the floor, don't you?"

"Yes, I do."

"Well, we'll put a mattress on the floor in your bedroom and you can sleep on it."

"Mama!" Sibyl clapped her hands. "That's wonderful!" She ran into the empty living room and threw her arms around her father and gave him a wet kiss. "Thank you, Papa!"

"For what?"

"That you're going to let me sleep on the floor!"

The beautiful furniture never came. Gradually the apartment was refurnished with pieces that didn't match. It began to look very colorful, even quite dashing, and Sibyl was delighted with it all.

Sibyl's parents hadn't always been poor. When they had married, her father had just inherited a considerable fortune and the first years of their marriage were free from all care. Her parents traveled to England, Spain, France, and Italy. Sibyl was born in Italy. Then they had settled down in an apartment in Berlin.

Her father had studied music. In his youth he had even composed. His teachers said he had talent and a promising future. He played piano beautifully; he played it all his life. When he came into his inheritance he stopped composing. He said he had to prepare himself for his first symphony. He spent four years preparing for it. It didn't matter how long he took because there was still plenty of money. Sibyl's father bought his wife jewelry and beautiful clothes because he loved her. He was a gentle lover and the marriage was good. But then the money was gone.

Sibyl's mother still believed she faced a bright future. She was confident that the symphony would be a great success. She believed every word her husband said. He said he knew Gershwin, Rachmaninoff, and Addinsell, and claimed they said he showed great promise. When the symphony was finished, it would be recognized world wide, on the strength of which the couple took out a bank loan. Sibyl's father said, "I'll start tomorrow."

But on the following day he fell down the stairs and broke his arm. It had to be in a cast for six weeks, and after that it took quite some time before he could play piano again. He said the six weeks weren't really lost because during that time he had developed the basic theme of his symphony. But his fingers were still too stiff to get it down on paper. Unfortunately he had broken his right arm.

During this period a movie director from UFA saw Sibyl's mother on the street and spoke to her. Actually he had something else on his mind rather than hiring her as an extra, but when he heard that she was married and in financial difficulties, he suggested that she come to see him in his office in Babelsberg. His name was Othmar Plüschke.

Othmar Plüschke became the family guardian angel. He engaged Sibyl's mother for four weeks at 27.35 marks a day as an extra in a motion picture called *The Congress Dances*. This was followed by other films. Her father regained the use of his right hand, but he still couldn't seem to get the basic theme of his symphony down on paper.

"Every artist goes through periods of crisis like this," he said. But this crisis lasted six months, and by then the money from the bank loan was gone. Sibyl's father played piano more beautifully than ever and Sibyl sat at his feet and listened, enchanted. Sometimes she saw her father take a bottle out of his pocket and drink. When he drank he played even more beautifully.

When the bank sent its first reminder, Sibyl's mother went to see Othmar Plüschke and asked him, "Couldn't my husband and daughter work as extras, too?"

"Sure!" said Plüschke. "Bring them with you, Magda."

They were making a film on Chopin. Sibyl, her father and mother worked as extras. Her father had brought along his bottle and took an occasional swig out of it and was friendly and polite to everybody. Sibyl adored being in the studio.

In the Chopin film there was, of course, a grand piano. During the midday pause, Sibyl's father would sit down and play. He didn't think there was anybody else in the studio, but there was. The producer who heard him loved music. He asked Sibyl's father, "What else can you do?"

"Nothing," said her father, "except play the piano."

"You can work here as a prop man," said the producer, "if you like." He knew that the family was in financial difficulties.

Sibyl's father was pleased with the job; her mother was pleased, too. During the next two years they were able to pay off the bank loan. Sibyl got a bar of chocolate every now and then and at Christmas—a doll.

Then, one day, two plainclothesmen appeared, showed their identification cards, and took Sibyl's father with them. "He's going on a little vacation," her mother told her.

He came back from this vacation three months later, pale and thin, but cheerful. Sibyl didn't find out what had happened until later. The prop men were in charge of considerable sums of money, for which they had to account at set intervals. Once, when Sibyl's father had to account for the money he'd spent, he couldn't do it. A quite large sum was missing. And it turned out that he didn't only play the piano but the horses as well. Sometimes they won, sometimes they didn't. When it came time to account for his expenditures, the horses hadn't won for a long time. Plüschke couldn't do anything about it. "We can pay it all back," Sibyl's mother assured the court. "We have fine carpets and furniture."

So they let Sibyl's father go, but they took his job from him, which surprised him, and they came for the furniture. That was on a hot day in August, while Sibyl was playing in the park. When she got home, her father was sitting on a crate, playing Chopin and smelling of cognac. He was playing more beautifully than ever. They had let him keep the piano.

28

The piano disappeared a year later at a time when neither the telephone nor the electricity were functioning. The gas was turned off, too. Something in the pipes had broken down, Sibyl's mother explained. After the disappearance of the piano, the gas and electricity functioned again, and the telephone rang.

Since there wasn't a piano at home anymore, Sibyl's father began to play in bars. He was paid a little for it, but he also drank a little while he played. Sometimes Sibyl's mother sent her out to bring him home. If Sibyl hurried there might be some money left. Sometimes she didn't get there fast enough. Then her father made a scene when he got home, her mother cried, and her father beat her mother. Sibyl saw him do it and hated him.

Her mother was still working as an extra, but she wasn't earning enough. Her father drank, her mother wasn't beautiful any longer. Plüschke said, "I'm sorry, Magda, but I can't use you anymore as a top-flight extra with evening clothes, but don't worry, I'll put you in the crowd scenes. Only I'm afraid all you'll get is fifteen-fifty. Can't your old man do *anything*?"

"Right now he *is* doing something," said Sibyl's mother.

"What?"

"He's writing his symphony."

Her father actually had begun to compose. In the following five years he wrote the first three movements. Then he was overcome by the despair that overwhelms all artists when they suddenly doubt the value of their work, and on a stormy autumn evening he lit a fire in the park and burnt his unfinished symphony. He told his wife and daughter, "I'll start again tomorrow. I have it all in my head."

Sibyl was 15.

Her mother said, "Other children your age are earning money. You've got to help me, *Liebchen*. I can't support us anymore, not by myself. Plüschke is dead, and the others—they don't always let me work."

"What do you want me to do, Mama?"

"Well," said her mother, "in Luna Park there are all sorts of attractions: the Shimmy Stairs, the Roller Coaster, the Death Leap, and so on. The man I spoke to said he hired girls who didn't have to do anything but go on all the rides and scream as loud as they could."

"Why?"

"Because it's such fun," said her mother. "They yell and scream and act crazy. And the people watching say, my, that must be fun, and they buy tickets. The girls also have to run around the park advertising the rides. Do you want to try, *Liebchen*?"

"Are the Shimmy Stairs free, too?"

"Everything would be free for you, dear, I'm not saying you've got to do it, but I would be grateful if you'd help out. So that Papa can finish his symphony."

"He's never going to finish that symphony," said his daughter. "But I'll be glad to help out."

So Sibyl went to work at Luna Park. A week later the boss told her, "I've never had anyone like you." Sibyl took her work seriously. She yelled and screamed and ran through the tents advertising the rides. Men stopped and stared at her, pop-eyed. She was very beautiful even then, slender, with big eyes, dark hair, and long legs. She worked from five in the afternoon until midnight. Then her mother came to get her and bring her home. In the morning Sibyl was very tired. Her school work began to suffer. She was left back and had to do one term over again. But the family could now count on a minimum of 80 marks from Sibyl. At the end of the season she asked for 100. Her boss agreed without a murmur, and her mother was dreaming of her perhaps getting 150 next season, but then something happened.

One night, on the roller coaster, when Sibyl opened her mouth to scream, all that came out was a hoarse scream. However hard she tried, that was all she could produce. She couldn't talk either, not above a whisper, and that with great difficulty.

"Her vocal chords are damaged," said the doctor they consulted. "She must be careful not to utter a sound until they have healed, or I won't answer for anything."

"So," said her mother, on their way home in the streetcar, "work at the amusement park is over. But never mind, darling; I have something else lined up for you. Tomorrow you go to the Scala. They're still auditioning there, for show girls."

"What do you have to do to be a show girl, Mama?"

"Nothing at all, darling. They give you a beautiful costume and you walk up and down some stairs or just stand still."

"And they pay you for *that*?"

"I should say so! More than in Luna Park." Sibyl's mother coughed and massaged her throat. "I must have caught cold. It hurts me to swallow, has for days." She took Sibyl's hand. "Come, we get out here."

"But it's a station too soon."

"We're going to pick up your father."

As they walked into the little bar he was playing the piano, a glass of cognac at his side. The bar was still empty. Sibyl's father was playing Chopin. "Doesn't he play wonderfully?" said her mother, folding her hands as if in prayer.

29

Two hundred girls turned up for the audition. Thirteen were hired, among them Sibyl. She still had on her bathing suit and her high-heeled shoes when the director of the new revue came up and shook hands with her. "Okay, Fräulein. Three hundred marks a month. Topless a hundred marks more, if you like."

"I'd like three hundred and fifty marks a month, and not topless."

"Three hundred marks is very good for a starter."

"I'll have to speak to my mother about it. I should be earning three hundred and fifty."

"You know what? We'll say three hundred and fifty. Okay?"

"Okay," said Sibyl.

"You have such an exciting voice, Fräulein."

"Do you think so?"

"Yes. It's so deep and husky. Have you always spoken like that?"

"Always," said Sibyl.

So now Sibyl supported the family. Her mother went to the studio less frequently, the inflammation in her throat became chronic. Her father went through another crisis. He was toying with the idea of giving up the symphony and trying to write a rhapsody instead. He complained bitterly that he missed his piano. "But I shall manage without it," he said confidently. "It's just a question of concentration. It's all in my head."

Sibyl liked her new job. A stage designer, a rich young man, fell in love with her. It was her first love.

"Is he nice?" asked her mother.

"The nicest fellow in the world, Mama!"

"Then ask him to give you the money to rent a piano, as his first present," said her father. "Tell him I'm going to teach you how to play."

The rented piano arrived. Sibyl's father didn't teach her anything. But he played again. Sibyl's mother took to her bed and listened happily. The doctor's first diagnosis had been wrong, now they knew what it was, not chronic bronchitis but cancer of the larynx.

Six months later Sibyl's mother died after suffering terribly. In the end she hadn't been able to eat any solids, only liquids. But she was always happy when her husband played Chopin; sometimes he also played some of his rhapsody—for instance, on the day she died.

30

In the following year there were two weddings. The first to marry was the young stage designer. He had to marry, he told Sibyl, to please his parents. It was a marriage of convenience and would take him to Düsseldorf. He wanted her to keep his engagement ring as a souvenir. He had the rental firm pick up the piano.

Soon after that Sibyl's father asked her what she would think of his marrying again. He introduced the woman, whom he had met recently. She was young and wealthy. She admired Sibyl's father because of his musicality. "I have enough money for both of us. With me, he will finish his rhapsody."

"I wish you every happiness," said Sibyl. "I shall go to Austria."

"Why to Austria?"

"I'm going to join a small company. They pay better than the Scala. And I want to travel." To her father she said "You don't need me anymore."

"I'm going to miss you terribly, *Liebchen*," he said.

"Only at first."

"No, always. You must come to see us often."

"I will, Papa."

He took Sibyl to the station. From the window of her compartment she looked down at him and said, "It's horrid of you to marry again, and so soon."

"I need someone to look after me."

The train whistle blew. "It's your fault," said Sibyl, "that Mama had to die."

Six months later, in Vienna, she met a man who had seen her on the stage. He lived in Hamburg and was in Vienna on business. His name was Rolf Brunswick. He was tall, blond, slim, and tanned. He said, "Fräulein Sibyl, I am not an adventurer. I want to marry you. I want a son, and a mother like you for my son."

Rolf Brunswick impressed Sibyl as refined and cultured. Not until she had married him did she find out that he was crazy.

The Brunswick Works in Hamburg made dust filters, gas masks, and air-raid shelters. Sibyl moved into her husband's big, gloomy house on the Innenalster. Instead of the paintings, hunting trophies or tapestries one usually finds in the houses of the rich, there were plaster painted heads, with real hair, wearing the various gas masks manufactured in the Brunswick Works.

Sibyl was introduced to Hamburg society. Her husband was one of the richest men in the city. Sibyl had beautiful clothes, valuable jewelry, and she grew lovelier every day, but she also grew increasingly nervous.

Since the First World War, her husband had fallen victim to the chronic fear that he would be murdered at night. He found it impossible to sleep in a bed. He always slept on the hard wooden floor, a revolver beside him, and Sibyl had to sleep at his side. He said he didn't want a weakling for a son. Sometimes he woke up out of a nightmare, screaming, and ran through the house, his revolver in his hand. On trips he never used any of his three cars but took his motorcycle. It had a sidecar in which he carried complete camping equipment, and he insisted that Sibyl accompany him everywhere. "You are my oxygen," he said. "I refuse to make a move without you. You bring me luck."

Sibyl sat on the hard little seat of the motorcycle behind him. In the evening he put up his tank. They slept at the edge of the highway, wrapped in blankets, in summer and winter, in snow and rain and storms. His son was to be a strong, healthy boy, said Brunswick. Sibyl found out that he had been married four times.

Her father wrote to her from Berlin. He was moving to the United States with his wife. The letter was forwarded to Sibyl in Cologne, where she was in the hospital with a severe intestinal ailment. She had caught cold on the highway. For weeks she had fluctuated between life and death, then the doctor told her, "In six months you should be fully restored. But you will never have a child."

They were divorced. Sibyl received 70,000 marks in cash. She moved back to Berlin and lived for a while in a hotel. Now she was independent, and she lived an adventurous life, until she met Peter Sparr, a young writer working for a newspaper, and fell in love with him. They rented a small house on the Wannsee and lived together. Sparr was a person who could only work at night, during the day he slept. Sibyl couldn't get used to it. "We have enough money," she said. "Don't write anything for a while. Rest. Try to think of a novel."

Sparr agreed, and for a while they were happy. The only trouble was, now the young writer didn't work anymore at all. They lived on Sibyl's settlement, and they lived on a lavish scale because they had decided that when the war broke out, they would die together. Sparr declared he preferred suicide to wearing a uniform, and Sibyl couldn't bear the thought that her frail, nervous lover should have to endure the indignities of barrack life. As a precaution, they bought some cyanide.

But the war took its time in coming. Sibyl's bank account shrank. She began to sell her jewelry, a piece at a time. When her friends reproached her, she told them, "Leave me alone. There's nothing I want for my money but Peter and his love. Besides, I like to live well, and when the war comes I shall commit suicide."

She decided that Peter's creativity had rested long enough and urged him to start writing again. He was perfectly agreeable. He told her that he had seen a beautiful antique desk in a shop on the Kurfürstendamm, and a matching armchair. "If you'd buy the two pieces, I'd start writing again. I know I could work marvelously on that desk."

Sibyl sold a bracelet and bought the desk and the chair, and Peter started to work. He worked on his novel for a year, and the manuscript got thicker and thicker. Sibyl sold her mink coat. They would be able to live on that for a long time, and by then the novel would be finished and sold.

But the novel didn't sell. The publisher to whom Peter submitted it, shook his head and said it was bloody amateurish. Sparr decided he was just another victim of fascism, and Sibyl declared it was the most wonderful book she had ever read.

She still had a fur coat and a few alligator bags, and the war was imminent. So she continued to live happily and with a certain fatalistic sense of security. Until she found out that Peter was deceiving her with a little blond salesgirl. He admitted it at once and promised to give up the girl, whereupon Sibyl forgave him.

At last the war broke out, and Sibyl said, "Our time has come."

"Tonight," said Sparr.

That evening he didn't come home. Sibyl saw him again only once, three years later, on the street, looking as young and sweet as ever. He had on the uniform of an air force lieutenant and was wearing the Iron Cross. The little blond salesgirl was with him. He introduced her as his wife. He said the three of them simply had to get together and have a long talk, especially about their childish behavior in the past, like their so-romantic plan to commit suicide together. He laughed heartily over that. And how was Sibyl?

"Just fine," she said. At the time she was living in a furnished room and was working as a secretary in the Foreign Office. "And you?"

"Great!" He was beaming.

"Peter has shot down eight English planes," Frau Sparr said proudly.

"Just luck," her husband said modestly. "Tomorrow they may get me. But I must admit, it's fun."

Sibyl began to laugh. "What are you laughing at?" he asked.

"Nothing, really," said Sibyl. "I was just thinking . . . when you didn't come home that evening, I took the cyanide. . . ."

"For God's sake, no! And what happened?"

"Nothing. I felt very sick and they took me to the hospital and pumped out my stomach. The man who sold us the poison was a swindler. It wasn't cyanide at all!" And all three of them laughed.

A year later Sibyl was sent to Rome on a mission for the Foreign Office. She met many men and had a few affairs. But none of these relationships caused her any unhappiness. Now she was the superior one; she was the one who would cause suffering. She got the reputation of being as fascinating as she was cold.

At a party, the young *chargé d'affaires*, Tonio Trenti, was introduced to her. Again Sibyl fell in love. All Rome talked about their affair. They were going to get married as soon as the war was over. They seemed inseparable. Sibyl spent many nights in Trenti's house, and all the people who knew them were shocked when they heard that Sibyl had betrayed her lover to the Gestapo after she had found out he was deceiving her with Petra Wend. How could it have happened? The two seemed to have enjoyed an exceptionally harmonious relationship. Neighbors recalled evenings when they had heard sounds of a piano playing coming from

Tonio Trenti's house. Trenti played piano beautifully, especially when he was a little drunk. He played a lot of Chopin. . . .

31

I was awakened by Sibyl, moving in my arms. I could feel her soft, fine hair on my shoulder and thought, why is Sibyl there? I opened my eyes. I was still lying on the floor, but Sibyl had put a pillow under my head and had covered both of us with a blanket. Now she sighed and woke up. We always woke up together.

"Beloved," I said, "did you—"

"Yes. At about five I woke up and noticed that you weren't in bed with me. I turned on the light and saw you lying here." She kissed me on the cheek. "You didn't notice a thing. You must have had a bad dream. You were restless and said a lot of confusing things."

"What about?"

"Mostly about Chopin."

"It was sweet of you to cover me."

"I love you."

"How's the weather?"

She got up, walked over to the window, and drew the curtains. The morning sunlight fell blindingly into the room. The sky was blue, the snow glittered.

"No more wind," said Sibyl. "The cable car's running. I can see it."

She stood there, bathed in the dazzling sunlight, and I could see her body through her thin nightgown. "Come to me, Sibyl."

She came quickly and slid under the covers beside me, and we made love on the floor. It was all beautiful and harmonious, and I felt as if I had been ill for a long time and was well again.

After we had bathed, we ordered breakfast. While we were waiting for it, we sat on the bed and looked out at the snow. The wind had piled up gigantic drifts, and where it had blown the snow away, you could see the stubble of frozen grass, black and brown. But in the sun, the snow was blue, yellow, violet, and white.

"After breakfast, I'll take the car down," I said. "I'll be back in a few days. You'll wait here for me, my sweet."

"Where are you going?"

"To Munich. Or Frankfurt. It depends."

"On what?"

We were sitting close together, my arm slung over her shoulder, and I could feel her warm breath on my chest. It was a peaceful morning. Everything was clear, simple, and final.

"I'll get you a false passport," I said. "Give me yours. I'll need it because of the picture. I'll call the office from Munich. I have friends there who know several foreigners. One of them will do it for me. Quite a few of them are under obligation to us."

"Like Frau Totenkopf?"

"Yes. I've got it all planned."

"When did you plan it? You slept like a log."

"I planned it in my sleep. They've been after me for some time, to take over the office in Rio, and I've always turned them down because of you. Now I'll ask for the position. We'll fly to Brazil. I'll fly alone and you'll fly alone. We'll take Pan Air do Brasil. I have friends at the airline, too. And in Rio we'll get married. It's a big country. We won't attract attention there."

"Paul?"

"Yes?"

"You're going to stay with me?"

"Yes. And I'll never leave you."

"But I shot a man. You said you had to leave me because I had committed murder."

"That was yesterday."

"And today everything's different? Why?"

"Because I love you," I said. "And I don't want to live without you. And that's all that matters to me."

"It's what I want, too, Paul."

After that we didn't speak anymore. We sat there, hand in hand, looking out at the snow and the little cars of the cable railway going up and down. Now it was in perpetual motion; many skiers were coming up. They made a lot of noise and fooled around in the snow.

A friendly waitress brought our breakfast. We had ordered ham and eggs, orange juice and coffee. The coffee and ham smelled great. After the waitress had

gone we sat down at the table. The girl had brought
up the Munich paper. It lay beside my cup and I gave
it a cursory glance. Then a headline on page one
caught my eye. "Witness in Trenti Murder Case Says
Sibyl Loredo Is Alive!"

32

The article was based for the most part on Petra
Wend's statement at Salzburg police headquarters. The
first thing I did was to scan hastily to see if my name
was mentioned. If it was, we were lost.

The name Holland was not mentioned.

Petra Wend had declared, "I am sure that the
woman who calls herself Sibyl Loredo is alive, and
that she committed the murder."

Question: "And what do you think she will do
now?"

Answer: "She will try to leave Austria. She may
even try to get out of Europe."

Question: Do you think she can do this alone?"

Answer: "She has devoted friends who will certainly
help her."

Question: "Would you give us the names of these devoted friends?"

Answer: "No."

That was all, and it was plenty, but I didn't want to cause Sibyl any anxiety. "Ridiculous!" I said. "They're trying to make a big thing of it because it's all they have. Pass me the salt, please."

"So what do we do now?"

"I'll go to Vienna. It says here that Petra has gone back to Vienna. I can get your passport there and have a talk with Petra. The police will calm down when they see I've come back."

"But if we try to leave the country?"

"Nobody can stop me from flying to Rio. I'm going alone, on business. You fly alone with your new passport. Everything's going to be all right." That's what I said to calm her. I didn't tell her that by now her picture was undoubtedly posted at all airports, railway and border stations. But there were ways to get around that, too. She would have her hair dyed and wear it differently. The passport picture could be retouched. But I had to see to it that Sibyl didn't panic. If she did, we'd never get away.

"I'll call you every evening," I promised before I left an hour later.

"Every evening? How long do you plan to be away?"

"Only a few days. Try not to worry."

"Come back soon!" she implored me. "Please! Please! I'm so frightened."

"I'll come back as soon as I can."

As the car started down, I could see Sibyl at the

window of our room, waving. I waved back until the car had descended so low that the mountaintop, the house, and Sibyl at the window had disappeared.

I returned to Austria the same way I had come: in one of Alice Totenkopf's coffee trucks. I called her from Trauenstein, and she sent a car for me. All went well. The day remained clear and bright until evening. I took the midday train to Vienna and ate lunch in the dining car. I was hungry and felt marvelous because I knew exactly what I intended to do. The man sitting next to me pointed out the roadbed of the new Salzburg-Vienna autobahn, which was in the process of being laid. The bare reinforcing wires showed black in the snow, and I saw many cranes and bulldozers and men working. Once I saw a new overpass, bright orange with rust-protective paint.

I went back to my compartment and read for a while, then I grew sleepy. I had drunk half a bottle of wine. I fell asleep and dreamed of Sibyl. In my dreams we had arrived in Rio and were lying on the Copacabana beach in the sun. Sibyl had on a white bathing suit and was tanned. All the men were looking at her. There were many beautiful women on the beach, but for me Sibyl was the most beautiful of all. In my dream I told her so and she replied that for her I was the most desirable man. She wanted nobody else.

33

In Vienna I took a suite at the Ambassador Hotel
because I had always stayed there and been treated
very well, but also because I wanted to make my reap-
pearance in the Austrian capital conspicuous. I was
given a room on the fourth floor, in which I am now
writing these lines, the room with the red wallpaper,
the white and gold furniture, and the green-tiled
bathroom.

I drove straight to the police station and asked for
the officer on duty at homicide. I showed him my passport in which, thanks to Alice Totenkopf, there was no
exit or reentry stamp. I protested angrily about Petra
Wend's statement. I said that the words *devoted friends*
were undoubtedly aimed at me, with the purpose to
cast suspicion on me. The officer assured me that no
one suspected me of anything, and he could understand
my indignation very well. He respected my devotion to
the woman who had disappeared. What was I planning
to do in Vienna?

"I want to speak to Petra Wend."

"So you also believe Sibyl Loredo is alive?"

"For God's sake!" I cried hysterically. "What do you mean—believe? How do I know! Is it a crime when I try to find some sort of assurance? What would you do in my place? Go home and forget all about it?"

My hysteria paid off. He assured me that I had his sympathy, which was what I had been aiming at. I asked, "What do the police think?"

"We have no proof that Frau Loredo is dead."

"Nor that she is alive?"

He raised his hands and let them fall again.

"Is that supposed to mean no? Except, of course, for Frau Wend's statement."

"A statement isn't proof," he said.

I drove back to the hotel. It had started to snow again. The snow muffled the sound of the traffic. I found it very quiet in Vienna.

In my room I wrote a letter to the directors of my agency, asking to be moved to Rio de Janeiro. After all that had happened to me, I wanted to leave Europe. The office had frequently expressed the wish to have me in Rio. I spoke Portuguese, the climate agreed with me. . . . I considered for a while whether I should say more about the pain Sibyl's disappearance had caused me but decided I had said enough. The three were older men; love didn't mean much to them anymore, it only made them nervous. So I remained businesslike and reminded the gentlemen that I had done good work for the agency in Brazil in 1947 and 1948. I could leave anytime. . . .

By now it had grown dark. I sealed the envelope and thought of Sibyl. Was she sitting at the window, looking out at the snow? Was the cable railway operating? I lifted the receiver of the phone. The hotel operator answered. "Herr Holland?"

"Please connect me with Frau Petra Wend."

"Do you have the address?"

"No. But there can't be too many with that name."

"Hang up, Herr Holland. I'll call back right away."

A minute passed. If Sibyl was sitting at the window, the light wasn't on in her room. She liked to sit in the dark. So did I. We had often sat in the dark together, looking out into the night.

The telephone rang. "Hello?"

"This is Petra Wend." Her voice was dry and cool.

I said, "This is Paul Holland," after which there was a short pause.

"You're in Vienna?"

"Didn't you expect me?"

"I? Why should I?"

As usual, she was making me nervous. "I want to talk to you. Would you have dinner with me?"

"Certainly."

"May I come for you in an hour?"

"I'll be pleased to see you," she said, and gave me her address. "Have you heard anything about Sybil?"

"No. Why?"

"I was only asking. So . . . in an hour, Herr Holland," and the conversation was over.

I ordered whiskey and ice, and went into the bathroom to shave. Then I changed. It was snowing harder. The room was warm, and I sat down and drank a glass of whiskey, after which I wasn't nervous anymore.

Petra Wend lived in Grinzinger Allee. The taxi driver swore constantly because the snow interfered with his visibility. His wipers couldn't cope with it. I was reminded of the drive through Bavaria. Alice Totenkopf's driver had had the same difficulty. There was a lot of snow that winter.

Petra Wend lived in a house that had a large garden. I arrived at eight. Lights were on in the villa, they shone yellow on the snow. A man, a woman, and a little girl were snowballing each other. They seemed to belong to the villa. The woman and the little girl chased the man around the garden, laughing and breathless. He fell, they pounced on him and rubbed snow on his face. They were having a great time. Then father and daughter chased the woman through the snow. She didn't see me, and bumped into me. "Oh . . . I'm sorry."

"It's perfectly all right," I said, smiling. But she didn't smile. Instead she stepped back, and the little girl went over to her father, who put his arm around her. He said hello, and I went into the house. Inside the door I turned around once and looked back at the happy family, who were playing in the snow again. They were strangers, but I knew Sibyl would have liked them, too, and I thought: as soon as we get to Rio, we'll be married. I wanted a wife and a home. I wanted to live in peace at last.

34

Today, as I try to explain what happened that evening, I mustn't forget to mention that Petra drank a lot. She was never drunk; she only pretended to be. She knew exactly what she was doing, but I only realized this afterwards, when it was too late.

We ate in a restaurant that was located on the second floor of a house opposite St. Stefan's Cathedral, a large restaurant, too brightly lit. The stark light didn't do a thing for the women. It made them look pale and sad. The place was famous for its exotic hors d'oeuvres; the chef had made a science of the aperitif.

Petra had on a tight black cocktail dress that left her shoulders bare. Two bands crossed over her breasts, otherwise the dress was plain. She had made up her eyelashes, her lips were red, her white hair was brushed straight back. Under the merciless light she looked weary in a rather exciting way, but it didn't excite me. I didn't care what she looked like.

Before the hors d'oeuvres we drank two martinis,

with the dinner a bottle of Burgundy, and two cognacs with the coffee.

Over the filet mignon we declared a truce. She said, "I didn't know the police were going to pass on the information I gave them to the press."

A waiter came and picked up the basket with the bottle of Burgundy. "A little more wine, *gnädige Frau?*"

"Yes, please." She waited until he was gone, then she went on. "But I do believe that Sibyl is still alive, and there's nothing wrong with my saying so, is there?"

"And it's your opinion that I would help Sibyl to escape, isn't it? Because I'm such a devoted friend."

"I would be very disappointed in you if you didn't." She drank. "I'm—I had no intention of offending you when I used the word 'devotion.' On the contrary, I find your love for Sibyl touching, something really quite wonderful."

"I don't love Sibyl anymore," I said in a loud voice. "After the things you told me, I have to believe that she killed Trenti. It's dreadful. I hope the police don't find her, I hope she gets away, but I would never help her to do so."

"I thought you loved her."

"I don't love a woman who has committed murder. And I wouldn't help her." I told myself that I had to say it over and over again, primitively. Then she would think of me as a primitive person, and that was fine.

"Then you don't know how to love."

"That's possible."

"I think my husband would help me if I committed murder."

"You're married?"

"Yes. And I have a son. Didn't you know?" Nonchalantly, while cutting her meat, she added, "My husband lives in Paris. I don't see much of him. He's very busy. Tommy is seven. He's in a very good private boarding school. You can't look after a child properly when you're working, can you?"

"I suppose not," I said, and foolishly began to think that I had overestimated the damage this woman could do.

After dinner I took Petra to a bar I hadn't been to before. Here the lighting was dim. It was a lot like Robert Friedmann's bar on the Kurfürstendamm. There were the same red plush chairs and candles and red wallpaper; even the bar was like the one at Robert's.

After two whiskeys nothing meant very much to me. Suddenly I felt very sure of myself as I noticed that Petra grew less and less steady. A woman who got drunk that fast couldn't pose much of a danger.

"Herr Holland?" Her eyes were shining, her lips were moist. We were sitting at the bar, side by side, close, although there was plenty of time. It was Petra who had moved so close. I could smell her perfume, her skin. Pleasantly. The whiskey warmed me and I thought of Sibyl and the beach in Rio, and felt very secure.

"Yes, *gnädige Frau?*"

The cigarette between her fingers trembled a little. "You're a nice fellow, Herr Holland," she said.

"Thanks."

"Just now . . . I lied to you."

"You did?"

"When I spoke about my husband," She moved closer. Her blue eyes were open wide. The piano was nearby. Nobody could hear what we were saying. The redhead tending bar was interested in a man at the far end. There weren't many guests that evening and the ones that were there were quiet.

"I said I didn't see my husband often."

I nodded.

"That was a lie. I don't see him at all. I haven't seen him for three years." She laid her hand on mine. And now I'll get the intimate details, I thought. This was the confessional hour. So what? Let her talk, I thought. That meant I wouldn't have to. I could drink and smoke and pretend to be sympathetic. Every hour brought me an hour closer to the time when I would leave everything behind me and be with Sibyl forever. . . .

"My husband is an architect," said Petra. "Please don't think I want to speak badly of him. I don't. As long as we were living together we had the happiest marriage in Vienna. Everybody said so. An exemplary couple. We never quarreled, he was good to me always, and he loved Tommy. He was a good father." She twirled her empty glass between her fingers and I called over the redhead. She filled our glasses. "Not too much soda," said Petra, smiling at the woman.

"Not too much soda, *gnädige Frau*."

Petra drank. The dim lighting in the bar helped a lot. Now she looked fine, her cheeks had color. "But then he got this assignment in Paris. A high-rise house, together with Corbusier. He asked me whether he should accept it. I told him of course, he had to! You only get a chance like that once in your life. Don't you agree?"

"Certainly."

"So . . . off he went. At first he wrote to me every day. He wanted me to join him in Paris. But then he met this woman—Ramona Leblanc."

"The actress?"

"You know her?"

"Only from her pictures."

"He's been living with her for three years, and he's not coming back."

"Why don't you get a divorce?"

"He says he doesn't want a divorce. He says he loves me and the child."

"Does he send you money?"

"Oh, yes." She threw back her head. "Why am I telling all this? Let's dance."

"I don't dance very well. My leg . . ."

We danced. The piano player smiled and nodded as we waltzed past him. The redhead smiled. The other dancers smiled. Everybody seemed to like us. I liked all on them, too. I held Petra in my arms. She felt soft and warm, and she pressed her body against mine. Once she stumbled. I said, "I'm sorry."

"It's not your fault. I'm drunk. Please take me home."

"If that's what you want."

"Come upstairs for a minute, for a cup of coffee."

"That'll be nice."

"You're nice, Herr Holland. Very nice. . . ."

35

She lived on the top floor of the villa. An attic had been transformed into what would have been called a penthouse apartment in a higher building. It had a roof terrace, kitchen, bathroom, bedroom, and a large studio with sketches and modern paintings on the wall. The furniture was low, carpeting and upholstery were in light colors, and a lot of bright pillows were scattered on the couch. When we walked into the studio, Petra let her coat drop off her shoulders. I picked it up.

"You know," she said, "there's really no point in drinking coffee now. It'll just keep us awake."

"That's right." I was determined to agree with her on everything.

"You like whiskey. I have a bottle. Would you like another drink?"

"Sure."

"Then come along."

We went into the kitchen, got the bottle of whiskey, glasses, and soda; Petra took a tray of ice cubes out of the freezer compartment. "Give it to me," I said, and held the tray under the warm water faucet. She passed her hand across my cheek. "Your skin is so smooth. . . ."

"I just shaved three hours ago."

"What's your first name?"

"Paul."

"I bought some new records the other day, Paul. You'll like them."

A small lamp with an orange shade was the only light in the studio. We sat on the couch and drank and smoked, and the new records turned out to be recordings by Harry James. The trumpet made me nervous, always did, with its long drawn-out cadenzas.

"Marvelous, isn't he?" She was looking at me.

"Great!"

All the same to me. Everything. I loved Sibyl and God protected lovers. Who had said that? I couldn't remember. Didn't make any difference anyway. When I got back to the hotel, I'd call Sibyl.

Petra sank back onto the cushions. Her dress hitched up and I saw her legs. Beautiful legs. The ice cubes tinkled in my glass and there was a lot of whiskey left in the bottle.

"You know something, Paul?"

"What?"

"You really disappointed me tonight when you said you wouldn't help Sibyl. My husband would help me, still, in spite of everything."

"Your husband must love you more."

"My husband wouldn't help me," she said, and drank. "He doesn't love me at all. Men can't love.

They're egotistic and mean. They all want the same thing, we let them have it, then they get tired of us. You're just the same, Paul."

"Perhaps."

"But nice."

The record was finishing. "Let's have Gershwin next," said Petra.

"Which record?"

"Whatever you like. I have them all."

I got up and went over to the stand that held her records and looked through them; she remained stretched out on the couch, watching me and drinking. I wondered if she drank regularly. She didn't look like an alcoholic. A piano solo . . . a saxophone, joining in plaintively. . . . "Beautiful." This time I meant it.

"Wonderful!" she exclaimed. "Now there's a man I'd go straight to bed with."

"I don't know a woman who wouldn't have gone straight to bed with Gershwin."

"Dreadful. That he had to die so young." She stretched, her lips parted; I drank. "You have complexes, don't you, Paul?"

"Not that I know of."

"Because of your leg." She touched my healthy knee with the tip of her high-heeled shoe. "You shouldn't have any complexes, Paul. You really shouldn't."

"I don't have any."

"All of us have complexes." She got up and came over to me. The piano solo was ended, the orchestra came in.

"Would you like another drink?" I asked.

"Yes, Paul." Her lips were still parted.

"There's no more ice."

"I'll get some."

She took the ice bucket and left the room. The door closed behind her. I lit another cigarette and listened to the music, and thought: the last time I was in Rio, they'd just started working on a housing development next to the golf course. They build fast in Rio. When I get back there, the work on the houses should be well advanced. I could probably rent a small one. Sibyl and I didn't need a large house.

"I got up and went into the kitchen. "Petra?" No answer. The bathroom was empty, too. I walked across the white tiles, past the tub, to the door of the bedroom. A lamp was lit on the bedside table. Petra was lying on the bed. Her body was very white and beautifully proportioned. I saw her large breasts with their rosy nipples, her long legs, her narrow hips. She was naked. She looked at me seriously and said, "Come, Paul."

36

I knew that the main post office in Vienna had a counter that was open day and night. It was still snowing when the taxi that had brought me from Petra's apartment into the city stopped in front of the big building. I told the driver to wait.

I walked through the snow to the lighted entrance. Not a soul in sight, and it was snowing, uninterruptedly, inexhaustibly. In some spots I sank up to my knees in drifts.

The clerk was old. He yawned, and I saw a lot of gold teeth. "What do you want?"

I told him what I wanted, and he said, "Have a seat."

There were stools in the post office lobby. They were fastened to the floor and stood in front of writing desks. There were seven people in the lobby, besides the clerk and me. All seven were poor and fast asleep. Five had sat down on the stools and were asleep with their heads and arms on the desks, the other two were asleep standing.

"Here's your call. Booth ten."

I went into the little booth and lifted the receiver. A night clerk answered. I asked for my wife. I had decided to always call from a post office, not from the hotel.

"Hello?" Sibyl's voice sounded very near, very clear and sweet.

"Forgive me for keeping you waiting so long."

"It doesn't matter. I was reading. How are you?"

"Fine."

Through the glass door I could see a policeman come into the lobby. It startled me, but then I saw that he was interested only in the sleeping vagrants. He woke them up, one by one. It was evidently forbidden to sleep in the lobby.

"How long are you going to stay in Vienna?"

"I don't know yet."

"Have you seen Petra?" Now the policeman was talking to a man leaning against the radiator. The man had to show his identification. I said, "I spent the evening with Petra."

No answer.

"I've just come from there. I don't think she's going to make trouble for us."

Again Sibyl was silent; the open wire hummed.

"She was very friendly at first and quite sensible. But then she got drunk and asked me to sleep with her."

"So?"

"I was a little drunk, too, and I didn't want to antagonize her. It would have been an impossible situation. . . ."

The police officer gave the man back his ID card and left the lobby. The seven men immediately went back to sleep.

"Did you sleep with her?"

"I tried."

"Oh," said Sibyl, then she was silent again; then, suddenly, she laughed. "Forgive me, Paul."

"Yes."

"I think it happened because I was thinking of you all the time."

"I'm sure it did," she said, "and I'm touched."

"She said it must have been the whiskey, and I wasn't to attach any importance to it. She wasn't going to."

"Are you going back to her now?"

"No."

"Are you going to see her again?"

"I don't know. Perhaps. We didn't mention it. She fell asleep quite suddenly."

"Paul, I miss you."

"I miss you, too."

"When you see her again, will it happen again?"

"No."

"Hurry," she said. "Hurry back to me."

"Yes."

"I love you."

"And I love you, too."

"There's something else I must tell you," she said.

"Yes?"

"I've had such headaches lately when I read. Today I took the car down and saw an eye doctor. I'm far-sighted. I have to wear glasses."

"You can get very pretty glasses."

"I won't have to wear them all the time. Only when I read."

"You can wear them all the time. I won't care."

"Paul?"

"Yes?"

"Farsightedness is a sign of old age. I'm getting old."

"You'll never get old," I said.

BOOK THREE

1

"Herr Holland?"

It was the desk clerk calling. The sun was shining and it wasn't snowing any more. The sky was a brilliant blue. I had breakfasted and was going to leave my room to call Frankfurt. I had to talk to Kalmar. He could give me the number of a passport man.

"What is it?"

"A lady wants to speak to you. Frau Wend."

"I'm on my way down."

At this time of day the lobby was usually empty. Petra waved to me from the far end. She was wearing a navy-blue coat and no hat; she looked elegant and rested. I kissed her hand. She smiled and said, "I want to apologize."

"If anybody should be apologizing, it should be me."

"No. Listen to me. I was drunk last night. I behaved abominably. I'd like both of us to forget it, please."

"But of course."

"I want to forget it because I'd like to see more of you while you're here."

"So would I," I lied.

"What are you doing this evening?"

"Nothing. Why?"

"Would you like to go to the opera with me? Our opera house has been completely restored, did you know? They're playing *Rosenkavalier*. I could get two tickets."

I forgot to be wary of Petra. Instead, I began to think I had been unfair. That she had come to me with an apology and proposed we got to the opera together, which was nice of her.

"Thanks, Petra. I'd like to go."

"The curtain's at seven."

"Then I'll call for you at six-thirty and we'll have dinner afterwards at Sacher's."

"Have you ever eaten there?"

I had eaten at Sacher's many times, but to please her I said, "Never."

"Oh, that's wonderful. You'll love it!" All Viennese were convinced that every foreigner would adore the restaurant in the Hotel Sacher.

Petra had to go to a conference at the film studio. After she had gone, I waited a few minutes, then I left, too.

This time I phoned from a different post office. Kalmar helped me out at once. "Fuchsberger. Eugene Fuchsberger. Alseggerstrasse 174. He won't overcharge you, and he's fast."

"Thanks."

"Paul . . ." Kalmar sounded serious. We'd known each other since the end of the war and had experienced quite a few things together. "I'm not asking any questions. You know I'm your friend. But Paul . . . be careful."

"I will."

I took the streetcar along the Rhine, cleared by now of snow, then changed to a car that went to Hernals. I stood outside on the platform and breathed deeply. It felt good because the air was so clean and dry. The snow piled high on the sides of the street was still white. I saw no one, and it never occurred to me to wonder if I was being followed.

Alseggerstrasse ran along the top of a hill that led to the Vienna Woods. I walked uphill for at least half an hour. Here the villas stood in large gardens. There was no wind and it was quite warm. Below me I could see the city houses, and the higher I walked, the farther I could see. Half an hour later the Prater Ferris Wheel loomed up on the horizon, the largest ferris wheel in the world, and the spire of St. Stefan's Cathedral, and the Danube, shimmering in the sunlight, looking like a broad ribbon of liquid lead.

Alseggerstrasse 174 was a small house with a concrete foundation and a wooden structure on top. It stood all by itself on a slope. I rang the bell on the gate but nobody answered, so I sat down on a snowbank and waited.

A little while later an old woman carrying a net shopping bag came slowly up the hill. Sitting on the dry, hard-packed snow, I could see her from far off, coming nearer and nearer. There were vegetables in her shopping bag—light yellow turnips and small, thin, sandy potatoes—a few small paper bags. She was wearing a black bandanna and a gray coat with a worn Persian lamb collar. I got up. "Frau Fuchsberger?"

"Yes." She looked at me suspiciously. "What do you want? Two of you were here last night."

I felt apprehensive. "I'm not from the police, Frau Fuchsberger."

"No?" Her voice was high-pitched and thin, like the voice of a frail child. "You must excuse me, but since they arrested him, they keep coming back."

"Your husband was arrested?"

"Well, yes. Last week. On top of everything else, that had to happen. If you're not from the police, then what do you want?"

"I wanted to give your husband a little job. I need a passport. . . ."

She looked startled. Her face twitched. "A passport? I don't understand. You're not from around here. You talk so differently. You're a Reichs-German!"

A Reichs-German. It was a Viennese explanation left over from 1938.

"Yes, I'm German, Frau Fuchsberger. I take it your husband was in trouble with the police as far back as 1945."

She nodded anxiously.

"It was that business with the forged passport, wasn't it?" I said. "There was this Reichs-German journalist in Vienna. . . ."

"Yes. Herr Kalmar!" Now she seemed more at ease. "He was a good man. He provided my husband a lawyer who got him out of that mess in court."

"I know. Herr Kalmar is a friend of mine. He sent me here. I need a passport."

"Oh dear. That's too bad." Frau Fuchsberger looked sincerely distressed. "And now they've locked Eugene up." She clicked her tongue. "And he always said he'd like to do something for Herr Kalmar, or any friend of his." She was swinging her market bag. "So now what do we do?"

"Is your husband still held by the police?"

"No, no. He's back in jail, awaiting trial. He won't be back for a year."

"It's terribly important, Frau Fuchsberger."

"Let me think. . . . Now who could—?" She stuck the forefinger of her left hand into her toothless mouth, and seemed to be giving the matter some thought. "Yes. Franz," she said then. "He might do it. But you can't go to him. I'll have to talk to him first, and he'll call you. . . ."

"But I don't have much time!"

"I'll go see him right away, soon as I've eaten. I'd do anything for a friend of Herr Kalmar. It's really too bad that they had to lock up my old man right now!"

2

"Hello?"

"Good evening, my sweet. I'm late again. Sorry I was at the opera, and after we had dinner together."

"How was Petra?"

"All right. Friendly. She only drank two glasses of wine. And I took her home right after dinner."

"What was the opera?"

"*Rosenkavalier*. With an enormous Marschallin. I can't stand Hofmannsthal."

"You can never follow the text."

"The whole production was pure Hofmannsthal. But the house is beautiful. Listen, I have good news. The man came to see me this afternoon."

"So?"

"Everything's fine. He'll have it ready for us this week. He only needs three days, four at the most."

"And then you'll come?"

"At once!"

"That's beautiful, Paul. You know, I'm not nervous anymore. I'm not afraid."

"Are they nice to you at the hotel?"

"Couldn't be nicer."

"I'm going to rent a car tomorrow morning. Petra's son is in a private school near Vienna. She usually goes to see him on Wednesday, but tomorrow she has to be in the studio. So I said I'd get the boy and bring him to Vienna."

"But she still cleans her teeth herself?"

"Only three more days, darling!"

"Maybe four."

"Maybe four. But certainly not five."

3

The name on the place nearest to the private school was Rekawinkel. It was a village in the Vienna Woods, about an hour's drive from Vienna. I wasn't in a hurry. The road was clear and dry. Sometimes it ran beside the woods, then along the tracks of the West-bahn, glistening in the sun. I kept having to look at them because in a few days I would be riding across them to Sibyl.

The school was in a big old building. The wallpaper

was dark, so was the furniture, and there were a lot of antlers on the walls of the room where I waited for Petra's son. From a nearby classroom I could hear a chorus of boys' voices reciting the multiplication table: " . . . Three times three is nine; four times four is sixteen; five times five is twenty-five. . . ."

The door opened and a young teacher brought in Tommy. "There you are. That's the uncle who's going to take you to your mama."

Tommy looked at me curiously. "What's your name?"

I told him my name and we shook hands. He was small and frail for his age, but he had an intelligent, sensitive face and beautiful dark eyes. His hair was brown and thick. It was time he had a haircut. A lock of hair kept falling across his forehead and he pushed it back with his hand.

"Have you come by car?"

"Yes, Tommy."

"Great! May I sit beside you?"

"Of course."

"You'll bring Tommy back this evening, Herr Holland?"

"Oh, yes."

Tommy walked proudly with me through the hall. Quite a few children were standing around. One little girl said, "Hi, Tommy!"

Tommy stopped and introduced us. "This is Michelle. Michelle, this is my uncle Paul. We're going to Vienna by car!"

"Oooh!" said Michelle. "May I watch you take off?"

"Sure," said Tommy.

In the car he was silent for a while, looking intently out the window. He had beautiful hands and very narrow wrists, an attractive child, I decided. I was feeling like a man looking forward to a vacation. With every day I was drawing nearer to the day when all this would be behind me; with every hour I was nearing the time when Sibyl and I would be together again.

In the village I stopped in front of a store. "Let's get you a chocolate bar."

"Oh . . . I don't know." The boy sounded hesitant.

"What's the matter? You don't like chocolate?"

"Yes, I do. But if Mama says anything, you must tell her I didn't ask for it."

A well-behaved boy. As we drove on he chewed happily on his chocolate bar. "Milk chocolate with nuts is my favorite."

"It used to be mine, too." I was smoking a cigar and felt wonderful. "Are you looking forward to seeing your mother?"

"Yes. Have you known her a long time?"

"No. Not very long."

"Are you going to marry her?"

"Your mother is married already."

"No, she isn't."

"But she is, Tommy. She told me so herself. Your father is living in Paris."

He looked angry. "Did she tell you that?"

"Yes."

"Did she also tell you that he's a famous architect?"

"Yes."

"And that she was very happy with him?"

"Yes."

"And that he sends us money regularly?"

"Yes."

"None of it's true."

"What do you mean?"

"That's what she tells everybody. I think it's because she's ashamed. But I know the truth. I know what it was like when my father was there. They fought all the time and there was never any money." His little face twitched; he had even forgotten his chocolate bar. "A great architect!" he said scornfully. "At school the children showed me a picture, in a magazine. My father was in it, with this actress. It's because of her he left Mama."

"You saw the picture?"

"Yes. And I've kept it. It's in my footlocker, under my bed. My father is the meanest man in the world! I never want to see him again! Never!"

"And what would you do if you saw him one day?"

"I'd look away."

"And if he spoke to you?"

"I'd kick him in the shins!" And I thought how much this child had to be missing his father to speak about him like this. "Watch it, Paul," I said. "Your chocolate's going to fall into your lap."

He retrieved it and bit off a square. "And he doesn't send us any money. He hasn't sent us any money since he went away. That's why my mother has to work."

"I didn't know that," I said.

"Well, how do you suppose she pays the school?"

"I guess you're right."

"When we get there, don't tell her I talked about it. That always upsets her."

"I won't say a word."

"Thanks." He looked down at my right foot on the gas pedal and mumbled. "Constant companion!"

"What do you mean . . . constant companion?"

"That was under the picture. 'The French actress Ramona Leblanc and her constant companion, the Austrian architect, Clemens Wend.' "

4

I drove Tommy to the film studio on the Rosenhügel, which had once been seized by the Soviet military. Now the Austrians had their State Treaty, reestablishing the Austrian republic as "a sovereign, independent, and democratic state," the occupation was over, and the studio belonged to them again. In the hall, facing the entrance, you could see a light square on the begrimed wall. Only a short while ago a picture of the Father of All Proletarians had hung there, and before Stalin, undoubtedly, Adolf Hitler. Right now the spot was empty.

Petra worked in a small room above the cafeteria. A

lot of colorful sketches were lying around. Tommy hugged his mother. "Hello, Mama."

"Hello, Tommy. How are you?"

"Fine! Uncle Paul said he'd take us to the movies this afternoon. To *When a Father and His son.*"

"But you've seen that!"

"It's such a good picture, Mama. I'd like to see it again."

So we went to the movies, and after that to a coffee house, and Tommy had hot chocolate and ate a lot of cake. Every now and then I could see Petra looking at me thoughtfully. She was probably thinking of Ramona Leblanc's constant companion and her own little incomplete family.

"Another piece of cake, Tommy?" I asked.

"No, thanks. I don't think I can. Besides, you're spending too much money on us." He turned to his mother. "Uncle Paul bought me a chocolate bar on the way here, but I didn't ask him to."

"That's right," Petra said seriously. "We mustn't ask favors."

We took Tommy back to school. It was a pleasant evening. For a brief moment I felt like a family man. Back in Vienna, I drove Petra home. She thanked me.

"You have a nice boy."

"I know. I love him. There was a time when I hated him because I felt that with a child I'd never get another man."

"And now you don't feel that way anymore?"

"Now I don't care."

I turned in the rented car and went back to my hotel. The desk clerk handed me a letter. From Frankfurt. My hands trembled as I opened it. The directors agreed to my transferring to Rio. They had booked a flight for me with Pan Air do Brasil, for March 28, 7:30 A.M., from Berlin, Tempelhof Airport. It was the same plane I had taken last time.

I was filled with a wild feeling of joy. March 28. Only a week away! In a week it would be all behind us!

"Somebody is waiting for you in the lobby, Herr Holland," said the desk clerk. It was Frau Fuchsberger. She was sitting at the far end of the lobby, tiny and gray, her feet pushed under her chair as if she wanted to hide them. She looked as if she wanted to hide everything—her hands, her face—she was looking at the wall as if she believed that if she saw no one, no one would see her. She was wearing an old brown imitation fur coat, and her hands held a shabby muff. As I came up to her she smiled a toothless smile. "I've been waiting for you for two hours, Herr Holland," she said.

"Has anything happened?"

"Nothing," she whispered. "On the contrary, Franz finished earlier, and since you wanted it as fast as possible, I've brought it with me."

Everything was going well. Things were running smoothly. If there is such a thing as God, I thought, then thank you, God. You really are protecting us.

"Let's go outside."

She rose quickly, as if she were glad to get away. In a quiet side street, in the entrance to a building, where I was sure no one could see us, she gave me the passport. It was a masterful forgery, with an incontestable stamp by the Vienna police. Sibyl had a new name, different dates, different birthplace, and there were several entry and exit stamps. It wasn't absolutely clean and looked as if it had been handled. One of the corners was slightly dog-eared. All as it should be. And it was valid until 1959.

"Where is the visa for Brazil?"

"On the next page, Herr Holland." Frau Fuchsberger was beaming. "Franz is so proud of it. I think he did a good job, don't you?"

I found the big rectangular stamp on the next page: *Consulado do Brasil em Vienna Visto. No. 115. Bom para embarcar parao Brasil até 26.4.56.* The visa was valid until April 26, 1956. The name of the consul who had granted it was *David Linés.*

"He did all right, didn't he?" said Frau Fuchsberger.

"Excellent, Frau Fuchsberger." It was dark in the house entry, only the feeble light of a street lamp fell on us. I gave the old woman the money for the forger. "And this is for you."

"No, no, Herr Holland! I can't accept it!" She pushed my hand with the money away. "For Franz, all right, but nothing for me!"

"But Frau Fuchsberger—"

"I won't hear of it! You're a friend of Herr Kalmar. I'd do anything for him, but not for money. Herr Kalmar is a good man." She came closer. "Lean down a little." I did, and she made the sign of the cross on my forehead with her cold, hard forefinger. "God protect you."

"Thank you, Frau Fuchsberger."

My mother had sometimes made the sign of the cross on my forehead. She had died five years ago and since then nobody had done this to me. I said good-bye to Frau Fuchsberger and walked through the snow to the main post office. It was a little before ten P.M. and the streets were empty. Every now and then a car passed by. I was very happy that evening. I think it was my happiest evening in years.

I got my connection at once. "Darling, it's all settled. I'll take the next train and be with you in the morning."

"All settled?" Sibyl's voice petered out.

"In Frankfurt they've said yes, and I have the passport. We'll leave a week from today."

There was no answer.

"Sibyl! What's wrong?"

"I—I don't know what to say. I—I didn't think it was going to work out."

"But it is, my sweet. I love you."

"You know what I'm going to do now? Order a triple whiskey and drink it neat."

"And I'll do the same thing."

"I guess I'm going to grow old after all. You know something . . . I feel sick."

"Order your whiskey, darling," I said, and laughed. "I'll be with you in a few hours. And brace yourself for our *Wiedersehen*. We won't get out of bed all day!"

"I'll be looking for you, Paul. You're in my heart, and someplace else, too!"

" 'Bye, darling. Until tomorrow."

" 'Bye, Paul."

As I hung up I was smiling. I was smiling as I left the booth. Then I stopped smiling. Petra Wend was standing in front of the booth.

5

She looked like a clown. Her face was white, her lips were painted a brilliant red, and there were blue shadows under her eyes. She didn't look alive. Her voice sounded strange, metallic. Her words were profoundly shocking. "From now on you will do only what I tell you to do, Paul. You understand?"

I didn't answer. There were a few people in the lobby but nobody was paying any attention to us. The man at the counter said, "Charges for overtime in booth three."

Petra said, "The glass door is thin. I heard every word."

"You've been following me."

"For hours, Paul. For days." Now she was smiling, a venomous smile.

"Booth three!" the man at the counter cried.

"Excuse me—"

"What's the matter with you? Fifty-four schillings overtime."

"It's my fault," said Petra. "I was talking to the gentleman. Please excuse us."

I paid.

"Let's go," said Petra.

"Where to?"

"To your hotel."

She took my arm, we left the post office and walked through the snow on Fleischmarkt to Rothenturmstrasse. We must have looked like a pair of lovers.

"I thought you must have taken Sibyl to Bavaria," she said. "It was the smart thing to do."

"I don't know what you're talking about."

"You know exactly what I'm talking about." Now her voice was tender; if she had been a cat, she would have purred. "We don't have much time. I want you to understand that I'm desperate and determined."

"Determined about what?"

"If you leave me for a moment, if you don't do exactly as I say, just once, I'll call the police and tell them where Sibyl is. You understand?"

"No."

She removed her arm and began to walk away. "Where are you going?"

"To the police."

"No, you're not!" I grabbed her and brought her back.

"That's better," she said. "That's a lot better. And now please let go. You're hurting me."

I let go of her.

"Let me take your arm again."

I did.

"We'll go back to your hotel. I need a drink, and I want to explain your situation to you."

"I don't understand."

"Yes, you do, Paul. So please drop it. I'm only human, too."

6

Half an hour after having left her, I was sitting in the large, pleasant lobby of the Ambassador Hotel again, Petra Wend opposite me, and a waiter was taking our order. "Whiskey," I told him.

"Scotch?"

"Yes. Two doubles."

The waiter went off. "What do you want?" I asked.

"First of all—your passport."

"No."

We stared at each other for a moment, then she said, "You must want me to go to the police."

I gave the passport.

"And now Sibyl's. The forged one."

"I—"

"I saw the old woman give it to you. I want it."

I gave it to her. She leafed through it, nodded. "To Brazil," she said. "That's what I thought, too."

"Petra! What did I ever do to you?"

"You never did anything to me. That's not the point."

"So what *is* the point?"

"I'll tell you in my good time." She was wearing a leopard coat, slung across her shoulders now. She had on a woolen dress underneath it. She was smoking. A waiter came with the whiskey. "Thanks."

"Is there enough ice?"

"Yes."

"I can bring more."

"Herr Franz"—I closed my eyes—"There is enough ice."

"Very good, sir. It melts so fast because it's so warm in the lobby. And when the whiskey isn't cold, it doesn't taste good. Am I right, *gnä' Frau*?"

"You're quite right, Herr Franz," said Petra, and Waiter Franz left us.

Petra poured soda water into her whiskey and drank. I drank, too. Two Frenchmen were seated at the other end of the lobby, talking loudly and laughing. I felt ill.

"And now you will call Sibyl again and tell her to come to Vienna."

"She wouldn't come. She'd just grow suspicious!"

"You'll tell her your plane is leaving from Vienna. She trusts you. After all, she loves you."

"Yes," I said. "And that's why I won't tell her to come to Vienna."

"Oh, yes, she will."

It's all a bad dream, I told myself. Any minute now I'll wake up. I said, "Petra, be reasonable. What do you think you're doing? I thought you were afraid of Sibyl."

"I am. Very."

"So?"

"I am in a position that forces me to do just what I am doing."

"What sort of position?"

"I'll tell you when Sibyl's here."

It was no dream. I was awake.

I got up. Petra didn't move. "Where are you going?" she asked.

"I've listened long enough."

"Herr Holland, the minute you leave this lobby without me, I shall go to the telephone over there," she gestured with her head.

I said nothing, but went on walking toward the exit. I counted my steps. At 14 I had reached the door and turned around, and saw Petra rise and walk over to the booth. I got there ahead of her.

"Petra, please!"

"Don't make a scene," she said. "Do you want witnesses?"

"Please! Petra!"

She said, "We'll take the forged passport to the post office at the Westbahnhof and send it off registered, special delivery. It will be in Bavaria tomorrow, and Sibyl can take the noon train." She spoke calmly and quietly. She had it all planned.

"You've thought it all through carefully, haven't you?"

"I didn't have anything else to do these last few days, Paul, but to think it through carefully." Now I was "Paul" again. "But before we send off the passport, you'll call Sibyl and tell her to come to Vienna."

"My voice would give me away. She'd notice. She'd know something was wrong and she wouldn't come."

"That would be too bad," said Petra.

We had gone back to our table, and now she finished her drink. "There's a second receiver in every booth. I'll listen in and decide after you've spoken to her whether to send her the passport or go to the police. So see what you can do with your voice."

"For God's sake, Petra! Don't you realize what you're asking me to do?"

"You said you didn't love her anymore."

"I was lying."

"I know."

"Why should I tell Sibyl to come here? If she does, she's finished."

Petra shook her head. "She's finished only if she doesn't come. If you do as I say, everything could still turn out all right for you. Then you can fly to Rio, for all I care—both of you, with my blessing!"

"You're acting out of hatred. You hate Sibyl and you want to torture her."

"I do not hate Sibyl." Petra picked up her gloves and bag. "We'll go up to your room now, and pack."

"What do you mean . . . pack?"

"You and Sibyl will stay with me. It's the only place where they won't look for her after the statement I made. Anyway, it's only for a few days. I'll explain everything when Sibyl is here."

I tried desperately to think of some way out, then it came to me. "You can't come up to my room with me, not in this hotel."

"Yes I can. I asked. You don't have a room, you have a suite." She took my arm again. "Come on, it's getting late, and we don't want to wake Sibyl."

7

"Sibyl?"

"What is it? Why are you calling again? Has something gone wrong?"

I was perspiring profusely. The booth was small and Petra was standing close beside me, listening on the second receiver. She didn't move, she didn't make a sound, and she never took her eyes off me.

"No, darling. Nothing's happened. What makes you think so?" The sweat was running into my mouth. I managed a laugh. "On the contrary—everything's going very well. Only . . . I can't talk about it."

"Over the phone. I know." She sounded reassured. I noticed that I was crying. Petra's body was pressed against mine.

"Listen, darling, the Berlin plane is sold out. An hour ago I managed to get two seats on the Vienna plane. We've got to take it or we lose too much time."

"Yes, of course." Sibyl's voice, the voice I loved, sounded eager. "But how do I—?"

"I'm sending you your passport right now, special delivery. You'll have it in the morning, and you can take the noon train."

"If you say so, Paul. I'll do anything you say. You know what we have to do."

"Yes. I know."

"And Petra?"

"What about Petra?"

"She's in Vienna, isn't she?"

"We won't stay in the city. I've found a place. It's going to work out all right." And all the time I was worrying about my voice. If only it would ring true in Petra's ears and false in Sibyl's! Sibyl knew me better. I was no actor, and I was afraid, terribly afraid.

"Thank God everything's all right," said Sibyl. "You know, I was startled when you called again."

"Don't be silly! Would I tell you to come,"—I had to cough—"if everything wasn't all right?"

Petra laid a hand on my receiver. "Tell her you love her," she whispered, and took her hand away again. "I love you," I said.

"And I love you," said Sibyl.

"I'll be at the station tomorrow evening."

"Yes, Paul."

The sweat was running into my eyes; I had to close them. I was wet from top to toe; my clothes were stick-

ing to me. I looked at Petra and thought: so that's
what it's like when you have to kill somebody. . . .

"Good night, beloved."

"Good night, Paul."

I hung up. "Well, how did I do?"

"Very well," she said. "You've got talent."

"So you're not going to the police."

"No. I think Sibyl will come. Now we'll mail the
passport."

She stood beside me and watched me address the
envelope. Then she took it away from me, sealed it,
and took it to the counter herself. I stood behind her
and looked at her slender neck under her white hair
and thought that the best thing would probably be to
strangle her before Sibyl came. She lived alone. If I
was lucky, they wouldn't find her for several days. Nobody at the house had ever seen me. No. That wasn't
right. I remember the happy family playing in the snow
and thought—if I go crazy now, too, then it's all over.
To kill her wasn't the answer. What I needed was time
to think things over. Who could tell what Petra was
really up to? The thing to do right now was to be
friendly, very friendly. . . .

"Nine schillings twenty," said the clerk. He stamped
the envelope with the forged passport in it, Petra gave
him a 10-schilling note, he gave her 80 groschen
change. She put the coins in her purse. "Will the letter
be there tomorrow morning?" she asked.

"Yes."

"Are you sure?"

"Absolutely sure. Unless there's a train accident."

I thought how funny it would be if there was a train accident. . . .

"Come, Paul."

She took my arm again and we went back to the taxi, where I had left my suitcase. "Seilerstrasse 10," Petra told the driver. The taxi started down the Mariahilfer-strasse, toward the Ring.

"Who lives at Seilerstrasse 10?"

The glass between us and the driver was closed; he couldn't hear us. Petra took my passport out of her bag, added a piece of paper to it, and slipped both into an envelope which she sealed carefully. Then she said, "My lawyer has his office there. You see, Paul, it is quite possible that you—and in due course, Sibyl—might want to get rid of me." She sounded like a teacher trying to explain the Pythagorean Theory to a dense pupil. "I don't want to be murdered like Emilio Trenti. That's why I'm going to leave your passport with my lawyer. I shall go to see him every day from now on, at four P.M. If ever I don't turn up at four, he will open the envelope two hours later, find your passport in it and read the instructions on the paper enclosed."

"And what are those instructions?"

"They read: 'This is the passport of the man who has murdered me,' " said Petra Wend. Now she was smiling.

8

It had started to snow again. The taxi passed under the archway of the Hofburg. I could see the tall caryatids that supported the balcony over the entrance. Snow lay on the heads and shoulders of the huge figures. "Every day at four P.M.," I said. "So if I kill you at five, I have twnety-three hours head start to get out of the country."

"You can't get out of the country in twenty-three hours, Herr Holland. And in twenty-three hours you can't get a forged passport."

Seilerstrasse 10 was a big old stone house. We rang, and a sleepy doorman opened for us. I went up to the second floor with Petra, to a door protected by a steel grille. The name of the lawyer was on the door, and below it a mail slot. Petra threw in the envelope. I could hear it fall on the floor on the other side with a dull thud of finality.

"Come on," said Petra, walking ahead of me, quiet and determined. She ran down the stairs in the damp, dimly lighted stairwell, with its ancient elevator that

surely hadn't been repaired since the war; she ran like
a woman who has just invested in a life insurance
policy.

We drove through Grinzinger Allee. The snow was
falling in thick flakes now, and it had grown warmer.
The streetlights cast yellow pools of light around the
lampposts. When we reached Petra's apartment, she
said, "Shall we go to bed right away, or do you want a
drink first?"

"Petra! I love Sibyl!"

"I know you do. I never doubted it."

"Please, Petra, Please tell me what you want from
us! I'll do anything!"

"I've told you—I'll explain everything when Sibyl is
here." She shrugged. "Don't make things more difficult
for us. So—do you want a whiskey?"

"No."

"All right. Then we'll go to bed."

"And where am I supposed to sleep?"

"In my bed. Beside me. It's wide enough."

"Petra," I said, "aren't you in the least afraid of
me?"

"I was never afraid of you, Paul. I don't think any
woman could be afraid of you." She yawned as she
took off her wool dress. I turned away. "No, I don't
want anything more from you. From now on ours will
be a strictly business relationship," and she walked past
me to the bathroom.

I sat down on the couch with the many cushions
while Petra brushed her teeth. She came back into the
room in her nightgown. "It's all yours," she said, ges-
turing in the direction of the bathroom as she walked

into the bedroom. I could see her lie down on the bed, a wide bed. A telephone stood on a small table beside it. Dear Petra. She had taken care of everything. There was an extra pillow and blanket.

I got my pajamas and toilet kit out of my suitcase and went into the bathroom. "Leave the door open," she said.

"Why?"

"The bathroom has a window, Paul."

So I left the door open, undressed, washed, used the toilet. Petra lay in bed, smoking and watching me. When I came back and lay down beside her, she said, "I bought a few magazines. I thought you mightn't want to go to sleep right away," and she shoved a few illustrated journals and magazines across to me. She had taken off her makeup and looked younger. I said, "Perhaps I don't care what happens to me. Perhaps I'll kill you after all, if only to give Sibyl a chance."

"You won't do that," she said, the ash on her cigarette growing longer.

"Why not?"

"Well, first of all, you don't have the courage, and secondly, you love Sibyl. You want to live with her. And you can't do that if you kill me." She took one of the magazines and opened it. "Always a story about the Hohenzollerns," she said, shaking her head. "Does anybody want to read about them anymore?"

I got up.

"What is it?"

"Where's the whiskey?"

"You see . . . I thought you'd want a drink. Everything's in the kitchen."

I walked to the other side of the bed, grabbed Petra by the hair, lifted her and struck her in the face as hard as I could. After the second blow, her nose began to bleed. The blood ran down her chin and onto her breast, above her nightgown. She said, "Do that once more and you're finished. Get a towel from the bathroom and wipe off the blood."

I got a small handtowel, wet it and wiped the blood away. "From my neck, too."

I did as I was told.

"And from my breast."

9

"This is the American Forces Network! AFN Munich now brings you Music at Midnight." A saxophone tuned in. "Glenn Miller and 'At Last.'" I had drunk half the bottle. I was lying in bed, my glass in my hand. The ice bucket and soda bottle stood on the carpet beside me. Petra wasn't drinking. She was reading a serial in one of the magazines. The music was coming from the radio beside the telephone, "At last my love has come. . . ."

I fell asleep. When I woke up it was two A.M. and the light was still on. Petra was still reading. I got up and her hand moved toward the phone. "Don't worry," I said. "I always get up once during the night."

I woke up several times after that, and whenever I opened my eyes, Petra was sitting beside me, watching me. "Aren't you sleepy?"

"No."

"Did you take something?"

"Pervitin."

In the morning she got breakfast and we drank coffee in her little kitchen. The weather had changed during the night. There was a strong warm wind, *"Föhn,"* she explained, and the snow was melting. The sky was a cloudy sulphur yellow. Petra spent the morning mending and sewing on buttons. She didn't talk much. I sat beside the window and wondered how long the Pervitin would remain effective.

We went out to eat, then we came back to the apartment. At four we drove into the city. Petra went to see her lawyer. She insisted that I accompany her. When I refused, she threatened me with the police again and I gave in.

It grew dark early. The streets were dirty and wet, the snow went on melting, cars splashed through the black slush. Sibyl's train was late. We stood on the platform under the electric floodlights swaying in the warm wind.

That evening I prayed. It occurred to me that it was low and humiliating to make my peace with God now, when I didn't know which way to turn, but I also thought, if there was a God, it would have to look like a victory to Him that I had found faith in the very moment when I hadn't been able to make any headway with my intellect. I begged God to protect Sibyl. I prayed, "Let her become suspicious. Don't let her come to Vienna. Let her stay in Germany with her forged passport. If Sibyl isn't on this train, I shall believe in You. Don't let Sibyl come to Vienna. Then I'll admit that You exist and that You heard me." That evening I was determined, against my better judgment, to believe that God was behind every act of faith.

"Attention, please! The Arlberg Express from Zurich, via Salzburg, arriving on track three."

I saw the lights of the diesel locomotive. Far away, between the signal lights I could see it coming closer. Dear God, if You help me now. . . .

The lights came nearer, nearer. Porters appeared with their dollies. The train rolled into the station and stopped.

"You stay here," said Petra, as she moved behind a column. The first passengers were coming toward us. Friends embraced. A child cried "Papa!" and broke loose from his mother.

Dear God . . . dear God . . . please. . . .

More and more people coming toward me and still no sign of Sibyl. My heart was beating fast. If God answered my prayer and I now had to believe in Him, then it would be my duty to go to confession.

The child who had cried "Papa" came running back, laughing and dragging a tanned blond man behind him. Sibyl was walking beside the blond man. I thought: so there is no God. But then I had to admit that perhaps there was, and He just hadn't chosen to answer my prayers.

A porter was carrying Sibyl's suitcases. I stepped forward. She embraced me. "Hello, darling. I had no trouble at the border. My passport—" She stopped. I knew why, although I couldn't see Petra. But I could feel Sibyl freeze in my arms and I said, "There was nothing I could do about it. She has been blackmailing me since yesterday." Then I turned around. Petra had stepped forward. The Pervitin had enlarged her eyes; the pupils were huge. She said, "Do you see the policeman over there, Sibyl?"

Sibyl said, "Yes."

I couldn't get over how calmly she took it. She looked at Petra thoughtfully, with no display of excitement. The porter had walked on ahead with her luggage.

"You will give me your passport, Sibyl," said Petra. "If you don't I shall call the policeman."

Sibyl opened her bag and the forged passport changed hands again. "Herr Holland, walk between us, please." I did, and both women took my arm. We walked to the exit that way, and I told Sibyl, "There was nothing I could do. If I hadn't told you to come, she would have gone to the police."

Sibyl nodded. I had the feeling she didn't grasp our situation yet. A banner was stretched across the station entrance: Visit Beautiful Austria!

10

After also depositing Sibyl's passport at the office of Petra's lawyer, we drove to her apartment. The warm wind had grown stronger. Sibyl's calm was eerie. She was apathetic, almost stupefied. She sat quietly in the taxi, looking straight ahead, never at Petra or me. Once she nodded to herself, slowly, thoughtfully; she also talked to herself a little, but so low you couldn't understand what she was saying.

"What is it?" I asked.

"Nothing," she said, and grasped my hand.

When we reached the apartment, Petra didn't keep us waiting. She was not a sadist. "I want the jewelry," she said, looking at Sibyl almost apologetically. "I am heavily in debt, Sibyl. One of my loans falls due the day after tomorrow, and I can't pay it. I'm up to my ears and don't know where to turn. I tried gambling, and lost. I'm desperate. My creditors won't wait any longer, neither will the bank. So give me the jewelry, Sibyl, and I'll give you back your passports right away, and you can leave."

Sibyl shook her head with an air of finality.

"You *will* give it to me!" said Petra. "You have time until tomorrow evening. That's a long time. Think it over."

"What jewelry is she talking about?"

"The jewelry Tonio gave her," said Petra. "He gave her rings and bracelets worth at least a hundred and fifty thousand schillings. All Rome was talking about it."

"I don't have it anymore," said Sibyl.

"What do you mean?"

"I had to sell it."

Sibyl spoke as if in her sleep, the words slurred, with no intonation, and her face was lifeless. What had happened to her? This wasn't the Sibyl I knew. This was a strange, sick woman.

"I sold it during the years after the war, when I too didn't know where to turn."

"You're lying!" Petra cried. "I know all about you. I took pains to find out."

"Then you were misinformed. I'm sorry to disappoint you, Frau Wend. I seem to be constantly disappointing you."

It was weird to see Sibyl grow calmer and calmer as Petra became more and more excited. "I don't believe it!" she screamed.

"You can search me. You can search my luggage and keep anything you find." Sibyl sat back in her chair and closed her eyes. I found the whole thing incomprehensible.

"What's the matter with you?" I asked.

Her smile was wan. She stroked my hand. "Nothing, my love. I'm just tired."

"Petra," I said. "You're mistaken. You really are.

Sibyl doesn't have any jewelry. I'd have seen it if she did."

Petra jumped to her feet. With trembling fingers she lit a cigarette. "You be quiet!" she cried. "You don't know what it's all about! Sibyl has lied to you from the day you met. What did you know about her before I told you everything? I'm telling you—she has the jewelry!"

Sibyl lifted one hand and let it fall again. "There's my suitcase."

"It's not in your suitcase," Petra screamed. "You've hidden it somewhere. Just wait a few hours and you'll tell me where you've hidden it. I've got to have it! And you've got to give it to me or you're finished!"

As if under the influence of a narcotic, Sibyl murmured, "There is no more jewelry."

"How much money do you need, Petra?" I asked.

"A hundred and ten thousand schillings."

That was almost 20,000 marks. I couldn't possibly get my hands on that much money. Part of it, perhaps.

"I'll call my office, Petra. And some friends. I'm sure I can get part of it."

"That's no good to me. You don't seem to understand my position. If I don't come up with the money, all of it, I'll be arrested. I'll go to jail. And I have a son! Who's going to look after him?"

"Frau Wend," said Sibyl, without opening her eyes, "would you please leave us alone?"

Petra's lips parted in a smile of satisfaction. "Certainly. I was waiting for that. You'll come round." She walked out of the room and I could hear her lock the door on the other side.

I went over to Sibyl and shook her. "What's the matter with you? Why are you behaving like this?"

"It's all over, Paul."

"What's all over?"

"Everything. We can't do it."

"I—"

"Let me finish. I knew yesterday, when you called a second time, that something had gone wrong. I could tell by your voice. But I came just the same."

"Why?"

"Because I wanted to see you once more."

"What do you mean . . . see me once more? We don't have time for that sort of nonsense. We've got to satisfy Petra. Somehow!"

She got up and walked over to her suitcase, released the lock and the top sprang open. When she stood up again, she was holding a revolver in her hand.

11

"Sibyl!"

I took a step forward, but she waved me back with the weapon. "Sit down," she said, "and listen to me.

And don't interrupt me. I know what I have to do. Up there on the mountain, Paul, I had time to think. We can't do it. I have killed a man. Another lost his life because of me."

"You say that . . . after all you've done to escape the consequences?"

"I needed time to realize what I'd done. Actually it was you who made me see things in their true light."

"I?"

"Yes, Paul. When you said you didn't care if I had committed murder or not. It was then that I began to realize there was no escape. And suddenly I didn't want to run away anymore. You know I believe in God."

The revolver kept moving in her unsteady hands. I was wondering if fear and excitement had deranged her.

"God is just, Paul. You can't deceive Him. If I run away with you, He won't protect us anymore."

"Stop talking about your God! We have to protect ourselves!"

"He protects us, Paul. He does! And one day you'll believe in Him. But I have to pay for what I've done."

"Damn it, Sibyl, stop talking such nonsense!"

"I've given it all a lot of thought," she went on, in that same monotonous voice. "If I go to the police and confess everything, I'll be given a few years in prison. When they let me go, I'll be an old woman. And I will have lost you. I don't want to go to prison."

"Who's talking about prison? Sibyl, I implore you, come to your senses!"

"This is the revolver," she went on, ignoring my outburst, "with which I shot Emilio Trenti. And I am going to shoot myself with it." I moved, and quick as a flash the revolver was steady again, aimed at me. "Don't move!"

She has gone mad, I told myself. I felt cold. I was more of a coward than I had realized—I didn't move.

I tried to reason with her. "Why do you want to kill yourself, Sibyl!"

"Because then God will forgive me. Then I won't lose you."

"And I?"

Her lips twisted in a mad smile. "Come with me, Paul," she whispered. "If you come with me, we'll be together forever. We'll never have to part again."

She came closer. My hands began to sweat with fear.

"I'll give you the revolver. You'll shoot me first, then yourself. And then . . . then we'll be at peace and nothing can part us, and God will love us again."

"Give it to me," I said. But I spoke too fast. She stepped back.

"You're not going to do it."

"I'll do it," I said. "Give me the revolver." I stretched out my hand; I took a step forward. She aimed the revolver at her own breast. "You won't do it, Paul. I know you won't. I've thought it all over for so long. There's no other way out for me. . . ."

I jumped. Wild with fear, I leaped at her, the two of us fell and rolled over on the floor. Sibyl screamed. "No, Paul! No!" The weapon was aimed at me now. "I love you," she whispered.

It was the last thing I remember. In the next moment she fired and I felt as if a gigantic hand had flung me to one side. It grew dark and I was falling down, down, into a black abyss.

12

A siren wailing. I was lying on a hard narrow cot that swayed slightly. I opened my eyes. A man in white was sitting beside me, drawing the contents of an ampule into a hypodermic syringe. I was in an ambulance, tearing through the streets of Vienna. The red revolving light on the roof passed fitfully across my face.

"Where is—"

"Don't talk," said the man in white.

There was another cot on the other side. It was empty. "Sibyl," I whispered. "Is she—"

"Don't talk," said the man in white, sticking the needle into my arm, and it became dark and I began to fall again.

13

That was on March 19 at 8:45 P.M. At 8:53 I was in General Hospital and they began operating. I recovered consciousness many hours later, and the police didn't come until the twenty-first, in the afternoon. They asked a lot of questions, after informing me that Sibyl was dead. For her the doctor had come too late. She had shot herself in the heart. They told me that her body was in the morgue and had not yet been released for burial. But they had found a handwritten confession in her suitcase that she had murdered Emilio Trenti.

"Go away," I said to the officers. But they stayed and told me I could expect an investigation since I had helped a criminal escape. They had arrested Petra. She was in jail, awaiting indictment. She had broken down and confessed that she had tried to blackmail us. Her creditors were filing suit.

"Please," I told the men, "go away!" But they stayed and told me they had notified my office and confiscated my passport. Then the doctor came in and insisted that they leave. They promised to come again. The doctor gave me an injection, and I fell into a deep sleep, and this is what I dreamed.

Robert Friedmann's bar was empty, not even he was there. Instead of the usual barmaid, an elderly gentleman was standing behind the bar. He bowed low as I came in. He had on a tuxedo. Sibyl was waiting for me in a corner, and after I had kissed her, she introduced me to the gentleman in the tuxedo. "This is Herr Holland," she said, and to me, "This is God."

"I'll take it you'll want whiskey, too," said God, filling a glass for me.

"Thanks."

Sibyl stroked my hand. "Did you have to hurry, darling?"

"There was a lot of traffic in Rio," I explained. "Nothing was moving. It was especially bad at the Copacabana Beach."

"I know that area," said God.

"I'm sorry I had to keep you waiting," I said to Sibyl. The piano player had grown older but he was still playing "C'est si bon."

"That doesn't matter. We had a lot to talk about, didn't we?" She turned to look at the old gentleman.

"Your whiskey's on the house," he said, nodding.

"Yes. Sibyl and I had a lot to talk about."

Now he was talking like Robert Friedmann and suddenly his face looked a lot like Robert's, kind and sad, with bags under the eyes.

"Sibyl and I are old friends, you know," he said. "We've been through a lot together."

"She's told me a lot about you, too," I said. "Only I didn't really think you existed."

"Sometimes I don't," he said politely. "In certain areas, for instance, and at various times. From 1933 to '45, I wasn't in Germany."

Sibyl said, "We discussed everything, darling. God says it's going to be all right."

"We're going to get our passports?" Suddenly I was very excited, because I remembered that God was the person who was supposed to give us our new passports with our residence permits.

"Of course," said the old gentleman. "Since Sibyl has shot herself, nothing stands between her and a passport. Nothing to it." He took the cap off his fountain pen. "There's a date missing in yours . . . just a minute . . . here." He put on a pair of tortoiseshell glasses and looked at me. "Where did you die?"

"A hundred and sixty miles east of Rio de Janeiro," I replied.

"Thank you. That will do." He wrote the information into my passport and gave it to me. It was a very elegant, brand-new passport. God was smiling. "This time I made it myself. Franz hasn't been too reliable lately. I don't want you to have any difficulties."

"All of us are getting old," said Sibyl. Then we drank and toasted each other. I thought what a good friend Robert was, Robert Friedmann from the Kurfürstendamm in Berlin.

"And how is your wound?" I asked.

"Completely healed," said Sibyl. "Would you like to see it?" She pushed her dress off her left shoulder, ex-

posing her small, taut breast. Under the nipple I could
see a little red mark. "That's all?"

"That's all," said Sibyl.

14

I was in General Hospital four weeks. For four
weeks a police officer sat in front of my door and the
men from homicide came to see me again and again.
They became more friendly; I became friendlier, too.
After all, it was their job to ask questions. Five days
after Sibyl had shot herself, her body was released.
They asked me if I wanted her buried in the Central
Cemetery, and was I willing to bear the cost. I told
them to cremate her. Sibyl had said once that she
wanted to be cremated.

Since Sibyl had no relatives or close friends and I
couldn't attend the ceremony, they cremated her on
March 29, at about two A.M. Next day I received the
bill and was told that the urn was in Box DL
7659/1956.

I was dismissed from General Hospital with the assurance that I would not survive if I did not spend the next two months flat on my back for the most part, and avoided all excitement. I moved back into the Ambassador Hotel, into the room on the fourth floor, with the red wallpaper and the green tiled bathroom. Here Dr. Gürtler came to see me regularly until he gave up his practice and moved into the Children's Hospital in Floridsdorf. Here, in the Ambassador Hotel, I began to write this story on the seventh of April. Flowerwomen in the street below were selling violets, primula and snowdrops, and it was already very warm in Vienna for April.

The two months stretched out to four. The investigation dragged on. I was more or less confined to the house; I couldn't leave the city. My office in Frankfurt granted me a leave of absence, the move to Rio was postponed. They sent me money, provided me a lawyer—they were most generous.

My wound healed satisfactorily, and I went on writing. It rained a lot that summer, and there were many thunderstorms. We didn't have any more beautiful days like those in spring. I drank pretty regularly during those four months, and took sleeping pills. I dreamed a lot, confused stuff, but never any more of Sibyl. That may have been because I was so totally absorbed with her when I was writing.

On July 17 a young man visited me. He introduced himself as Alfred Peter. He was wearing rimless spectacles and looked like an intellectual and a man of refinement. "Herr Holland, I work in a publishing house." He mentioned the name. "I've been told that you're working on a novel that deals with—with recent events in your life."

"Who told you?"

"One of the waiters here. His name is Franz. I eat there sometimes, and he knows me. I'm interested in your manuscript. When you're through, would you let me read it?"

"I don't know yet if I want it published."

"But when you began to write—"

"That was different. At that time I was still very weak. Now I'm much stronger, and I'm not at all sure that I'm going to finish it."

"Are you more than halfway through?"

"Two thirds, I'd say."

"Then you'll finish it," Herr Peter said confidently. "And when you're finished, you'll let me see it."

It was raining on the day he came to see me. I accompanied him down to the lobby, then I went to a record shop in the Kärtneerstrasse. It had several small booths in which you could play records. I thought it would be nice to have a record player. I chose one and went into one of the little booths and played the Rachmaninoff Piano Concert II. I smoked as I listened and tried to think of Sibyl. I laid the snapshot of her, which I always carried with me, on a small table in front of me and looked at her slender body in its bathing suit, at her shiny eyes and her big, laughing mouth. But the concerto didn't help. All I could think of was the metal urn at the Central Cemetery. The only thing that helped me was whiskey.

I left the booth and said to the saleslady, "Will you be angry if I don't buy the record player after all?"

"Of course not, sir," but she sounded annoyed. "You changed your mind?"

"Yes," I said. "I'm sorry."

15

Petra and I went on trial on July 4, 1956, in a small courtroom in the Vienna County Court. The only charge against me was possession of a forged passport. I refused to give the name of the man who had forged the passport for me, and the judge gave me a suspended sentence because I was a foreigner and because I had a good lawyer. But they threw the book at Petra.

She was charged with blackmail, extortion and fraud, and was sentenced to 18 months in jail. She was wearing a gray tweed suit and seemed calm, almost indifferent, when the judge pronounced sentence. A few of her creditors were present, and their animosity was apparent in the way they glared at her.

"Have you anything to say?" the judge asked.

I shook my head, Petra nodded.

"What is it, Frau Wend?"

"It concerns Herr Holland." For the first time she

looked at me. It was stifling in the courtroom. Black thunderclouds had been hovering over the city for hours and I was feeling sick and dizzy. Petra Wend said, "I'm sorry for what I did, Herr Holland."

I said nothing.

She went on, "I'm very unhappy about it," and stopped. I thought of something I'd read long ago: Sorrow and anxiety are at the root of all evil. I said, "All of us were at fault, Petra."

"Can you forgive me?" They were photographing as we spoke. I thought: What difference does it make if I forgive her or not, so I said, "I forgive you."

"Court adjourned," said the judge. "The defendant, Paul Holland, is to be released immediately." Then they led Petra past me and she nodded at me once more. She gave an impression of feeling safe and resigned. The state had taken over the care of her child, she would find a way to settle with her creditors, a year and a half of peaceful living lay ahead of her.

"Herr Holland?" It was Dr. Gürtler, the doctor who had operated on me. He shook my hand. "Congratulations."

"Were you at the trial?"

"Yes." He smiled. He was tanned and looked younger and full of confidence. "I came into the city for it. You're better, aren't you? So I thought I'd like to ask you to visit me in the hospital when you can. You promised you would."

"I'd like to very much."

"You wouldn't happen to have time now?"

I hesitated.

"I'd drive you there and bring you back to your hotel. I've got my car here."

I really didn't have anything else to do, so I agreed. The storm broke just as we were driving across the Danube Bridge. The rain came down so hard, we had to stop. Suddenly it was pitch dark. Lightning flashed across the sky, and the thunder was practically constant. A bad storm. But it passed quickly. Ten minutes later it was light again. The heavy downpour had turned into a light, steady rain. We drove on.

The Children's Hospital was situated on a long suburban street, between warehouses and factories. It was an ugly, red brick building, built at the turn of the century. Inside it was just as old-fashioned, but spotlessly clean. The floors in the corridors were laid with long, narrow, yellow tiles. The few children we met greeted us politely. They looked happy, but they were pale and thin.

"Of course I had a reason for bringing you here," said Dr. Gürtler, walking a little ahead of me. "Also for bringing you here today." He opened a white door. There were three beds in the room, but only one was occupied. A little girl was sleeping peacefully in it. Her age was hard to determine because she was wearing a broad black band over both eyes, and the greater part of her face was bandaged. She might have been ten years old. "Sit down," said Dr. Gürtler.

"But what about the child?"

"She won't hear us. She's just been given morphine. She'll sleep till morning. When she comes to again, she'll already be on the plane."

A teddy bear, his pink tongue sticking out, was

perched on the night table beside the bed. In her sleep the little girl was clinging to its left leg. The child had brown hair, and her name, I could read on the card above her bed, was Angelica Reimer. Something else was written on the card, but too small for me to read.

"Angelica is flying to New York. She has a very serious cataract which we can't operate on here."

"But doesn't that cost a lot of money?"

"A lot, Herr Holland." He seemed to be enjoying our conversation. Now he laughed, a short dry laugh, and began to clean his glasses. "A lot," he said again. "A specialist is going to operate on her, the only man who could be considered for this type operation, a Dr. Higgins at Bellevue Hospital. And an adult must, of course, travel with the child. Yes, yes, it will cost a small fortune. At least eighty thousand schillings. Angelica's mother is dead; her father is a dock worker."

"I see," I said. "You have a story for me."

"You're a reporter, aren't you? You told me once that only stories were important to you."

"That's right," I said. "Stories and facts."

"So listen to me." He puts on his glasses again and rubbed his hands. "The child's father brought her to us six months ago. Left eye very bad, right eye a little better. Opaque lens, visual disturbances, headaches, vertigo, and so on."

The sleeping child sighed and moved a little.

"We operated. Once. Twice. Then we realized what we were up against. There wasn't a surgeon in Europe who could do it. I forgot to mention that the father loves the child, more than fathers usually love their children. He's—one might say he's obsessed by her."

I began to sense what was on his mind and suddenly there was a bad taste in my mouth. Outside it was still raining.

"We told the father the truth," Dr. Gürtler went on, "and that it was a question of money. With a sum that size we couldn't help him. We might have been able to come up with it eventually, but not as quickly as it was needed. Angelica had to be operated on at once, if Dr. Higgins' intervention was to be successful."

I was sorry I'd come out here. I should have known what was going to be expected of me, and I was in no mood to listen to such stories anymore. They made me so nervous, I could barely control myself. And I had to control myself because, after all, Dr. Gürtler was the man who had saved my life. A good man, who wanted to help me.

"And then there was a miracle," I said, in an effort to bring the story to a conclusion.

"Yes, Herr Holland. We talked about God once," and here it comes, I thought! "I gained the impression that you didn't think much of Him."

"That's right."

"Herr Holland, the child's father believes in God just as little as you do. He is a passionate, outspoken member of the Social Democrat Party. So he didn't go to church to pray. Instead he gambled on the football lottery."

"And won."

Angelica let go of the teddy bear's foot and turned on her other side.

"No. Have you ever heard of anyone winning the football lottery?"

"So what happened?"

"The incident got into the papers. A lot of people read that Angelica needed help. An American airline company called up and donated two round-trip tickets to New York." He lowered his voice. "You see, God knows various ways to protect those who love each other."

"You mean the American airlines know various ways."

"I mean God," he said in the same low voice.

I turned away and looked out into the garden. "It's a nice story," I said. "Let's hope Dr. Higgins can save your patient. I have a feeling he will."

"There are various forms of love, Herr Holland. Your love for the woman who is dead was just one form. . . ."

"I don't want to talk about the kind of love it may have been."

He got up and laid a hand on my shoulder. "The sad thing about you, Herr Holland, is that you have more faith than any of us." I picked up my hat. "You depended on God more than any of us. Now you are angry with him."

"*Herr Doktor*," I said, "if you don't mind, I must get back to my hotel. I have to pack and write a few letters."

Outside, the children were playing in the garden. They were singing, "A little man stands in the forest, on one leg. . . ."

"You're going away?"

"Yes. I must go to Berlin. Three days later, I leave Europe."

" . . . He has a little coat on, all pur-ple red. . . ."
The children were playing on grass that was still wet
from the rain. Now they took hands and danced in a
circle. A little boy was standing on one leg in the center, his hands in front of his face.

"Where are you flying to, Herr Holland?"

"To Rio de Janeiro. I'm taking over our office in
Brazil."

16

"Attention, please! Air France Clipper 759 to Munich is taking on passengers at Gate 3. We wish you a
pleasant flight." The woman's voice came across the
P.A., fresh and bright.

It is 6:30 A.M., July 7, 1956. I am sitting in the
restaurant of the Tempelhof airport in Berlin, drinking
coffee. My plane leaves at 7:30. I have already registered my luggage and am writing these lines on the
same table at which Sibyl and I sat before my last
flight to Brazil. I have time. They'll call me when my
plane is ready to take on passengers.

"Attention, please! British European Airways Viscount 342 to Hannover and Hamburg is ready to take on passengers at Gate 1. We wish you a pleasant flight."

Here nothing has changed. Below me planes are being fueled in the morning sun, mechanics in overalls are working around them. I can see the EURAMA plane on which I am flying, number BRXK 56. Refugees from the East are still milling around the counters. It is summer, midsummer. A lot of Berliners are going on vacation, most of them flying south to Italy and Spain. There are a lot of extra flights, and I hear that all the planes are sold out. They are also flying poor Berlin children to West Germany. I can see an attendant marching a group of little girls to a four-engine plane. Each child is wearing a label with her name on it. Now they walk up the steps and disappear through the doorway.

It's going to be a hot day. The sky is a cloudless blue, a light east wind is blowing. I have two bottles of whiskey with me and I think I'll start drinking after Düsseldorf.

The waiters are very polite. All of them know me. One of them is setting tables somewhere in the background, just as it was then.

"Attention, please! Mr. Broome, just arrived with Pan American World Airways from Frankfurt, please come to the Pan Am counter. There is a message for you. Repeat: Mr. Broome from Frankfurt. . . ."

I had spent the night at the Hotel am Zoo. I didn't go back to Sibyl's apartment. I called the landlord. Since Sibyl had no living relatives I suggested that he sell all her things and rent the place again. He said he would use the money to repair the swimming pool. Did I think this would have met with Frau Loredo's approval? I said I was sure it would have. I threw the keys to Sibyl's apartment into the wastepaper basket in my hotel. I didn't need them anymore. I also gave up my room at the Astoria Hotel in Frankfurt. I gave my books and pictures, and the few other things I had there, to my friend Kalmar. My clothes are packed in two large suitcases. This time I needed two.

I flew from Vienna via Frankfurt. At the office they were very helpful and understanding. I had thought that the trouble I'd got into would have repercussions, but even the three directors didn't have a word to say against me. Just the same, I know they were glad to see me move on to Brazil.

It is 4:35. A half hour more and I'll be off. I think I'll order another coffee. When I'm through with all this, I'll put the whole manuscript into the manila envelope I brought with me, go over to the branch post office here and send it off to Herr Alfred Peter at his Vienna publishing house. It's a good house, with offices in Zürich and Hamburg. And Herr Peter impressed me as an intelligent man.

"Attention, please! Calling passengers Royce, Riddle, and Watts, booked with British European Airways to Hannover! Your aircraft is about to take off! Passengers Royce, Riddle, and Watts, please!"

The sun is so high now, its rays fall on my table. The waiter is bringing my second cup of coffee and I'll pay him right away. I'm thinking of Sibyl. We were here, in this restaurant so often—when I arrived, when I was leaving. Here I was sad and happy with her.

Here I held her hand, kissed her, asked her to marry me. And here Sibyl had told me that God would protect us as long as we loved each other truly.

Poor Sibyl! She should be leaving with me. Everything would have turned out all right if only she had listened to me. Now she is alone and I am alone, and we shall never meet again.

If the shot she had fired had hit me just a little higher, I would be with her now. I didn't believe in life after death, but it would certainly have been better to die with Sibyl than to live without her. I know that I'm much too much of a coward to take my life now. That's out of the question. I'll live on. In Rio, or somewhere else. . . .

"Attention, please! Air France Clipper 321 to Vienna is taking on passengers at Gate 1. We wish you a pleasant flight!"

Planes land and take off. So many in the summer. . . .

6:45.

They'll soon call me now. God can't be reproached, since He doesn't exist. That was the mistake Sibyl made. I can see it now. She believed in God. She believed that His power would protect us. A god who doesn't exist can't protect anybody. I should have seen it like that before, and perhaps I could have made it clear to her, too.

Since I have to live on, I hope I can succeed in forgetting Sibyl. They say that in time all things are forgotten.

Perhaps I shall find another woman. There are a lot of women, and some day I'm going to want one again.

They won't be like Sibyl—I realize that, but now that Sibyl is dead, I don't care how different they are. One loses a great many things in life that can't be replaced. I have lost my youth, one leg . . . and Sibyl. But I have learned that one can live without youth, without one leg. . . .

Poor Sibyl! I promised her I'd write a book about us, about our love. Now I've done it, and Herr Peter was right—I even managed to finish it. I can't do anything more for her. I remember how she begged me once, "If you write about me, please say that I had firm little breasts, not big ones." Since this is the only wish of hers that I can still fulfill, I shall close our story with this truth.

She had firm little breasts, not big ones. . . .

BULLETIN . . . BULLETIN . . . BULLETIN. Special attention all Western Press Agency offices. July 8. Rio. EURAMA Flight BRXK 56 crashed into ocean about 160 miles east of Rio early this A.M. All 45 passengers and crew of 10 presumed dead. Search planes located only large oil slick, no survivors. Plane was enroute from Berlin to Rio on regular scheduled flight. Cause of crash not known at this time. Among passengers was WPA correspondent Paul Holland, enroute here to assume charge of our Rio agency.

FREE
Fawcett Books Listing

There is Romance, Mystery, Suspense, and Adventure waiting for you inside the Fawcett Books Order Form. And it's yours to browse through and use to get all the books you've been wanting . . . but possibly couldn't find in your bookstore.

This easy-to-use order form is divided into categories and contains over 1500 titles by your favorite authors.

So don't delay—take advantage of this special opportunity to increase your reading pleasure.

Just send us your name and address and 35¢ (to help defray postage and handling costs).

FAWCETT BOOKS GROUP
P.O. Box C730, 524 Myrtle Ave., Pratt Station, Brooklyn, N.Y. 11205

Name_____
(please print)

Address_____
City_____State_____Zip_____

Do you know someone who enjoys books? Just give us their names and addresses and we'll send them an order form too!

Name_____
Address_____
City_____State_____Zip_____

Name_____
Address_____
City_____State_____Zip_____